Praise for Troy Cook's
47 Rules of Highly Effective Bank Robbers:

BOOK OF THE YEAR, ForeWord Magazine Finalist

'KILLER PICK,' Independent Mystery Booksellers Assn.

WINNER, Allbooks Reviewer's Choice Award

LEFTY AWARD, Best Humorous Mystery Finalist

"A hell of a book!"
— Ken Bruen, *The Guards*

"Troy Cook's debut novel is a rarity. From such an auspicious start, one can only imagine how good he may become. Did someone say Edgar?"
— I Love a Mystery

"Often touching…constantly amusing."
— Dick Adler, Paperback Mysteries

"The twists and laughs keep coming in this highly entertaining debut. A Pick of the Week."
— Sarah Weinman, Confessions of an Idiosyncratic Mind

"A fun book from a talented author."
— Crimespree Magazine

"Racy fun, peopled with strange and wonderful characters."
— Mystery Scene Magazine

"Will keep you turning the pages. This is no ordinary mystery."
— ForeWord Magazine

""Well written, clever, and laugh out loud funny - don't miss it."
— Stacy Alesi, Bookbitch.com

"In this hilarious debut, Troy Cook proves himself worthy to join the likes of such masters of the comic thriller as Carl Hiaasen and Lawrence Shames."
— I Love A Mystery Bookstore

"You'll find yourself cheering…a high speed adrenaline filled crime caper novel of the 1st degree. Exceedingly delightful…a resplendent job of weaving delightfully droll bits of humor throughout the story. A terrific debut."
— Spinetingler Magazine

"A fabulous first novel. Based on a cleverly cynical premise, from the first page to the last the story never bogs down."
— Gumshoe Review

"One of the most intriguing and original ideas for a mystery novel I've read all year!"
— Zoë Sharp, author of the Charlie Fox crime thriller series

"Cook can write crackling good dialogue and tell a damn good yarn."
— Reviewing the Evidence

"This is great crime noir, bleached by the Arizona sun."
— Mysterious Galaxy Books

"A fast and funny romp through the criminal world."
— Sleuth of Baker Street Bookstore

"A wild west romp of a novel."
— Maggie Mason, Deadly Pleasures

"Light-hearted, fast-moving fare—a good summer read."
— Mystery Morgue

"Cook writes with a director's eye, each scene choreographed for optimal effect. A cast of painfully funny characters weaves throughout the story… a remarkable fresh spin on the Bonnie and Clyde-style that was a pleasure to read."
— Futures Mystery Anthology Magazine

"Ground breaking. This first novel should be on all crime, mystery, or humor lover's list of summer reads."
— Front Street Review

for Cheryl and Ian

one

"IS this a great country or what? The geezer's heart attack bumped me three points in the Zogby poll." Odie Roberts cringed and covered his mouth. Had he really said that out loud?

In case someone was watching, Odie made the sign of the cross. "God rest his soul."

If I don't watch out, this politics crap will turn me into an asshole. He looked around for any witnesses to his indiscretion, but his faithful staff had vacated the offices a little earlier. With a start, he realized he was alone. In Hollywood. After midnight. When the freaks come out.

His campaign office had been broken into twice already. Druggies the first time and a wannabe actress turned hooker the second. Odie pulled open his desk drawer and rubbed his snub-nosed revolver, somewhat comforted.

He gave a little whistle and said, "Hey Jasper, come here boy."

His collie, rumored to be a descendent of the original Lassie, gave a bark and bounded over for a little attention.

"Good boy. Who's a good boy?" Odie rubbed Jasper's belly for a bit before catching a glimpse of himself on television. He paused for a little self-adoration. The boob tube was replaying the now infamous debate showing Crenshaw's fatal heart attack. For the fiftieth time that day.

As a participant in the debate, Odie'd had an up close and personal view of the fiery dispute. But he still smirked as he watched the video of Two-Bits, the rap-star candidate, disrespecting Crenshaw up and down the aisle. Poor Crenshaw had spluttered, red-faced, until he'd finally keeled over.

Odie shook his head. What a way to go. The media, already

enamored with the bizarre spectrum of gubernatorial candidates, was in the midst of a feeding frenzy with the "live death" of the front runner.

At the sound of a gunshot, Jasper barked and hurried out onto the balcony. Odie hesitated, then followed and glanced down at the crowd strewn across Hollywood Boulevard. Both the tourists and the hookers were still doing their thing. Business as usual. In fact, it looked like a transvestite was taking a leak on Odie's star on the Walk of Fame.

There was another shot, but this time it was obvious it came from farther north. Probably the drug dealers on Franklin. If he was elected governor in two weeks—and now that actually seemed likely—cleaning up Hollywood would be one of his top priorities. Well, that and getting California out of its massive deficit and helping the homeless and all that other stuff.

Odie stepped back inside his campaign headquarters and caught a glimpse of his four People's Choice Awards. He rubbed the third one from the left for luck, and then used his reflection in one of his framed movie posters to primp for a moment. Then he smiled his trademark smile—the one that had made him famous at the age of six.

His campaign platform was mostly built on freckles, red hair, wholesome apple-pie personality, and the same million-dollar smile that had endeared him to generations of viewers over the years. The hair had receded, of course, and the apple-pie thing had gone the way of the dodo, but the smile still worked wonders on the voting populace. He winked at himself and said aloud, "*Governor* Odie Roberts at your service."

"No kidding. Out of all these whackos running for office, you think you're the one gonna be elected, huh?"

Odie whirled around and found an impossibly thin man with buggy, Steve Buscemi eyes, walking through the front door. Odie stuttered for a moment before regaining his composure. He carefully placed his smile into its proper position. "Absolutely. You're interested in my campaign, I take it?"

The thin man shrugged. "Yeah, I guess."

Odie narrowed his gaze at the lackadaisical answer and

tried not to show his fear. The thin man looked distinctly apolitical. And with the man's Brooklyn accent, Odie assumed the worst.

He thought about the revolver in the desk. "Are you a Little Odie fan?"

"You're Little Odie?" The thin man smiled. "Jeez, you are. Abso-friggin-lutely. Heck, I grew up on that show you did when you were a little pup. No kiddin', *Back on the Farm* was my all-time lights-out favorite."

Odie heaved a sigh of relief. Just a fan. He pulled an autographed head shot from a stack on the floor and offered it to the thin man.

"Oh, hey. This is pretty cool. Thanks."

Odie's relief came to an abrupt end as an enormous black man slipped sideways through the door, scraping his back and belt buckle on the doorframe. After popping a few buttons, the big man squeezed past and closed the door.

Odie stammered, then found his voice and called out, "Hey. Leave that open, would you?"

The big man grunted and locked the door.

He locked it! Odie shivered. "What do you guys want?"

The thin man said, "Well, I truly am a fan, Odie. I want you to know that. But I'm afraid I got some bad news for you. And maybe just a bit of good news." He pulled a gun from behind his back and waved it around casually.

Odie's eyes widened.

"The bad part is we gotta kill ya. And for that I apologize."

Odie backed away, glancing quickly around. *This can't be happening!* He glanced toward the balcony but promptly dismissed it. He was four stories up. "And what's the good news?"

The thin man gestured with the gun. "I read in some rag that you were partial to heroin in the old days, so we picked you up some killer stuff to O.D. with."

Odie backed into his desk and stopped. His head whipped back and forth from the gun, to the buggy eyes, to the behemoth advancing toward him. His breaths came fast and furious. "That's the good news? I haven't done heroin in twenty years."

The big guy grunted and reached for Odie.

The thin man held out his hand to stop his partner. "It's not like you got a choice, Odie." He held up a syringe. "And I hear this shit is da bomb, so why not take it like a man. It's called blonde angel. You'll go out flying like a kite."

Odie abruptly started to cry.

Impatient, the thin man stamped his foot. "Hey. It could be worse."

Odie wiped his nose with his sleeve. "You're going to kill me. How could it be worse?"

"Well...like if we lit you on fire."

Odie felt the tears flowing like a river down his face. "You're not a Little Odie fan!"

The thin man reached out and patted Odie's head. "I really am. And in point of fact, your last series—the one with you pretending to be a priest so you could live with all those girls—well, that was a friggin classic. I'll watch that one in reruns forever."

Odie slid from the desk to the floor. "Then why are you going to kill me?"

"It's not personal. It's just politics."

Odie stared in disbelief. "I haven't even been elected yet."

The thin man shrugged and held out the syringe.

Odie said, "I can't."

The big man grunted again, then hauled him up and onto the desk, laying him flat. Odie squirmed, but the big man held him firmly and growled, "You do it, Barry."

Odie looked in surprise as the big man spoke for the first time. His right eye was twitching fiercely. Odie found it oddly fascinating.

The thin man, Barry, grabbed hold of the syringe and aimed it at a vein in Odie's arm. With grim determination, Barry used a stabbing motion and poked the arm with the needle a couple of times, but couldn't seem to find the vein. It kept rolling away.

THE ONE MINUTE ASSASSIN

Odie grimaced and turned his attention back to the big man's twitching eye.

Barry tossed the syringe onto the desk and rubbed the sweat off his forehead. "Crap! I can't do it, Nails. I never done nothing like this before."

Odie felt the needle come to rest by his right hand and thought about his gun in the drawer below his left hand. Maybe he could stab Barry with the needle, then go for the gun.

Nails said, "I think you're supposed to tie that rubber thingy around his arm to make the veins pop out."

"Even if there was a bull's-eye showing me where the veins are, I don't think I could do it," Barry said. "It's Little Odie, for crying out loud."

Odie felt a glimmer of hope until he looked at Nails standing above him. *Not* an Odie fan. Nails' eye was twitching overtime now.

"You do it or I'll do it, Barry. Makes no difference," Nails said. "But either way I need the money."

Odie gasped. "You're killing me for money? Well that's easy then. I'll give you double whatever they're giving you."

Nails' eye twitched again, causing Odie to burst out, "*Triple!*"

Odie quickly turned to his favorite fan, Barry, who appeared to be giving the offer some serious thought. "Please. We can go to the bank as soon as it opens."

Barry said, "Five hundred thousand and we got a deal."

Odie blinked a few times and said, "Done."

Nails pulled Odie from the desk and set him roughly on his feet. Odie flinched as Nails twitched again.

Barry said, "Hey. To seal the deal, would you mind doing that line from *Back on the Farm*? You know…the one you said every time you got in trouble."

Odie grinned, then paused for dramatic effect and said, "Aw, shucks."

Barry smiled. "That's the one."

Odie turned to Nails and cringed when his eye did that thing again. "Would you mind putting on some sunglasses or something? That eye twitch is freaking me out."

Nails' face reddened and Barry shouted, "He didn't mean anything by it, Nails."

Odie wondered what the fuss was about as Nails rumbled toward him. He stopped wondering when a four hundred pound body slammed into him with the force of a freight train.

Odie felt himself being lifted into the air and flung backwards toward the balcony. He caught a momentary glimpse of his dog Jasper and a saddened Barry as he sailed out and over the railing.

As Odie dropped like a stone toward Hollywood Boulevard, he quickly pondered his death and the likelihood of his becoming more famous than ever after going out in such a dramatic fashion. And, having been trained in the art of using a good exit line, he called out his trademark "Awwwww, shuuuuuucks" on the way down.

The last two things Odie saw was what he hoped was an adoring crowd gazing up at him—and his own urine-soaked star on the Walk of Fame.

two

JOHN Black stared at his clients and said, "I think you and your daughter would be safer staying at a hotel tonight."

It wasn't the kind of comment he would normally make in a Starbucks. Then again, he wouldn't normally be caught dead in a place like Starbucks. But you couldn't throw a stone in Los Angeles these days without hitting one—along with a couple dozen yuppie patrons chatting on their cell phones, another thing he hated.

Unfortunately, his clients had requested it, telling him they felt comfortable here. Something about the smell of the fresh roasted coffee. Either way, John wanted to make them happy. The poor things could use a little happiness.

John hesitated, giving Mrs. Allen and her fourteen-year-old daughter, Laura, a moment for the news to sink in. Their emotions were fragile, at best. "I'm afraid your husband is on his way here to L.A."

With a shudder, Mrs. Allen said, "If you think a hotel is the best course of action, Mr. Black, we'll find a place for the night."

"Better safe than sorry," John said. "My partner and I will set up surveillance on your house and pick him up the instant he shows his face. Then straight to prison. Do not pass go—do not collect two hundred dollars." John gave them a small smile, but neither appreciated his attempt to lighten the mood.

Laura sniffled and another tear streamed down her cheek.

John resisted an impulse to wrap his arms around her and hold her tight. Crying women usually had that effect on him.

"Hey, don't cry, hon." He knew he didn't do compassion well, but decided to give it a try anyway. "Laura, you're going to be safe now. I won't let him near you, and that's a promise."

She used a napkin to wipe away her tear. Then she smiled and said, "Thanks."

How about that—he said the right thing. She actually smiled. He'd inherited some of his family's genes after all.

Mrs. Allen said, "Laura, would you mind waiting outside for a minute? I've got something I need to talk about with Mr. Black."

Laura said sure and took her double grande cappuccino outside. John frowned, pretty sure fourteen-year-olds weren't supposed to be drinking coffee, much less by the gallon. But what did he know, right? He'd never raised any rugrats of his own, though he had spent a lot of time with his niece after his sister's husband had passed away.

"Mr. Black...John...I'm not really sure how to say this."

John could see her squirming in her chair. Uncomfortable for some reason. "Please don't be nervous, Mrs. Allen. Just come straight out with it."

More squirming. "Well...the thing is...I've talked to a lawyer. And he says my husband will probably only serve a year or two. Tops. And that's just unacceptable to me."

"Tell me about it," John said. "The prisons are too damn crowded. Guys I've put away that deserved twenty years get out in three."

"Exactly, John. I knew you'd see my point." All at once she stopped squirming and her face hardened. "And I have to protect my daughter for much longer than that."

John groaned, wishing he'd seen it earlier, but now he had a pretty good idea where she was headed.

Mrs. Allen leaned in close and whispered, "I want you to kill him."

There it was. She wasn't so fragile after all. John shook his head. "I can't do that, Mrs. Allen."

"I know it sounds harsh, John. But he's a sick man. I have to protect my daughter. I *need* you to kill him."

Now John squirmed. "Mrs. Allen. It wouldn't be right. You

can't just kill people because they've wronged you."

"People do it every day."

She started to puddle up and John felt his protective instincts kick in. Twice in one day his heartstrings were being tweaked.

"John, if I wanted a Boy Scout, I would have hired a private investigator instead of a...whatever you are. I need something extra. And your reputation..."

His eyes closed to a squint. "My reputation is for protecting children."

"Of course. And please don't take offense. But my friend, the one who recommended you, said you sometimes use unusual methods to get results for your clients. *Unorthodox* methods. And that's just what I'm looking for."

John sighed. "That doesn't include killing people." It was amazing how far people would go when they were pushed. *Hell hath no fury...*

He made a mental note not to scorn women. A good rule to live by.

He was saved from answering when their conversation, along with everyone else's in the coffee house, was interrupted by a large, overly muscular man with a set of nice, sparkly white choppers. He made his grand entrance with a well-dressed posse in tow.

"Hallo everyone." His booming voice echoed off walls. "Tis good to see you all. Wit da nice faces and da happy smiles and da utter tings like dat."

His goon squad moved quickly, passing out colorful buttons and bumper stickers to everyone. John read his with amusement. *Arnold 'The Mountain' Schwarzkov for Governor. If 'The Mountain' can pulverize 'The Rock' in the wrestling arena, imagine what he can do to the State Assembly.* Ah, yes. The Hungarian / Pro-wrestler / B-movie star turned wannabe politician. A fan rushed up, eager for an autograph.

Resisting the urge to gag, John muttered under his breath, "Three-ring circus."

The Mountain continued, "Rememba to vote for me in two veeks. And since you peoples can't come to da mountain, da mountain has come to you peoples. Are der any questions you would have for me or tings of dat nature?"

John gave one look toward the man's bulging muscles and decided he couldn't resist. "Yeah. Does 'The Mountain' believe steroids should be tested for and banned from all professional sports?"

"Dat is a goot question, sir. A very goot question." The Mountain flashed his pearly whites again. "And yes, of course dey should be banned. No one should ever use da steroids or utter tings like dat. Your body is a temple."

John frowned. Schwarzkov had actually said that with a straight face. He might be a politician after all.

Another question was shouted from the other side, and when The Mountain's attention turned elsewhere, Mrs. Allen leaned toward John, bringing him back to their conversation. "So will you do it, John? For Laura?"

"No, I'm sorry. I told you I can't do that."

Mrs. Allen pushed her chair back and stood up. "Then I'm sure I can find someone else. I mean...this is Los Angeles. I read in the *Times* that L.A. ranks third in the nation in hired killers. Just behind Miami and New York City."

John looked out the window at her daughter, Laura, and was immediately reminded of his girlfriend in high school. He could even smell the soap she'd used.

He took a moment to gather his thoughts, pushing out the twenty-year-old memory of her murder. Still watching Laura, he said, "I'm sure you're right, Mrs. Allen. There are plenty of killers here. Hired or otherwise."

Mrs. Allen pursed her lips.

He tried to shake it off. It had been a while since he'd remembered Beth this strongly. He turned back to Mrs. Allen. "I can see you've got your mind made up, and I know how you feel. Really. But I'm not going to do it."

She started to walk away.

"Wait. Why don't you hear me out?"

Mrs. Allen turned around and slipped back into her chair, a hopeful expression on her face.

"I won't kill him because that wouldn't be right," he continued. "And I don't want you to have him killed. But I've got something better in mind—*unorthodox*, as you put it, but probably better. Now, this'll be up to you and your husband... he'll have a say in the matter, too. But it might actually work out for everyone involved. Especially Laura."

John leaned in and began telling her the idea.

BARRY PULLED TO A STOP IN FRONT OF THE LONG DRIVEWAY, RUBBING his eyes, wishing for the hundredth time he was a morning person. "Jeez. This is some swank house. You sure this is the right place?"

Nails looked down the rain-slicked street and checked the address carved into a marble pillar curbside. "Yeah, this is it." Nails looked around at the mansions surrounding them and grunted. "We're like the Beverly Hillbillies in this jalopy. We stand out."

"Well what do you want to do about it? My cousin's junk-yard don't carry no Rolls Royces." Barry turned off the motor to the rusted-out van, thinking his partner was a friggin ingrate but knowing it was safer to keep the thought to himself. The van sputtered for a couple of minutes before dying in a cloud of black smoke.

"We could steal one," Nails said.

"Oh yeah, right. My skills are confined to scamming people and yours are limited to smashing people. So what, now you know how to hotwire a car? Somehow, I doubt it."

Nails grunted in agreement.

Barry looked at the target house for a moment, its Roman-styled architecture seeming out of place in the civilized world, and lit a cigarette with a skull and crossbones style Zippo. "You ever think we shouldn't be doing this?"

Nails looked at him sideways. "You growing a conscience?"

Barry squirmed in his seat and shook his head. "Nah, I've always had one. But I got a special closet in my brain that I use to lock it up when I need it to quit bugging me."

"A closet?"

Barry shrugged. "A figure of speech. Anyway, you know this lady we're gonna whack? I heard her on TV last week. Eleanor Black. She's got an old name but she's not really that old, maybe pushing forty is all. She sounded pretty smart, like she knew what she was talking about. In fact, I bet she'd actually make a pretty good governor."

Nails smirked. "You probably would bet on that."

Barry reddened, wishing for a moment that Nails wasn't more than twice his weight. But when Nails' eye twitched, Barry snapped, vividly remembering Odie's death. Five hundred gees of Odie's money lost 'cause of the twitchy freak sitting beside him. "At least I'm not some science experiment gone awry."

The moment the words left his lips he knew he'd made a severe mistake. There was a rumble and Nails reached out with a beefy hand, fingers outstretched, stopping just short of Barry's pencil-neck.

Barry looked down at the seatbelt restraining his partner. *Heck. Seatbelts* do *save lives!* And here he'd always thought it was a way for the government to keep people under their thumb.

Quickly, Barry said, "Hey, Nails, I'm sorry. That was out of line. I know you can't help all that crap that happened to you."

The fingers receded, but Nails still looked fairly agitated, his eye twitching steadily, like a metronome.

Barry tried again. "You know, that idea you had back at Odie's place after he went jumping without a 'chute? Well, that was plain genius. And heck, typing that note that said 'Awww, Shucks,' just like he said on the way down, and leaving the drug stuff by the note—well that was inspired. No one even suspected it wasn't suicide."

Nails relaxed in his seat, the metronome slowing down, so Barry relaxed as well. That was too close. What the heck was Mr. S thinking, hooking him up with this four hundred pound psycho?

There was a rumble from the street as two trucks from a

party rental store and a couple of roach coaches pulled into Eleanor Black's driveway.

"What the...?" Barry dropped his cigarette in his lap and had to fish it out before crisping his privates. "What are all these people doing here at six in the morning?"

"Looks like they're setting up for a party."

"Well that's it then. We're gonna have to call this off."

Barry cringed when Nails turned the full force of his gaze toward him.

Barry said, "I'm serious. How can we cut her brakes with all these people around?"

Nails rolled his eyes, and the twitch started up again. "You don't do it now and it won't be your job anymore. Mr. S will sic the Russian boys on you. Anyway, your job just got easier, not harder. The security gate is wide open...and with all these people around setting up for a party, no one will even notice you."

Barry looked down the drive. "You think so, huh?"

Nails grunted an affirmative.

Barry grabbed his knife from under his seat. An eight inch Rambo style with serrated edges for serious cutting, kept in its sheath so he wouldn't do himself any accidental damage. Barry had never used it before, but he'd loved it since the day he'd bought it 'cause it looked so friggin cool.

He tucked it inside his coat, opened his door, and started up the driveway. He heard Nails call out after him, "Hey, don't take too long. I don't want to be here when these Bel Air security guys do a drive-by down this street."

Barry kept on, trying his hardest to look like he belonged. That was the secret to a good scam, looking like you were supposed to be there. He passed by people in white coats, bringing in chairs and whatnot, wishing he had one himself to blend in. But after one sphincter-clenching minute near all the people, he went past the trucks and further down the drive, behind the house.

He noticed a black Mercedes parked in front of a garage. Maybe it was a garage. He wasn't sure because the thing was four times bigger than his house.

Jeez! It was a garage.

And there was a friggin Olympic-sized pool with naked Greek statues and shit pissing into the water. He'd been feeling bad before about whacking a lady who might actually be good at running this state. But now, no friggin way. "The witch is rolling in dough while I'm up to my ears in debt. West Coast, money-grubbing skank."

Barry pulled the knife out and scrunched under the car, appreciating for the first time that his frame was thin and substandard. No one he knew could have fit underneath the car, and he wondered for a moment if he'd missed his calling. Maybe he should have been a thief, slipping into places no one else could.

But if there was one thing he'd learned over the years, there was always someone better at stuff than he was. If he'd tried a little breaking and entering, then some circus freak or Chinese acrobat would have come along and taken his job—just like every other job he'd ever had. No. Better to just take what came his way and wait patiently for an opportunity for the big score.

He looked around for the brake line, thankful his cousin had showed him what to look for back at the junkyard, and started sawing away. After a couple of minutes with the jagged knife not doing much to the line, he tested the edge on his finger and almost sliced it off. He muffled a scream as blood spurted onto his clothes and the driveway.

He started whacking away at the brake line, using the knife like a hatchet, and finally cut through the line. Brake fluid squirted into the gash on his finger, causing him to scream again.

He shuffled out from under the car and squeezed his wound closed, hoping to staunch the bleeding.

"Hey! What are you doing to my mom's car?"

Barry jumped, regained control of his bodily functions, and turned to see a young, bikini-clad hottie rushing his way. Jail bait. This was the last thing he needed, what with his finger bleeding all over the place and him having just committed a felony. He pulled the big knife out, hoping to scare her away, but when he did, he heard an ear piercing shriek to his right.

Jeez. Another one. He charged the new bikini-girl, since she was blocking the drive, and saw her dive out of the way as he ran past. Huffing and puffing, wishing he didn't smoke two packs a day, he raced down the cement road.

All the caterers must've been inside because he didn't see another soul till he got to the van. And never had another man looked so good.

Nails shook his head. "You're such an idiot."

three

WHERE is this idiot? Drumming his fingers on the dash-board, John rolled down his window and took a deep breath, enjoying the short hiatus from the smog and forgetting, for half a second, about the child molester he was hunting.

Los Angeles cleaned up pretty nice, he decided—once the filth of humanity was temporarily washed away. Of course, it took some major help from a summer storm—and around midnight it would turn back into a pumpkin—but right now things seemed perfect. The unpolluted air was brought about by negative ions sweeping the sky clean, or so he'd read. Some-thing positive from something negative—which was good any way you looked at it.

He kept watch on the overpriced West Hollywood houses off Sunset Boulevard as the mauve tint from the rising sun made the swanky neighborhood look even better than usual. Like looking through rose-colored glasses. Probably why no one around here figured they had to worry about this kind of security issue, like they didn't get child molesters in *their* neighborhood. Then again, maybe they simply weren't pay-ing attention.

John watched the joggers with their three hundred dol-lar running shoes, and the people walking their dogs—and shook his head. With all the money these people made, you'd think they could come up with a better way to remove their dog's steaming piles of crap than a plastic baggie that covered their hand. Not that money ever made anyone smarter.

As he surveyed the area, the clumsy gait of the approaching jogger put John on alert. It was a little too spastic, like the guy had never been jogging before in his life. And if it was John's guy, he probably hadn't. His type was more into liposuction than physical effort.

John reached over the seatback of his Suburban and lifted the binoculars off his snoring partner, Harley. Through the glass, he noticed a price tag hanging off one of the running shoes and a fake mustache hanging off the guy's lip. John grabbed the dossier and compared the picture to the pseudo-jogger. Facial hair notwithstanding, it was him. Rodney Allen—asshole extraordinaire.

Score one for the good guys, John thought. He felt goose bumps forming on his arms. No matter how many times he and Harley turned the tables on a predator, it felt damn good every time.

John started as his leathery, white-haired friend woke with a flatulent expulsion that doubled as a natural alarm clock. Nice.

"Crikey. Kick open a window back here, would ya John?"

John hit the windows, as Harley requested, but kept his eyes trained on Rodney Allen as he hurried up the driveway. John cracked a smile, glad he'd sent Laura and Mrs. Allen to a hotel for the night.

"Must've been that buffalo steak I et last night." Harley leaned forward and followed John's gaze. "That the 'Father of the Year,' is it?"

John gave a tiny shake of his head at Harley's dark, Aussie sense of humor. "Yeah, that's him."

"How you want to play it with this sick bastard?"

John thought about it for a bit, then said, "Well, probably like the Phoenix job five years ago. Mrs. Allen wants to go the 'therapeutic' route, if Rodney's up for it. If not, she's going to hire someone to kill him."

"She said that?" Harley scrunched up his eyebrows. "This bloke'll never go for the therapy. Jus' look at 'im. He thinks he's smarter than everyone."

John shrugged. "Then we'll have to convince him it's the smart choice." He put his hand on the door, ready.

The moment Rodney entered the house, John left the cover

of the Suburban's tinted windows and headed up the drive. He thumbed the safety off his .38 and paused behind an oak tree, allowing Harley time to get in position at the rear of the house.

After a five count, John slipped through the unlocked door and stopped in the tiled entryway, listening for any sounds. Nothing. To his left was Rodney's den, sporting a young doe on the wall and a couple of stuffed foxes and squirrels. The mighty hunter.

On the desk was a picture of Rodney Allen shaking hands with the President. And another of him shaking hands with fellow lobbyist Richard Steel, one of the frontrunners in the current gubernatorial recall election. So Rodney Allen was a lobbyist *and* a child molester. John shook his head. That's two strikes.

There were a couple of thumps from above and John heard Rodney heading down the stairs. John hid his gun behind his back and pulled out his ID.

Rodney froze, two steps from the bottom, spying John by the door. On his head he sported girl's pink panties for a hat.

John halted when he saw the panties, attempting to get his emotions under control. *Sick bastard.* Out loud, he said, "Mr. Allen, my name is John Black, of Black / Harley Enterprises. Your wife hired me..."

At the word "wife," Rodney Allen shrieked and fled down the hall, ripping the panties from his head in the process. *Typical.* John took off after him, following close behind. At the end of the hall, Rodney ran through the mudroom and grabbed the door handle for the back door.

John said, "Rodney! Don't open that."

Rodney flung open the door, then shrieked again as the doorframe splintered from Harley's three quick shots from outside. Rodney slammed it shut and turned toward John. When he saw John's gun, his eyes bugged out and he shut the door between the hallway and the mudroom.

John groaned. "Rodney. Come out of there."

"No! And don't come in here! I've got a gun!"

"Hey. Settle down. If I've got to dig you out of there, things are bound to get messy."

"No way! I didn't do it!"

"Look, Rodney, I've seen the evidence your wife has gathered. And it sickens me. I'm personally going to make sure you don't get away with it."

"You want to kill me!"

John sighed, thinking things would be a heck of lot easier if he was willing to kill Rodney. But no. It was time to sweet talk him—keep this from getting out of hand.

"Well, of course I want to kill you, Rodney. Who wouldn't? And if you'd touched my niece the way you touched your daughter, we wouldn't even be having this conversation 'cause my partner would've plugged *you* three times instead of the doorway."

"*What?*"

Of course, sweet talking wasn't his strong suit.

Harley's voice, muffled from outside, was still discernible. "I wouldn't mind killing this bloke now."

"What? Oh, my God!"

John tried again. "Your wife didn't hire us to kill you." *Though she wanted to.* "She just wants her daughter safe. No one has to die."

Rodney quieted down, sniffling, and John had a hard time making out his muffled voice from behind the door. John was pretty sure he said, "How do I know you're not lying?"

Because I'm not one of your buddy politicians, John thought. Not that he was bitter about politics.

He pulled out a business card and slipped it under the door. "Take a look at my card, Rodney. Tell me what it says about our specialty."

Sniff. "It says 'Black / Harley Enterprises specializes in Child Protection Services.'" Sniff.

"That's right. That means we track down deadbeat dads mostly. A few times a year we catch a parent who has kidnapped the child from the other parent. And thank god *this* kind of disgusting job only comes around maybe once a year."

Sniff. "What's that supposed to mean?"

Another trait John knew he lacked was patience with idiots or scumbags. He pounded once on the door. "It means if you don't get out here in three seconds, your wife will end up collecting on your life insurance policy."

The door opened a crack. "I didn't want to do it. I can't help it."

John grimaced. "Do I look like your therapist?" They always tried to tell their side of the story—which was easy to ignore since they always lied. "Slide your piece toward me."

Rodney raised his hands as he stepped through the doorway. "I don't have a gun."

"Oh, you're a tricky one, are you?" Harley said as he slipped inside, his Colt .45 and homemade silencer trained on Rodney.

Rodney jumped, apparently unaware that Harley had snuck up behind him.

Harley said, "You know, Rodney. You can consider yourself lucky this is John's deal. I would've taken you out and not thought twice about it. Personally, I think the world would be a better place without you. In fact, maybe you can't tell, but it's taking me a mighty heroic effort just to keep from pulling this trigger."

Rodney's eyes popped out, attempting a grand escape from his skull.

Harley gave him a crocodile smile. "But no worries, eh? I've got plenty of willpower. You're in good hands."

John watched as Rodney started shaking. Harley often had that effect on people when he spoke from the heart. John found it kind of endearing.

Harley gave a nod to him. "Well done, John." With a grin, he said, "You know you've got a smooth tongue when you want to. Must be genetic, eh, mate?"

There was that Aussie humor again. Five years of training under Harley and fifteen partnering with him, and John still didn't appreciate his sense of humor.

Rodney looked at his feet and mumbled to himself, "I don't want to go to jail."

John smiled. *Now comes the hard part.*

Harley took his cue, cocking his thumb toward Rodney. "Hey, John. You haven't told him about my keen therapy idea?"

"Nah. There's no way he'll do it. He's not the brightest bulb on the tree."

Rodney perked up a bit.

"Well, obviously, mate. But all his options are shitty right now. And even idiots don't want be caged."

Rodney looked back and forth between them, a hopeful expression on his face.

John decided to turn it up a notch. "I know he doesn't want to go to jail. But does he want to stop the stuff with his daughter? That's the question. You know as well as I do that there's no way he could take the treatment if he didn't really *want* to stop."

Rodney broke in. "Hey, I do want to stop. I'm up for it. Whatever you're talking about, I'm in."

Harley clapped his arm around Rodney. "See, John, I told you he's a gamer. He can take a little pain to stay out of prison. Am I right, Rodney?"

Rodney frowned. John gestured toward the kitchen table and they all took a seat. A nice comfortable conversation.

John said, "I'm not gonna bullshit you, Rodney, the treatment is going to hurt. But Harley's therapy has a ninety-five percent success rate, so it's worth doing if you're man enough."

Rodney stammered, "What...what is it?"

John looked him in the eye. "You don't have any good alternatives, Rodney. With the evidence your wife has, your best case scenario is going to prison. With overcrowding, you'll probably serve a year...maybe two."

Rodney said, "That might not be so bad."

John frowned, wishing Rodney would use his brains. "You're not thinking things through. First off, your career as a lobbyist will be over. What big corporation or politician will come near you with a conviction like that? And second, you'll never see your family again. You'll be a pariah. Trying to get a job at Burger King with a severe criminal record and not having much luck."

Rodney shivered.

John continued, "Look, for some reason your wife still loves you. She's mad as hell, and wants things fixed, but she still cares about you. That's why she wants you to try our program. It'll leave you changed, maybe even broken. But not destroyed."

"But what is it?"

John paused. Rodney was just about ready for it. "Did you know that child molesters have the highest rate of recidivism compared to any other criminals?"

When Rodney looked confused, Harley piped up, "That means they repeat their crimes almost every time. Even after they go to prison. Like they can't help themselves."

"That's right," John said. "And that burns us up. So Harley came up with a radical idea when he was in 'Nam. A modification to the harsh punishment they used in a village over there."

"Trying to make something positive out of something negative," Harley said.

John blinked. He'd been thinking the same thing a little earlier. Probably why they were good partners.

Rodney turned from Harley to John. "But what is it?"

"It's painful, Rodney, that's what it is. But the treatment works, so shut up and listen," John said. "When I was seventeen, and first started working with Harley, I thought he was some ex-military whacko. You know, one of those guys the army had trained a little too well. But when I met a couple of his success stories—people just like you, Rodney—I got off my high horse. Harley's methods are crude, but effective."

"What did they do in the Vietnamese village?"

Harley piped in, "Same as in lots of countries. Chop off the offending parts of people's bodies. Like cutting the hands off a thief."

Rodney recoiled and shoved his hands under the table, instinctively covering his privates. "You want to cut off my... hands?"

"'Course not," Harley said. "Crikey, we're not barbarians. That's a bit harsh for thieves, I would think. But you're not a thief now, are you?"

Rodney nodded. To his credit, John thought he looked ashamed.

"There's two parts to my treatment. Part one is physical," Harley said. "Since you used your hands for your evil misdeeds...and not Mr. Winky...I put a bullet through each palm. And after a few months of healing, you'll get the use of your fingers back. But they'll *always* hurt when you move 'em. A little reminder, like, not to use 'em for the wrong things."

Rodney hesitated.

John read Rodney's body language and decided he needed a little more of a push.

"It's purely voluntary, Rodney, but we're hoping you go for the treatment. And not just for your daughter's sake. Or society's. It'll be better for you in the long run, too. Child molesters don't do well in prison. Once word spreads in there, you'll either be dead, or wish you were."

Rodney shuddered. "Okay. I'll do it."

With an easy smile, John said, "Good choice. My partner will even patch you up afterwards."

When Rodney looked skeptical, John added, "He's a trained field surgeon."

John pushed some papers in front of Rodney. "Of course, you'll have to sign these divorce papers granting your wife full custody of your daughter. You'll have supervised visitation only, when and if your daughter is ready for it."

"Of course." Rodney gave it a cursory glance and signed it. As he did, Harley tossed a thick envelope onto the table. Rodney glanced up. "What's this?"

Harley said, "That's part two of my treatment. Those photos raised my success rate with you guys from fifty-five percent to ninety-five percent, so you better take a look at 'em."

Rodney opened up the envelope and gasped. Then he started to retch. "What the hell is this?"

"That's what happens if you ever do it again," Harley said. "That poor bastard failed the treatment program. And failure is unacceptable, if you take my meaning. I take it personally."

John winced, feeling a moment of sympathy for Rodney. He'd looked at the photos once twenty years ago, when Harley had been trying to scare him out of working with him. And they still gave him nightmares.

Harley leaned in, a glint in his eye. "That's what I'll do to you if you mess up. You believe me?"

Rodney nodded violently. He stopped retching long enough to spit out, "Let's get this over with before I lose my nerve."

"Don't worry. It'll turn out." John pulled a dishtowel off the stove and tossed it to Rodney. "Stuff it in your mouth. It'll help to have something to bite down on."

Harley said, "Yeah. And it'll muffle your screams."

Rodney whimpered for a moment before a calm seemed to come over him—like he'd accepted his penance. He shoved the rag in till his cheeks puffed out like a chipmunk.

Harley grasped Rodney's left wrist, held it on the table, and placed the muzzle about six inches from Rodney's palm. Harley gave him a wink, then thumbed the hammer back.

Rodney turned away and screwed his eyes shut.

Instead of a shot, they all heard the electronic sound of 'N Sync, or some other boy band, coming from John's cell phone. It was hard to tell which one. John looked at his phone in disgust. He'd programmed the thing with Beethoven's Fifth.

A snigger from Harley got his attention. Aussie sense of humor.

John saw his niece's number on the caller ID and immediately started worrying. She *never* called him on the cell because she knew how much he hated using the darn thing. "Sorry, Rodney. I've got to take this. You mind holding on for a minute?"

Rodney sighed, apparently happy for the momentary reprieve.

John took a couple of steps away for a little privacy and hit the green button on his phone. "Hey, Hillary. Everything all right?"

John heard her sobbing.

"No! Someone tried to kill Mom this morning."

John almost dropped the phone. "Is she okay?"

"Yeah…she's fine. But she's being stubborn as hell." Another sob. "I need to talk to you, Uncle John."

"I'm on my way. Where are you?"

"The Rose Café."

"I'll be there in twenty minutes. Hang on till I get there, Hillary. Okay?"

Sniffles. Then, "Okay."

John hung up the phone and started pacing.

Harley said, "Is she all right, John?"

"Yeah. I think so. But I've got to go. Can you handle things here…and stitch him up?"

"Yeah, sure. No worries."

John turned to Rodney. "I hope I don't see you again, Rodney. Do it right this time."

Rodney nodded. John grabbed the divorce papers off the table, then turned and ran to the front door. As he reached it, he heard the sound of a muzzled shot and Rodney's muffled cry.

four

JOHN turned off Santa Monica Boulevard, doing fifty, then squeaked past a Hummer wallowing in the right lane. A BMW darted in front of him, blocking him in, and he had to brake to avoid squashing the Beamer like a bug.

He told himself to relax, then dried his sweaty hands on his jeans and decided to ease off the gas. After all, Hillary had said Eleanor was all right.

He racked his brains, trying to find a reason someone would try to kill his older sister, but came up empty. Eleanor was the respectable one of the family—smooth, likable, and an all-around friendly gal. Hell, that's what got her where she was today. According to statistics, the most likely suspect would have been a disgruntled husband, if she'd had one. But as a widow, she hadn't had the pleasure of a nasty divorce.

That left one likely prospect. Politics. Fucking politics.

Breaking from his reverie, John was pleasantly surprised to find a parking space a half block from the restaurant. After feeding the meter, he chirped the alarm on his car and hoofed it to the door, taking in the wonderful, salty smell of the beach one block over. That smell always brought him back to his childhood.

"Hey, Uncle John. Over here."

John stopped at the door and turned back toward the patio dining area. His niece, Hillary, waved from a table by the street. He'd run right past her. *More worried than I realized.*

When he got a closer view of Hillary, he had to suppress a frown. His fifteen-year-old niece had enough skin showing to be in a Victoria's Secret catalog. Skimpy shorts that seemed to be cut below her hips and an extremely revealing top. Seemed like yesterday she was playing with her Barbie doll, not trying to look like one.

Hillary gave him a hug and a peck on the cheek. "This is my friend, Amber."

Amber reached over and gave him a hug, too,surprising him. There was something familiar about her appearance, but he couldn't place her. John quickly averted his gaze. Her clothes were even more revealing than Hillary's. "Where's your mom, Hillary? Did she drop you off?"

"No. Amber brought me. She just got her license." Hillary's eyes began to fill with tears, but she blinked them back. "Mom doesn't even know I'm talking to you. She's pretending nothing happened."

John frowned. Eleanor was always the stubborn one. "Exactly what did happen?"

Amber's eyes sparkled. "Just your everyday, typical assassination attempt."

Hillary rolled her eyes, but John ignored Amber's obvious enthusiasm and motioned for Hillary to go on.

"Well, I was crossing the backyard, headed for the pool like I do every morning when it's summer, when I saw this really creepy looking man with buggy eyes slide out from underneath Mommy's car."

John's brow furrowed. "From underneath? There's not a lot of clearance on a Mercedes."

"This man was skinny, Uncle John. Flagpole skinny. String bean skinny."

Amber added her two cents. "Thinner than an anorexic supermodel."

"You saw him, too?"

"No doubt." She leaned forward and put her hand on John's thigh. "He was creepy skinny."

John jumped, then reached out to remove her hand, but she moved it away first.

Hillary said, "Amber was late for our swim date, as usual."

"I'm not following you," John said.

"That's okay, John." Amber giggled. "But better late than never. Right, Hillary?"

"No shit," Hillary said. She quickly covered her mouth. "Sorry, Uncle John. What I meant was…if she hadn't shown up, I might be dead right now."

John threw up his hands. On a good day, conversation with a teenager was hit and miss. Talking to two of them, one with roving hands, John felt out of his league. "I'm still not following you. Except for the fact that there was a string bean under the car."

Amber giggled again.

Hillary said, "What happened was I ran over to confront the guy."

John gave her his hard fatherly look, or a reasonable facsimile. "You charged a stranger who was lurking around your house?"

"You know, looking back, that doesn't seem too bright, does it?" Hillary said. "Especially when he pulled the knife."

Amber put her hand on John's knee again. "And that's when I arrived, John. I saw the knife and screamed bloody murder. The thin man took off like a jackrabbit."

As she gave him a squeeze, John firmly pulled her hand away.

Hillary said, "Jeez, leave him alone, Amber. Sorry, Uncle John, she's a little oversexed these days."

John frowned. "At sixteen?"

Amber leaned back in her chair, crossed her arms, and started to pout. John smiled. That probably worked on guys her own age.

"That's when I looked under the car and saw a big puddle," Hillary said. "Mom tried to keep it from me, but I overheard her tell her campaign manager it was brake fluid."

"Okay, now I'm on the same page. But why doesn't your mom know you're here with me?"

"Because she doesn't want to 'derail her campaign' or lose focus." Hillary rolled her eyes in dramatic fashion. "You know how she is. She's ahead in the polls and doesn't want the attempt to distract voters from her 'message.'"

John thought it over. "So she doesn't want me to know about it, either. Eleanor probably hired a couple of extra goons from the security company she uses and thinks she's taken care of it."

"You got it."

John shook his head. "Sometimes it's hard to believe she's the smart one in the family."

Hillary started to puddle up. "On Tuesday it'll be six years...*six* years since Dad died."

John reached out to hold her hand. "I know, honey."

Hillary stopped crying and brushed away her tears. "Uncle John, please do something to help Mom. Please."

"You know I will. But your mom can be stubborn sometimes. She's not going to want my help."

Hillary sniffled. "I know." She thought about it for a moment. "We're having a huge fundraiser at the house tonight. What if I got you on the guest list?"

John smiled. "That would be great. And who knows, maybe if your mom sees me hanging around she'll decide she wants my help."

Hillary leaned in and gave him a hug. "Thanks, Uncle John. I can always count on you."

Amber reached around and gave them both a hug, momentarily grabbing his rear end. This time, John had to laugh. The girl was tenacious.

Reddening, Amber said, "We gotta ditch, Hillary. Places to go...people to see..."

Hillary giggled. "Oh, yeah. Keith and Rick. Yum."

John frowned. "Yum? Who are Keith and Rick?"

Now Amber giggled as she dragged Hillary down the street toward her red convertible. "Bye, John. Nice to see you again."

"Does your mom know about Keith and Rick?" John called out after them.

The girls ignored him and took off, leaving John alone with his thoughts. *There goes trouble.*

He turned his thoughts to his sister's predicament, trying

to figure out a way to help her. His mind bogged down almost immediately as a beater car, with a stereo worth ten times what the car cost, pulled up next to the café, the bass booming from inside. Apparently deaf teenagers were driving, because the sound was deafening to John from outside the vehicle.

By itself the noise pollution would've been enough to distract him from clear planning, but when the occupants spilled out, their boxers showing and their pants down around their hips, John decided it was time to head back to the nice, quiet, solitude of home.

And figure out a way to help his sister whether she wanted his help or not.

five

BARRY thrashed around on the couch for a moment, murmuring "No, Odie, no," before his eyes popped open and he screamed out, *"Lassie, go home!"*

He looked around wildly, but couldn't find either the collie or his first official homicide victim. Just the same rundown hole of an apartment where Nails lived—if you could call it living—piled high with pizza boxes and beer cans, the kitchen so full of them that you could barely reach the fridge.

Barry wiped the sweat from his brow and gave a quick prayer to Buddha or Jesus or whoever might be listening, begging for normal dreams once in a while.

Nails grunted, then clicked the TV volume up a few notches and turned away, his eye twitching something fierce. "Dude. You're messed up. You're the only guy I know who can have a nightmare while taking a nap."

Barry blinked a few times. "This from the walking, talking, refrigerator-sized, medical experiment."

The second he said it, he knew he'd blown it, like stepping off the curb right in front of a Mac truck. As Nails heaved his bulk from the sadly indented couch, Barry started to panic. Visions of Odie's swan dive danced in his head. "No. I don't mean you, Nails. This was the dream I was talking about. The dream! There was this giant Petri dish, right? This science experiment gone whacko…"

Nails sat back down on the couch, tossing an empty can toward the pile in the kitchen. He popped open a fresh one. "I don't wanna hear about it."

Barry relaxed back into his couch, glad to have dodged the bullet, but wondering how the heck an ex-pro football player could be so friggin sensitive. Probably time to get his meds adjusted again. "Hey, Nails. You think my dream was trying to tell me something? Like something psychological?"

Nails snorted.

"I'm telling ya, those two hot girls by the Mercedes—the ones that kept us from killing Black—they were in this dream. See, I was making out with 'em when they turned into Odie and some kind of Lassie look-alike. Naturally, this had me freaking out, but when I tried to shoot 'em they started screaming like those teenage girls."

Barry paused. "I'm serious, man. Lassie was screaming like a girl. You think that means something?"

"Yeah. You're a nutcase. Now shut up."

Barry shook his head. "No, that ain't it. I think it means there's something wrong with the way we're doing this. Like we need to change things up."

"No kidding. We had a hard time with Odie, and then a complete miss on Black. We don't get her taken care of soon... Mr. S and the Russians will be all over us like priests on an altar boy."

Barry felt his stomach lurch. "Look, we definitely gotta make 'em happy. But I'm just saying we should be looking for a bigger score here. You heard what Odie offered us before he made that unfortunate comment about you. Five hundred gees is big time."

Nails grunted.

"Maybe we should try to blackmail these guys before we kill them."

"That's extortion, not blackmail."

Barry shrugged. "Whatever. They got money is what I'm saying, whether they was born with it or they got it for their campaign. And I'm tired of being the peon with barely two nickels to rub together. We're making peanuts here while Mr. S is gonna make millions off of this deal."

"Fifty thousand a pop ain't peanuts."

"It ain't millions, either." Barry watched Nails' face as he thought it over, hoping Nails would see the bigger picture. "The boss always makes the money while we always take the risk. Just like every other business in the world where the little guy—the workers—get screwed. Since we can't unionize on account of what kind of jobs we got, we need to find a way to take a little extra for ourselves."

Nails' alarm on his watch went off. His eyes lit up as he shut it off and pulled a little satchel from under the couch. Barry watched the familiar ritual with mild fascination as Nails grabbed four blue prescription pills, popped them in his mouth, and then grabbed a syringe with a four inch needle and jabbed it into his right knee. Barry winced as the needle went in, wishing he'd waited to tell Nails about his idea until the happy juice had done its job.

"First of all," Nails said, "Mr. S would find out about it."

"How would he? As soon as the mark pays up, we kill him. Dead guys are famous for keeping their mouths shut."

"But there'd be a record of all that money missing."

"So what? It could've been their campaign manager, their wife...who knows?"

"It's gambling, Barry. Which is what got you into this mess in the first place. It's not..."

Nails stopped in mid-sentence and began to smile as the juice kicked in. Barry smiled right along with him, knowing he'd be a little more agreeable now.

"Everything in this world is a gamble, Nails. We just got to make sure this is a safe bet we're talking about. And we only gotta make it work with one of 'em and it'll be like winning the lottery."

Nails' smile widened and his eyes glazed over. "Yeah, maybe."

"Look, I'll work on a plan. If I come up with something that I think will work, I'll let you know."

Nails leaned back onto the couch, his weight causing it to bend backwards until it pushed against the wall. His eyes jolted open for a moment. "But we got to take care of Black right away. No more screw-ups."

"I got an idea for that already."

"We should burn down her mansion while she's eating dinner."

Barry grimaced. "That's cold, man. I already told you I

didn't want to do anybody with fire. It's hard enough killing all these people. We got to make it as painless as possible if I'm gonna be able to do this. That way I won't feel so bad about it."

"Pansy."

"Whatever. It's what helps me sleep at night. Quick and painless, like cutting her brakes for a quick car crash, or the heroin we were gonna give Odie."

"They're still dead."

Nails started nodding off from the pills. Taking a deep breath, Barry decided to quit arguing and tell him his plan before Nails passed out.

"I got this buddy who does special effects in the movies," Barry said.

Nails rubbed at his face, scrunching his cheek. "Like computers?"

"No. Like mechanical effects on the movie sets. He's a pyro guy—loves to blow stuff up. I met him when I was doing a one year stretch for armed robbery. He doesn't have his pyro license anymore since he went to the joint, so now he's an assistant, but he still knows what he's doing. And he's got a rig that'll blow a tire by remote control while the car's doing sixty miles an hour. Blammo—car crash all over again."

"Sweet."

"Yeah." Barry thought about it for a moment. "But we'll still need a backup plan. 'Cause if we blow it again, we're dead meat."

six

JOHN turned off Topanga Canyon onto the private dirt road leading toward his home, windows open on his Suburban, soaking up the solitude like rays of sunshine—appreciating, as always, the only perk he truly enjoyed about being born into a wealthy political family. His two-bedroom 'shack on stilts' that lay hidden in the hills was probably worth close to a million these days, something way out of the range of his own personal wealth. But the natural forest and stream surrounding his place were the only things that kept him sane sometimes.

It wasn't that he detested the horrific traffic when driving anywhere in L.A., or the jerk-offs that peppered the landscape like so many bird droppings. Who didn't? But those were facts of life in SoCal. The problem was that he could only stand so much of it before he needed to decompress. Recharge his batteries.

He pulled into his carport and shut off the engine, half-listening to the raucous noise of the blue jays nearby, but mostly worrying about the danger his niece had been in this morning. Thinking about possible suspects that might wish his sister dead. As he stepped out of his car, the blue jays abruptly stopped screeching. In the silence, at the edge of his vision, he noticed a dark shape launch from the roof toward him.

Out of reflex, John moved away from the kick aimed at his head, avoiding most of the impact but taking a small glancing blow to the chin and rolling with the force, away from his attacker. He tried to regain his balance, but barely raised his head when the figure came at him with a series of Hapkido-style attacks.

John ducked under the first blow, turned aside the second, then switched to Tae Kwon Do when the assailant did as well. Between defenses, John managed a peek at the face of his black clothed, silver-haired attacker.

Silver-haired?

With a sigh, John quickly stepped back three paces, leading his adversary forward and building momentum. When his foe rushed toward him, John used a Judo move, along with the momentum of his attacker, to throw him onto the front porch. Harley crashed into the front door and lay there panting.

John panted along with him. That Aussie humor again.

"That gets really old, Harley."

"Crikey. I almost had you there, John. I trained you better than that."

John rose and gave Harley a hand up, then walked inside and sat down, wincing as his back cracked. The Pink Panther training exercises had been exciting as hell when he was a teenager and had first met up with Harley. Hell, he'd actually been looking for violence after Beth's ugly death, and probably searching for a father figure as well. And there it was in the form of Harley, ex-sniper for the army, martial arts expert, and most important—the private investigator who caught Beth's killer.

John shook his head. *But that was then.* Even in his twenties the fight training had still been fun, but at thirty-seven, everything hurt for days after one of these training episodes. He frowned at his solid oak door. "You gouged my front door."

Harley grinned. "Price you pay for success, eh mate?"

John couldn't help but grin back. The psycho grandpa from hell had grown on him over the years.

Harley grabbed a beer from the fridge and called over his shoulder, "How's little Hillary?"

"She's all right, I guess. A bit shook up from her run-in with the homemade assassin."

"Homemade?"

John mulled it over for a bit. "Well, I don't think this guy is a pro. If he'd been casing the place, he'd have noticed that Hillary swims at the same time every morning—that she walks right past the garage to get to the pool. And cutting the brakes? That's right out of a movie."

"Much more of a sure thing to pop 'em from two hundred yards with a deer rifle. That's the way I do it."

John hesitated. Joking, right? "Eleanor's security team is for shit, but she won't want me around making a mess of her campaign."

Harley snorted. "Like you did with your Mum's senatorial campaign?"

John frowned. "The press blew that way out of proportion."

Harley stopped snorting long enough to spit out, "I know. Sorry, mate. But it would be hard to make a mess out of something as ridiculous as this recall election. Every movie star, rap star…Crikey, even ladies of the evening and their pimp-daddies seem to be running. A hundred and twenty-three candidates was the final tally, right?"

John shook his head. "One hundred and twenty-one, now. Two have died in the last week."

Harley raised a bushy, silver eyebrow.

John met his gaze. "It could be murder, but I don't think so. The first candidate died of a heart attack on live television. That's way too sophisticated for a killer who cuts car brakes with a Bowie knife and runs from two screaming teenagers."

Harley snorted his agreement. "What about Odie? I loved that show he did when he was kid."

"Suicide note and enough drugs to O.D. at the scene." John hesitated. "But I guess he could have been helped off the balcony. It's possible anyway. Why don't you check with your buddy at the precinct. Let me know if there's any doubt about the cause of death that hasn't leaked to the papers."

"No worries, John. I'll take care of it."

John thought about it some more. "Most likely it was one of the bastards she blocked on the city council. Or one of the developers they're working with. As mayor of Los Angeles, Eleanor probably needs to go with the flow more and quit trying to buck the system."

Harley chuckled. "Only if she doesn't want to die."

John ignored the attempt at humor and sighed, knowing his partner was right.

NAILS TRUDGED ALONG BEHIND BARRY, GIMPING ALONG AS best he could, weaving his way through stacks and stacks of junked cars. Apparently, the town of Sunland, California, was where cars wanted to go when they died. Besides the thousands littering the junkyard owned by Barry's cousin, there were a dozen more car cemeteries in a five mile radius.

Nails grunted. What the hell was the matter with everybody? Treating cars like they were disposable diapers. Filling landfills with giant hunks of steel. What the hell would they do with they ran out of room for all the dead cars? He'd read that Los Angeles County alone had twenty-three million registered cars on the road. Not even counting all the cars with no tags driven by the illegals and whatnot.

There was a pause in Barry's monologue, which Nails hadn't been paying attention to, so he gave Barry a grunt for a response.

"When you meet this pyro guy, try to be cool," Barry said. "He's a little touched. All those guys are."

"Whatever," Nails said, ignoring Barry again. That skinny cracker could talk non-stop till the twenty-second century. Not for the first time, Nails wondered why the hell Mr. S had partnered him with this fool. Homeboy was so skinny, he reminded Nails of a rectal thermometer, which was the last thing he ever wanted to think about.

To get his mind off the subject, Nails looked around for one of those cool crushing machines that squished the cars into cubes the size of small refrigerators. He'd seen one on cable last week and thought it was pretty awesome. But even with the way they compacted 'em in those machines, it would still take a place the size of Las Vegas to store all the dead cars and other garbage.

Whatever. It ain't my kids that'll suffer. Kids weren't in his future, courtesy of the side effects of the latest experimental medication he was on.

With a grimace, he remembered when he got out of the shower last month—a moment that could have given him nightmares like that idiot, Barry—the moment when he looked down and couldn't find *any* of his private parts. He'd about had a heart attack.

For a man of his girth, it was hard to see his goodies on any given day, but bend as he might, he couldn't find a damn thing. Approaching panic, he'd punched out the mirror on the medicine cabinet and held a sliver of the glass next to his privates, angling the reflection until he could see them.

And there they were, not gone, but maybe just as bad. His grapes had shrunk and shriveled till they turned into raisins, and his hot dog had turned into a cocktail wienie. He'd bawled like a baby for three straight hours, cursing his bum knee as well as the half-dozen quacks who'd given him experimental pain meds over the last decade.

Nails grumbled, "Messed up world if a man's gotta choose between his pecker and walking."

Barry stopped in his tracks. "Come again?"

Had he said that out loud? Nails snapped his mouth shut and moved past Barry into a little clearing, surrounded by mountains of cars on all sides. As he took a step into the clearing, a wild-eyed Jethro missing three fingers on his right hand came running toward him, screaming at him like a cop or something.

"*Stop!* Don't move!"

As the man raced toward him, Nails grabbed him by the throat and casually lifted him off the ground. "And why should I give a rat's ass what some wimpy little redneck wants me to do?"

The man sputtered for a second, gasping for air, before managing to squeeze out, "Because you're about…to step on…a two gallon…gasoline bomb…mixed with…a little Remex flash powder."

Nails looked down at his right foot, which was only a couple of inches from a device that did indeed look like it might be a gasoline bomb—four large baggies filled with liquid, an electronic device with colored wires sprouting from it, and a small baggy packed with a sparkly powder sat surrounding the electronics.

Nails felt his eye start to twitch—like it always did when he was stressed, courtesy of an earlier experimental medication—as he put the guy down and stepped quickly away from the thing. "Sorry, dude. My bad."

As the man coughed a couple of times, Barry came up and clapped him on the shoulder. "Hey, Sparky. Good to see you."

Ahh, the dude they were here to meet for the tire gizmo.

Sparky turned to Nails with a look approaching adoration. "That was amazing, the way you picked me up like that. Like you were Darth Vader or something."

Nails grunted. A sci-fi nerd with explosives. His luck was getting better and better. "Why the hell were you building a bomb in this junkyard?"

Sparky's brow furrowed. "Well, you guys were late...and I like to keep busy. You know how it is."

The guy was a freak and a geek. "Not really," Nails said.

"Hey, Sparky," Barry said. "You might remember Nails here from the Raiders. 1996 Rookie of the Year..."

"...Denny Nalen! Oh, man. You were awesome. You won Rookie of the Year by a landslide, despite blowing out your knee in the fourteenth game. That's how great you were. It's an honor to meet you, Nails."

Sparky rushed up and pumped his hand a dozen times. Nails actually found himself smiling, something he couldn't remember doing in years, and felt a little shame for his snap judgment about the guy. Even freaks had their good points. Something to remember.

Barry said, "I hate to cut into the love fest here, but you got our gizmo?"

"Yeah, it's over here."

Sparky led them to what looked like a sixties Mustang, though it was hard to tell with all the body damage. He reached underneath the one good fender and tugged hard to remove something. He pulled out a contraption of little pipes, like a pan flute, and set it on the hood.

"This was my invention, but some asswipe assistant of mine patented it before I knew what was what. So instead of it being called a Sparky One Thousand, it's called a Pipe Shooter. Original, huh?"

"That's tough, Sparky," Barry said. "How's it work?"

"You loosen these knobs on the side to adjust the aim. It doesn't have much range of motion, but so long as you stick it by the front of the tire or toward the top of the fender, you should have no problems. It's got a strong magnet, so you just stick it on the right spot on the car."

Sparky absentmindedly scratched his privates and continued, "Then you use this remote here to set it off. You switch this to arm the pipe shooter, then push the red button to shoot the nails out of the pipes. Blammo. Tires in instant shreds. If it's going fast enough, the car will roll a couple dozen times before stopping."

Nails raised an eyebrow, revising his opinion of the freak yet again. "They pay you to think up stuff like this?"

Sparky's eyes lit up. "Heck, yeah! Movies are the real deal for us pyro geeks. I get a thousand bucks a day, minimum, to blow stuff up. Stuff I'd pretty much blow up for free if they'd let me. But we're lucky. We got a pretty good union."

Barry frowned. "That's what we need, Nails. A friggin union."

Nails stared at the crazy cracker next to him, wishing the dude wasn't serious. An assassins' union? He clenched his fist, but refrained from pounding some sense into the fool.

Barry said, "Thanks for the gizmo, Sparky. I'll pay you next week if that's all right. I'm a little short right now."

"I've got a better idea," Sparky said. "If your cousin will let me come in here a couple more times, I'll let you have the pea shooter for free."

"Yeah?"

"Why would you do that?" Nails asked.

Sparky gestured at the mountain of cars surrounding them, grinning like a fool. "This place is perfect for blowing shit up. On the movie sets I only get to work a couple of days a week. Then there'll be fourteen hours of standing around with my thumb up my butt before I finally get the chance to blow something all the way to Mexico."

Barry said, "You know what, Sparky? I'll bet I can work something out with my cousin."

Sparky danced around like he'd just gotten a puppy for Christmas. Nails chuckled, amazed to be experiencing amusement twice in one day. The little freak was starting to grow on him.

"And as a bonus, Barry, for introducing me to Denny Nalen, I got a good tip for you. A sure thing. Pushing Daisies to win in the fourth race at Santa Anita."

Now Barry was looking like it was Christmas. Nails shook his head. What kind of name was that for a horse?

Sparky gestured at his gasoline bomb and pulled out a little remote switch. "You guys want to stay for the fireworks?"

Nails eyed the device with trepidation and started to back out of the ring of cars, remembering vividly a humiliating propane accident with his mom's double-wide. "We'll catch you later, Sparky."

Nails rumbled down the path as fast as his knee would let him, not caring one bit if Barry could keep up. He wanted to put as much space between him and the bomb before it blew. He wheezed, limping along down one row of cars before Barry caught up with him.

"Pushing Daisies. That's perfect, ain't it Nails? That's what we're doing for a living these days, putting people in the grave, and that's what the horse's name is. That's what you call a grade-A top dollar tip. There's no way that nag's gonna lose."

Nails stopped short, amazed that Barry hadn't learned a damn thing from how he'd gotten into this mess in the first place. Nails was thinking about pounding some sense into his partner's skull when the bomb went off.

His heart skipped a couple of beats, and his bladder emptied.

But worst of all, he fainted.

seven

JOHN followed the trail of limos and expensive automobiles toward his sister's mansion, which was one of Bel Air's finest, and marveled at Eleanor's ability to throw an intimate party for a couple hundred of her best donors. Business owners and real estate developers working hand in hand to pillage society—part of the wonderful world of politics. And the family business.

Not something he missed.

As he pulled up to the valet, he noticed an electric microcar and a couple of hybrids scattered amongst the Mercedes and Ferraris and thought, *this must be a Hollywood fundraiser.* Ecologically-minded celebrities driving glorified golf carts and raising awareness about hemp products—John laughed. Actors would do just about anything for their cause, or to get themselves in the news.

Then he frowned, momentarily reliving an ugly memory from when he was about twelve—when he'd come across his favorite movie actor, pants down, and crapping on his family's front porch. All in the name of saving the environment.

The sight had scarred John for years, and was a political statement he hadn't really understood. Still didn't.

He gave his keys to the red-jacketed valet, idly wondering how parking cars could be an actual job. Was it too much to ask for people to park their own cars? As he hurried up the steps, he heard a round of applause from inside the mansion and felt damn glad he was an hour late for this shindig. With any luck he'd missed most of the grandstanding.

John noticed two security guys on the front lawn, staying out of the streetlights and watching the exterior of the house, and three more at the door, one demanding his name and identification.

"John Black."

Members of the security team were dressed in dark suits, with tiny earpieces, of course. Probably CIA wannabes.

They gave him the once over while he checked them out in return. They were very thorough patting him down, one guy frisking, one guy watching the new guest with his hand on his weapon, and the last guy looking out the front door for unexpected friends.

Not bad.

John looked through the foyer and into the ballroom and picked out four more dressed in black and at least two pretending to be civilians. Surprisingly, all of them appeared to be doing a decent job. John nodded as they waved him through, figuring Eleanor had hired a new security team.

John smiled, hoping it was true. *Maybe Eleanor has been listening to me for a change.*

At the sound of applause, he stopped in the doorway, bracing for the bullshit like it was a frigid Nor'easter. With a senator for a mom, and various uncles and grandparents fouling the political waters over the last fifty years—a dynasty surpassed only by the Kennedy clan—he'd suffered through more of these events than any human ever should.

And while he figured he had enough experience dealing with the political maneuvering and backstabbing to glide through the muck with practiced ease, being around the corruption day in and day out had always had the opposite effect on him. Instead of being easier to deal with, it felt more like being submerged in a giant vat of excrement up to his nose—unable to take even the littlest bit more without drowning.

John took a deep breath and then stepped into the grand ballroom.

Eleanor stood at the podium, situated in the middle of a long banquet-style table, spouting off as she normally did, and generally encouraging yet another bout of frantic clapping.

He had to admit—Eleanor was a pretty impressive speaker, one of the best he'd ever seen. But even better, Eleanor *tried* to do the right thing, which was unusual for politicians at the top levels, and a hard task to accomplish. Like swimming among sharks—with an open wound.

And while his older sister's policies were refreshing, John knew sooner or later the political cronies would corrupt her. They did it with everyone, turning their teeth on those who didn't play ball.

John ignored the oration and spied a nearly empty table to his right with an attractive woman sitting there. She was about thirty, with long brown hair. And not actress pretty, like the rest of the crop in the ballroom, but real-world pretty.

What made her interesting was that she obviously wasn't a politician or an actress, and didn't belong here anymore than he did. And what's more, she wasn't really paying attention to the speech. Unquestionably the right kind of person to be stuck with, at least until Eleanor's speech was over.

AFTER CLAPPING ON CUE WITH THE REST OF THE BUNCH, SIERRA Rodriguez tuned out Eleanor Black's speech once again. Black's ideas were mostly fabulous, and Sierra wished she could muster a little more enthusiasm since she *loved* politics and it was, in fact, her job. But she'd heard this discourse at least a dozen times before and even her excitement for political discussion couldn't withstand the steady barrage of platitudes and pontifications.

Her BlackBerry vibrated with an incoming text message and she looked at the thing with annoyance and a bit of dread. Sure enough, it was her scumbag ex, leaving yet another disturbing and haunting message: *You should have worn your black lace panties tonight. They're my favorite when they smell…*

She quickly looked away. There was more to the message, and more disgusting, to be sure, but she hit the delete button and sighed. Since the divorce, Gil's favorite pastimes were tormenting her and figuring out new, unique ways to get out of paying his child support.

And she'd actually married the bastard. Sometimes she still couldn't believe it.

She turned to her left and noticed a man looking in her direction—checking her out—and she felt herself reddening. It had been a while since someone had noticed her in a way that didn't make her skin crawl.

Lately, it had been old fart politicians playing a little grab-ass while she interviewed them. Not a real ego boost. And of course her producer sometimes had to be beaten back with a stick, or the threat of a sexual harassment lawsuit. Sometimes both.

But this guy seemed different. And out of place, which she found intriguing. *Maybe a story there.*

As he walked toward her, she fixed a picture of him in her mind so she could find him in the database later: six foot, late thirties, rugged and good-looking with thick, sandy-blonde hair. And he carried himself with self confidence, as though he took care of things instead of talking about them incessantly.

Definitely interesting…and definitely not a politician.

"Hi, I'm John."

"Sierra Rodriguez. And you're late, John." There was another round of feverish clapping from the audience as she waved her hand toward the podium. "You just missed the part about giving Hollywood special tax incentives to combat the evil Canadians."

He took the seat next to her, sporting a wry grin. "Even billion dollar corporations need a tax break sometimes."

John laughed after he said it, and she found herself laughing right along with him, drawing harsh stares from the neighboring tables. But to her, it was a great opening line—an icebreaker. She waved an apology to the other guests and whispered, "We probably shouldn't laugh. Runaway film production is a really big concern here."

"They should be concerned. It's a real problem. But that doesn't mean *we* have to be politically correct. Being P.C. isn't all it's cracked up to be, unless you're one of these guys."

Sierra smiled, liking the banter, and decided to give a little back. "Well, they've got a good reason to act that way. Film and television production is the number one industry in the state. It influences everything. Even politics."

"And that's a good thing, right? People who make stuff up for a living influencing politics?"

"Kind of like the blind leading the blind?"

Now it was John's turn to smile. "Yeah. Something like that. In the 1850's the big industry was gold. Then it was citrus, and then aerospace. A little more substantial. But now it's narcissistic screen icons. And we export them all over the world. Makes you proud to be a Californian, doesn't it?"

Sierra's eyes lit up, enjoying the easy conversation, but for some reason her reporting instincts kicked in. There was something she couldn't put her finger on—something about him that she recognized. "You look familiar. But you're not a politician, are you?"

John shuddered. "Absolutely not. Can't stand 'em. I've known too many over the years."

"Is that right?" *Now that's interesting.* "What about this one? Eleanor Black?"

John smiled and said, "She's one of the few good ones. Deserves to be the first female governor of California."

"I think so, too. And it looks like she'll win, so score one for the good guys."

For some reason, his smile grew wider when she said that. Sierra looked him over, trying to figure him out. "You're not a politician...and I don't think you're an actor..."

John snorted.

"...and yet you're here at a fundraiser for the Hollywood elite. So what *do* you do?"

After a moment of hesitation, he said, "There's no job description for what I do. But private investigator comes close."

Her eyes lit up again, but John shook his head.

"It's nothing glamorous," he said. "People have the wrong idea about PI's, that it's exciting or something. Anyway, private investigator doesn't accurately describe me, but it's easier than getting into some of the more unusual aspects of my profession."

Sierra raised an eyebrow.

John continued, "Without getting too detailed, I'm hired to help people—to fix things. But most of the time I track down deadbeat dads and persuade them to pay their child support."

"Persuade them?"

John shrugged. "I help them think things over. Come up with some better ways for them to behave."

Sierra thought about that until her BlackBerry vibrated again. She glanced down to find yet another sordid message from Gil. *Scumbag! Why does he have to keep torturing me?* She wanted to scream, but knew Gil would've *loved* that reaction.

"I hate to admit it, but I've got someone who needs that kind of persuasion."

John leaned toward her. "What's the problem?"

She hesitated, wondering if she should tell him. Her instincts told her she could trust him, and when she looked down at the disgusting message on her PDA, she just about lost control. She needed to talk about it.

"Gil-my-scumbag-ex-husband." She said it too fast, running the words together, and saw John's confusion. Sierra grimaced, hating that Gil still had an effect on her life when he wasn't even around.

She inhaled slowly a couple of times. "Sorry. Every time I think of Gil, the word 'scumbag' pops right out of my mouth, which is better than it was last year. I used to say an even nastier word, back when I first found out he was screwing his nineteen-year-old intern, doing stuff I've never even imagined doing." She shuddered. "But I've mellowed lately."

John smiled. "I can see that."

Sierra reddened and turned away, wishing she didn't blush so easily. She hoped he didn't think she was a nutcase. "Gil's depravity is way out there. I've seen the pictures that they took of themselves...you know...in the act." She shuddered again before getting herself together. "I'm sorry. I shouldn't be telling you these things. I guess the important part for you to know is that even though he's got money,he hasn't paid his child support in months."

"It's okay. I've heard worse. Unfortunately, your story's not unusual," John said.

Sierra sighed. "I wish it was unusual. Because I know the nasty messages and the stalking are pushing *me* over the edge. I wouldn't wish that on anyone."

John paused, focusing completely on her. "Do you think he might hurt you?"

The concern in his eyes was real, and Sierra felt herself melting. She made a quick decision. He was definitely the right kind of man to hire for something as personal as this. She'd check his background tomorrow, of course, but she was pretty sure how it would turn out. In fact, she had a feeling John would start her case right now if she was in danger.

But she wasn't—Gil was a wuss. And she didn't want to mislead John. "No. Gil's a scumbag, but he's not the violent type."

"Okay. Well, I've got something I'm working on for the next couple of weeks, but I'll be able to take a look after that."

Everyone around them rose for a standing ovation as Eleanor stepped away from the podium, waving and smiling before she left the room, surrounded by her security guards. Sierra and John blended in, rising and clapping along with the rest of the audience. The crowd surged together, pressing John up against her back, and Sierra caught her breath. She shook her head to clear the feeling. Like she needed another complication in her life.

She tried to think of something that might get John on board with starting her case. "You know, going after Gil would be like hitting two birds with one stone."

"How do you figure?"

"Well, you go after deadbeat dads and you can't stand politicians, right? Gil is both. A Los Angeles City Councilman is a low-level politician to be sure, but he's still a politician."

John perked up. "City Council? Buddies with Eleanor, I take it?"

"Well, I wouldn't say buddies. But they work together. Gil's specialty is condemning perfectly good buildings for shopping centers and the like. Wielding eminent domain like a weapon of mass destruction. And he's pretty good at finding new ways to take bribes without being caught. Eleanor mostly tries to stop him."

"I'm in," John said. He looked over her shoulder and frowned.

Sierra turned and found two bulky, security types approaching their table.

John leaned in and whispered, "I don't have a business card on me. Why don't you meet me at the Hamlet on Sunset Boulevard at noon tomorrow and we'll go over the details."

She nodded as one of the security guards put a hand on John's shoulder and told him Ms. Black would see him now. John gave Sierra a wink and shrugged off the guard's meaty paw, but then followed him out, leaving Sierra to wonder again about her mysterious new friend. With a sigh, she realized she'd have to put her journalistic talents to use tonight and find out who he was. Or she wouldn't get any sleep at all.

JOHN FOLLOWED THE GRUNTS TO THE LIBRARY, THINKING ABOUT MISS Rodriguez and how her problems could be connected to his sister. Sierra's ex-husband was a possible suspect.

Even if the job wasn't related, at the very least—while he was persuading Sierra's ex of the error of his ways—Gil could provide him with information about the other city councilmen.

John took a seat, looking at the rare books surrounding him—estimating that they cost more than the furnishings in his whole house—and only half-noticing that Eleanor was glaring at him from behind her desk. But when Eleanor hung up the phone and appeared to collect herself before speaking, John had to sigh.

"Come on, Sis, I'm always on your side. You don't need to worry about what you say to me. Or even how you say it. Leave the political speeches out of it, okay?"

"I know, John. I'm sorry. It's hard to turn off the politician side of me."

"Well, please turn if off anyway." John rolled his eyes. "And when you do, you might rethink the idea of giving tax breaks to multi-billion-dollar media conglomerates. They make plenty of money without your help."

Eleanor frowned. "Why don't you leave the politics to me, all right?"

"All right," John said, "But that's not why I'm here."

"Hillary told you what happened?"

"She's worried about you. Losing her father to cancer is more than any little girl should have to deal with. The last thing she needs is for her mom to get killed 'cause she's too stubborn to get out of the rain."

Eleanor laughed. "*I'm* too stubborn? Every time election season comes around, you disappear."

"All right. We're both stubborn," John said, ready to meet her halfway. "Have you any idea who's behind this?"

Eleanor shook her head. "Not a clue. I've got enemies, but so far as I know, none of them hate me enough to kill me."

"What about the City Council? Any of them got a beef with the Mayor?"

"Well, sure they do. But they still get filthy rich, even with me around."

"How about this election? Any of the other candidates seem like they've got something against you?"

"How would I know? There are a hundred and twenty candidates, and I've only met a dozen of them. Ever since 'The Body' Ventura and the Terminator were elected to governorships, the roaches have come crawling out of the woodwork. Everyone figures they can run. Crackpots, drug addicts, you name it."

John sighed. "I'm going to need more than you're giving me if I'm going to be any help in this."

Eleanor narrowed her gaze and stopped smiling. "You're kidding, right? Mom's first senatorial run was almost ruined by the atom bomb you dropped during her campaign. The last thing I need in this campaign is one of your wonderful sound bytes."

Jeez. As always, she was focusing on the minor indiscretions of his youth instead of the big picture. "No, Eleanor. The last thing you need is to be killed. And all I said, fifteen years ago, was that all politicians are scum-sucking bottom-feeders. Oh, yeah…and that the world would be a better place if aliens came along and snatched all the politicians away for display in an interplanetary zoo. Now which part of that isn't true, present company excluded?"

Eleanor rolled her eyes, her exasperation showing. "But you're the son of a politician. The brother of a politician. You can't say stuff like that."

John held out his hands in what he hoped was a placating manner. "I know. But that was a long time ago. I'll keep my sound bytes to myself, I promise."

"You promise?" Eleanor's eyebrows rose so high, they seemed to be trying to escape from her forehead. "Then why were you chatting with a reporter during my speech? What bomb did you drop this time?"

"What? Who? Sierra?"

Eleanor smiled icily. "Sierra…Miss Rodriguez…has been doing an in-depth piece on my campaign for the last week."

John's brain scrambled into overdrive, trying to remember if he'd said anything embarrassing. Luckily, he couldn't come up with anything.

"You didn't even know you were talking to a reporter," Eleanor said. "How can I have you around my campaign?"

At a loss for words, John figured he'd blown it before he'd even walked in the room. "You'll have to chance it, Eleanor. For Hillary's sake."

Eleanor stood up, the meeting apparently over. "No, John, I don't. I've got the best private security team working for me. Something you advised a couple of weeks ago, as I recall. They are well apprised of the situation."

John stood up, too. Eleanor was definitely the stubborn one in the family. And once she made her mind up, it was damn near impossible to change.

Eleanor said, "I'll tell Mom you said hello."

"Yeah, sure."

Reluctantly, John retreated, thinking he'd have to try again tomorrow. While it was true that Eleanor's security team was good, none of them were as good as Harley, or even himself. For Eleanor's sake, and especially Hillary's, they needed the help.

So the first thing to do was call Harley and get him over here to keep an eye on things, which would make John feel a whole lot more comfortable—and the security team wouldn't even know he was there. Then all John would have to do is figure out a way to talk Eleanor into letting them help. Somehow.

eight

HARLEY crept through the brush of Eleanor's estate, finger on the trigger, wondering if the inattentive security guard might benefit from a lead 'souvenir' to the buttocks. *Nah. Probably wouldn't teach him a bloody thing.* Blokes working security for private firms were notoriously slow learners. Otherwise they'd be earning them nice pensions you could get by working with the FBI or CIA.

FBI, he snorted quietly. After his tour in 'Nam, he'd been offered jobs by a couple of different government initials, but had turned them down, even dropping trou' and showing his backside to one particularly revolting recruitment officer.

He hadn't been impressed with the way things had been run during the war and figured that things with the government damn sure wouldn't be any better. The rodents in government practiced inefficiency and corruption till they'd turned it into an art form.

And yet here he was, crawling through the forested perimeter of a Bel Air mansion, protecting a politician, of all people. Not that he held anything against Eleanor. John's older sister was decent enough, for a rat bastard politician, but as far as Harley was concerned, if Eleanor wasn't related to John and sweet little Hillary, she could kiss her arse goodbye.

But he'd known John since the lad was a teenager. Over the years, John had risked his life to protect Harley—more times than he cared to remember—and Harley would do the same for John and his family. Like always.

Harley narrowed his gaze as the guard leaned back against a tree. Eleanor *would* be kissing it all goodbye if these worthless security guards were all she had between her and a premature death. *They couldn't guard the toilet they were sitting on.*

Harley decided that he'd have to set up a network of trip wires, with fireworks surprises, throughout the forested back yard. Then he'd be able to get some shuteye out here in the bush and still keep watch on the back. *Even the idiots guarding this place should be able to watch the open area in front of the house.*

Harley snorted. *Especially if I keep 'em on their toes.*

He took aim at the tree branch above the guard's head and fired three quick, noise-suppressed shots, severing the limb and dropping it squarely on the guard's head. With a cry of surprise and pain, the guard leapt into the air and twirled his gun frantically in all directions, looking something like a demented ballerina.

Harley chuckled quietly to himself as he eased back into the forest.

nine

BARRY pounded his fist into the windshield a couple of times before slamming his head into the steering wheel. "Son of a..."

Sparky had said the friggin horse was a lock. But Pushing Daisies' name had been perfectly justified. Dropping dead of a heart attack twenty feet from the finish line, Barry's twenty-to-one shot had gone down in a cloud of dust.

He shook his head in frustration. The second time in a week that he'd lost a six figure payout. It was like God himself was shoving a red hot poker up his rear end and stirring it around.

Twenty feet. Twenty friggin feet and he would've been through with the murder-for-hire biz.

The nightmares from the Odie job were coming every night, blurring with the screaming teenagers from the unfinished Black job, and giving him an ulcer. Barry lit up a smoke, attempting to calm himself down. Now he'd have to kill another candidate to make up for the ten thousand dollar bet! He opened a bottle of the pink stuff and sucked it dry. *Thank God for Pepto.*

His cell phone rang and he looked at the thing with trepidation. Sure enough, it was Mr. S calling. Barry thought about ignoring it, but figured he was in enough trouble without ignoring the boss. He poked a skeletally-thin digit at the answer button. "Hey, Mr. S. How you doing?"

"That's touching," Mr. S said. "Your concern for my well-being is very touching indeed."

Barry frowned, not buying the snake oil charm for a second. Charm was what Mr. S did, even if the hammer was ready to drop.

Mr. S continued, "I think you need to worry more about yourself, Barry. I understand you're not doing so well. Even Sasha and Lexi are disturbed with what's going on."

Barry gulped, then tried to steady his shaking hand. "Tell the Russians not to worry. Just put the ten on my tab. I'll take care of an extra one to make up for it."

"But that's the problem, Barry. You've only taken care of the first item on the list. So why would Sasha and Lexi believe you're capable of working off your debts?"

Barry took another drag. "You got my word, Mr. Steel. In fact, the second item will be taken care of tonight. I'm certain. We even got a backup plan."

There was a long pause before Steel finally said, "I hope you're right, Barry, I really do. And this time I hope you took more than a minute planning the job so you don't screw it up. I wouldn't want Sasha and Lexi coming after me."

Barry heard a click, followed by a deafening silence. He jumped a foot when Nails opened the door and squeezed inside the car.

"Hey, man. Let's roll."

Barry threw his cell phone on the dash and flicked his cigarette away. He sighed, watching it bounce off the carved granite sign next to the car: *Pfester Chemicals and Pharmaceuticals, We're there for you!*

*Great...*Stuck between the Russian Mafia and a major drug company fronted by Dick Steel. Talk about your rock and a hard place. Barry let out a deep breath, tapping his fingers on the steering wheel. If his friggin horse had come in, he wouldn't have to deal with all these rich crooked bastards.

Nails grunted. "Wake up, shithead. We got things to do."

Barry turned toward him, careful not to vent his frustration on the ogre sitting next to him. "What's with the friggin name calling? Is that really necessary?"

Nails gave him a baleful glare. "This from the guy who says 'friggin' all the time. There ain't no such *friggin* word as friggin. Like it's gonna kill you to use a curse word once in a while."

Barry flinched. Just the thought of using a curse word had him cowering in his seat.

His wife had been a rather large Italian woman with vicious right hook and a mean temper. She'd been bossy as heck, and never tolerated a single swear word in her house. It was a tough first six months of marriage 'cause all it took was one wrong word and the fists came out. He'd never gotten over it, either, even after providence had sent a Metro Bus to take to her to heaven. Or hell, maybe.

Nails interrupted his reverie. "Shithead is a much better word than friggin. It gets the point across with the minimum amount of effort."

Barry shook his head, unsure which was worse—someone who couldn't stop cursing or someone who couldn't start. He looked down at the bandage on Nails' knee and tried to change the subject. "Why you let these Pfester guys experiment on you? Pumping you full of chemicals and stuff? Have they made any real improvements to your knee?"

"No, nothing that lasts. But they make it feel good for a little while."

"So what's the point? So Pfester and Mr. Steel can get a new patent and get even richer while you're stuck with the side effects of the drugs?"

Nails rumbled a bit, apparently laughing. "Don't be such a retard. First off, with this good-paying job that Steel gave us, I'm the one who's getting rich. Which you would be, too, if you'd quit blowing it on the ponies. Secondly, when you weigh four hundred pounds and your knee doesn't work, you take whatever help you can get. At least until I can afford to have my knee replaced, which is getting closer every job. And third, Mr. S doesn't own Pfester. It's more like they own him. Hell, even the Russians probably got a piece of him. That's why they all want him to be governor."

Barry whispered, "I'm not a retard. I just can't stand the nightmares."

Nails paused for a moment. "Look. If we help Mr. Steel,

we get rich right along with him. And if we don't, they bury us. How hard is that to understand?"

Barry nodded, wondering how a beast of a football player could have such a way with words.

Nails grunted. "All right then. Have you got that electrical gizmo for Black's microphone?"

"Yeah. It's ready to go for the debate tonight. And you've got the pipe shooter for her car. One of 'em is bound to work, so Black is as good as dead." Barry looked down at his feet. "The thing is, I'm worried about the electrocution part. It seems like an awfully painful way to go. And we agreed to make it as quick and painless as possible."

Nails narrowed his eyes and clenched his fist. "If it's good enough for my brothers in the slam, it's good enough for politicians. Don't be a pansy."

Barry eyed the clenched fist and decided to change the subject. "What about our next guy? Two-Bits?"

Nails looked wistful for a moment. "Two-Bits is a god-damned musical genius. And it's a crying shame we got to bury the mo-fo. But this is business." Nails gave a little laugh. "You know, we might even be doing him a favor. His death will probably raise him to legendary status. Then he'll be the rap king for all eternity."

Barry felt confused. Were they talking about the same guy? "Hold on a second. How can a rapper be a musical genius? That stuff's not even music."

Barry felt a fist clamp around his neck, squeezing ever so slightly. Nails leaned in close and said, "The shit is poetry, man. Something a skinny white cracker wouldn't understand. So shut your mouth."

Nails released his grip and Barry slumped into his seat, rubbing his neck and thinking furiously. Was this a problem? Would Nails be able to kill his rap buddy? "Sorry, Nails. I didn't realize what his, ah, music, meant to you."

"Yeah, whatever."

Barry paused for a moment, giving Nails time to calm down. "You got any ideas for Two-Bits?"

"You kidding? A black rapper? We dress you in Crip colors

and bust a cap in his ass, gangsta style. The cops either think it's a Tupac or they think it's a gangland shooting. Either way, we're covered."

Nails said it with such calm that Barry shivered.

ten

SIERRA sipped a glass of white wine and looked around the restaurant for the tenth time. "Come on, John."

She caught herself tapping her heels together and wished she could put an end to the nervous habit she'd picked up as a child. Unfortunately, too many viewings of her favorite movie, *The Wizard of Oz,* had left its mark.

Another glance found that John still hadn't arrived. It went against her better judgment, but even now she hoped he would show for their lunch date—though she was dreading the moment she'd have to tell him she was a reporter.

She was pretty sure he hated reporters as much as he hated politicians. And she couldn't blame him—most reporters and politicians came from the same gene pool that spawned ambulance chasers and oil executives.

It had only taken a few minutes of research to discover that John was the infamous brother of Eleanor Black, something she wished she'd known without checking. But then again, who would have thought the reclusive and mysterious sibling would have shown up at a political fund raiser? John hated politics. In fact, he was famous for it.

Which made his visit all the more curious. She was positive there was a story there, and of course an interview with John would be a major coup since he was astoundingly and painfully forthright in stating his views.

Sierra sighed. Not that there would ever be an interview. She knew John would never even talk to her if it wasn't for her son and his deadbeat dad.

Which, unfortunately, made him all the more appealing. She found it way too easy to be attracted to someone who cared so much about protecting kids. That practically qualified as a knight in shining armor.

And from what she'd read, protecting kids was John's calling in life. She shuddered, wondering what John had felt like when his high school girlfriend had been killed by her own father. With a sigh, Sierra forced the thought from her head, shaking it off. John put her ex to shame.

"Penny for your thoughts."

Sierra started as John took a seat next to her. Then she blushed. "Maybe later." She took a deep breath. "Thanks for meeting me today. I can't tell you how much it means to me."

"I hope I can help," John said. "Why don't you tell me about your ex?"

"Well, first there's something important I have to tell you. I don't want to hide anything from you and after I found out you were Eleanor Black's brother…"

She paused, trying to figure out a way to break it to him.

John smiled and said, "Is this off the record?"

Sierra rolled her eyes. "'Off the record' is such a cliché." Then she raised an eyebrow. "How did you know?"

"That's my job."

From the sparkle in his eyes he was holding back laughter, which she found a bit annoying, but she felt more relieved than anything. He already knew *and* he had shown up anyway. A good sign.

"Actually," John said, "I've always had a soft spot for female reporters. And I can't tell you how many times that has come back to haunt me. So imagine my surprise when Eleanor told me you were a reporter. Like a sucker punch. But then I asked around to get the gruesome details. You might not know it, but you have a pretty good reputation at Channel 6 News. Not nearly as bad as your co-workers."

"Funny."

John grinned. "Maybe. But it's true. Or we wouldn't be having this conversation. Pretty isn't enough to get a free lunch out of me. You've got to be trustworthy as well."

Did he just call me pretty? "Thank you."

John seemed to be looking her over. "But one thing I heard did seem a little...odd."

Sierra wondered what he could have possibly dug up.

John said, "Your mother was a Southern Belle, an actual beauty queen, and your father was a champion Mexican boxer? Kind of an unusual combination."

Sierra laughed. "You really *did* do your research. Mom used to say that I was half Georgia peach and half jalapeno pepper."

John gave her an appraising stare. "Does that mean a fiery temper or something else?"

"Probably both."

"Interesting." John met her gaze for a second. "All right then. Before we get into the situation with your ex, there's something I need from you. I want your word that nothing I say gets used in any of your stories."

Sierra opened her mouth to speak, but John said, "Not for me—I don't give a rat's ass what the press or public think of me—but I don't want any of my comments hurting Eleanor's campaign."

"Of course."

She was interrupted by an electronic melody coming from his pocket. With an apologetic shrug, John cut off the tinny music by answering his cell phone.

Sierra said, "Wait a second. Is that a Britney Spears tune?"

"My partner has an odd sense of humor. Please excuse me a second."

Sierra listened in on John's side of the conversation and gathered he was talking to Eleanor Black's daughter. He kept it cryptic, but Sierra's curiosity was piqued by a couple of things. Hillary was extremely concerned about *something* related to her mother, about which John was as reassuring as possible. And even though Eleanor didn't want him to, John was still working on it, whatever that meant.

Plus, for some reason John wanted Hillary to tell him if her mother's schedule changed at all. Sierra sighed. Definitely a story there, and one that would probably help the exposé that she was working on, though she knew she couldn't use a single bit of it.

She stopped musing and noticed John had finished his conversation and was watching her. "I know," she said. "I won't use any of it. You can trust me. I won't even ask what's going on, even though my curiosity is eating away at me like acid rain on a Jaguar's paint job."

John nodded. "Thanks, I appreciate that. And I'm afraid I can't talk about it right now. But if and when I can, I'll make sure you get the story first."

Sierra smiled. "You would do that?"

"Of course. But I need a favor...regarding Hillary. And it's important enough that I'll cut my fee in half for dealing with your ex."

"In half? It's not illegal, is it?"

"Do I look like a politician, Sierra?" John held up his hand. "Don't answer that. Look, you don't know me that well yet, but I would *never* ask a favor that was immoral or illegal."

"You know, come to think of it, you do look quite a bit like Mayor Black. And you bear an uncanny resemblance to Senator Black."

"That's why I keep as far from politics as possible, Eleanor and the Barracuda included."

Sierra choked on her wine, practically snorting it out her nose. "The Barracuda?"

"A nickname the other senators have for my mother. It's not a slur—they use it with affection. Even reverence."

"I've got one of the senators on record saying your mom has balls of steel."

"Probably jealous," John said.

"You know, I think he was." Sierra looked him over. "All right. What's the favor?"

John hesitated for a moment. "I need a press pass to the debate tonight."

"A press pass. Can't Eleanor get you in?"

John shrugged.

"All right, don't tell me," Sierra said. She waited for him to say something, and when he didn't, she took her pass out of her purse and said, "Take mine. I'll get another one from the station."

"Thanks." John put the pass in his pocket. "Now tell me about Gil. Where he eats, where he sleeps, where he works, where he plays. His friends, his enemies. Everything. Then I'll see what I can do to turn him into a good father."

"Gil? That's kind of hard to imagine. He's never been much of a father."

"Then I'll just have to make sure he reaches his full potential. Everyone's got potential, Sierra. But sometimes they need a little nudge."

Sometimes they do. Sierra looked him over, seeing determination and certainty. *If anyone can nudge Gil in the right direction, it's this guy.*

eleven

JOHN pulled up to the old fashioned theater, his eyes drawn to the marquee: *Gubernatorial Debate. Two-Bits, Eleanor Black, Michael Sanchez, Arnold Schwarzkov, and Richard Steel.*

He chuckled quietly. A rapper with four platinum records and a colorful gang history, John's mostly left-wing sister, an Hispanic hardcore right winger, a pro wrestler with a belief system based on publicity and money, and a lobbyist for Pfester Pharmaceuticals—a company known for being both the largest single employer and the largest environmental polluter in the state. Might make for interesting politics for a change.

The old style movie house was a bizarre place for a debate, but then again, this was Hollywood.

He looked across the street, searching for a good vantage point for Harley, but found nothing. A quick turn down the alley took him to the rear of the theater and into a small adjacent parking lot. Spaces were reserved for parking the candidates' limos, but the lot was mostly filled with semi trucks full of lighting and video equipment, along with a segmented trailer with dressing rooms for each of the candidates. All-out star treatment for the wannabe politicians. John snorted. *Our tax dollars at work.*

He'd just spied a couple of good spots in the back when his phone filled the car with an annoying melody. It took a couple of rings to figure out the tune was *I'm Too Sexy,* by Right Said Fred, one of John's top ten least favorite songs of all time. With a start, he realized all the tunes coming from his phone were ones he detested. That infamous Aussie sense of humor.

He answered with an impatient stab at the phone. "How do you change the tune when my phone isn't even in your possession?"

John heard a couple of barks of laughter.

"Trade secret, mate. If I told ya, I'd have to kill ya."

"You think you could? You're getting a little old, aren't you?"

"Don't get cocky, John. I taught you everything *you* know. Not everything I know."

"All right, you win," John said. "Where are you now?"

"I'm following Eleanor and her so-called security detail to the debate. ETA is thirty minutes. Are you there now?"

"Yeah. When you get here, take the back alley and parking lot. There's a rooftop on an office building that'll be a good position for you. I'll cover the front entrance from the inside. We'll use the TK-11s to keep in contact."

"Ooh, the little headset radios. I'll pretend I'm FBI. No... ATF."

"Yeah, yeah. Funny. Hey, was everything clear at Eleanor's house?"

"Yeah, no worries. These security guys are dumb as Kiwis. Heck, I'm only driving two car lengths back and they haven't made me. Still, there's enough of 'em around to make a good show. One in the car with Eleanor and two each in a car following and a car in front, for a total of five. Eleanor's mansion is even better. Plenty of obvious security guys. If I were a smart assassin, I'd probably try someplace public where the security is harder to control—like the debate. So watch your back, mate. And Eleanor's."

John looked at the throng of people going in and out of the back doors and agreed.

"YOU WANT A DOUGHNUT? I THINK I WANT ANOTHER."

Barry looked across the cab of the truck and noticed the teamster's bulky frame. The guy held a cigar stub in one hand and was polishing off a chocolate glazed with the other. "I don't know, Bob. You think you should? You kind of look like a heart attack waiting to happen. No offense."

"None taken."

Barry turned away from his troll friend and gazed through

the windshield, taking in the view of the back doors of the theater.

Bob continued, "Hey, if sharing a cell with you and your irritable bowels didn't offend me, I don't know what could."

Was he serious? "You must be yanking me. Those were your bombs, Bob. Not mine."

Bob chuckled. "Oh, yeah. Speaking of which, I've gotta make a deposit at the old savings and loan, if you know what I mean."

As an angry stench reached his nostrils, Barry sat up straight and opened the door. "I'm reading you loud and clear. Let's head inside the theater. You hit the john and I'll hit the food table and pick you up some goodies."

Bob handed him a security pass and clipped one onto his own shirt.

Barry took a deep breath. *This is it.*

He checked out the swarm of people trying to get into the back entrance of the theater. Idiots reminded him of bees flying into a hive. Ignoring the swarm, he shuddered at the upcoming task, dreading the idea of killing Ms. Black. But he still found himself following Bob through the crowd and toward the rear door.

He fingered the innocuous-looking electric gizmo in his pocket and searched around for Nails, but couldn't find him anywhere. Then again, the limos weren't even here yet. There was plenty of time for Nails' part of the plan.

Approaching the security guards at the entrance, Barry felt his stomach start to churn and caught his subconscious warning him to slow his pace and check things out. He cracked open another bottle of the pink stuff. "Is this pass legit? How'd you get it on such short notice?"

Bob winked at him. "Of course it's real, boy. Everyone in film and television knows that you don't mess with the teamsters. I just told the production team that I needed to train another driver and that I needed another pass. They know if they piss me off, one of their camera trucks or lighting trucks is gonna get a flat tire on the way to the theater. Which would be inconvenient for a live, televised debate, wouldn't you say?"

Barry stopped dead in his tracks, mouth wide open.

Bob said, "You gonna catch flies that way, boy. What's the matter with you?"

"You're trying to tell me that *you* told the bosses what to do and they did it, no questions asked? I mean, I knew your union was strong, but…"

"Hey, man. We're the Teamsters. Hell, come negotiating time, Local 659 has even been known to crack a few skulls. On occasion."

Barry felt a moment of pure excitement wash over him—and clarity, like the sun burning off the fog. *Hot damn!* It was like an epidural…or an epiphany…or one of those e-words. It was like…a revelation. "I want to unionize my job. You think you can give me some tips on how to organize?"

Bob stared at him. "Don't you work for those Russian dudes? The ex-KGB guys?"

"Well, yeah. But they make crappy bosses."

Bob kept staring. The longer it went on, the more uncomfortable Barry felt—the sunshine disappearing and the fog settling back in.

Bob said, "You don't unionize the Russian Mafia, moron."

"Yeah, but…"

"But nothing. I think you've gone off the deep end. After this favor, we're square and I'm done. Don't call me no more."

Bob turned and marched up to the security guards, flashed them his pass, and walked on in. Barry followed along, showed his own pass, and entered the theater.

HARLEY FLEXED HIS LEFT CALF MUSCLE, CAREFUL NOT TO MOVE an inch, then progressed to his cramped thigh. *Crikey.* He was getting a little old to be sitting on an asphalt rooftop, pebbles cutting into his flesh, spying on politicians and security guards.

The worst part about working ambush, or sitting watch, was keeping completely still. Muscles tended to cramp something awful. But the slightest movement could call attention to your position, as he'd seen in 'Nam, so staying motionless was the name of the game. A necessity, really.

Night had fallen, which gave him the cover of semi-darkness, but with the half-moon shining away he didn't like to take chances. If one of the security team from the theater happened to be looking up at the roof at the right moment, Harley wanted to make sure they didn't see anything but the pigeons roosting on either side.

Harley's eyes darted from side to side, glancing around. *It really is a good vantage point.* John was certainly coming along with his training. It saddened him, but the young pup didn't really need him anymore, especially the surprise attacks to keep him on his toes.

And yet, Harley found that he didn't really want to stop jumping out from behind trees and sparring with John. First off, it was funny, and funny counted for a lot. It also kept Harley in shape. Without any real battle situations, it was too easy to become soft. Which would never do.

He glanced through the sniper scope and did a slow, methodical search of the parking lot and surrounding area, but there was still nothing. Though he had conflicting feelings about trying to save a politician, he tried to put them aside since the job had him sneaking through the forested grounds of the Black mansion and prowling through the asphalt jungle of Los Angeles, which would keep him sharp at the very least.

And it wasn't as if Eleanor was as bad as the other blokes that were debating tonight. The wrestler, Schwarzkov, worshipped at the altar of the almighty TV camera, while the hard core right winger, Sanchez, was known as much for raping the environment as he was for groping women.

Harley grimaced. Steel was the worst of them all—that bastard actually lobbied on behalf of Pfester Pharmaceuticals and Chemicals, the biggest toxin-spewing company in American history. Steel got favored tax breaks for Pfester, as well as exemptions from environmental regulations, by lining the pockets of congressmen.

A smile crept onto Harley's face. Maybe Pfester should be moved to the top of his list for mandatory environmental restitution. The company was certainly worthy of his extra attention.

JOHN PAUSED NEXT TO THE PRESS BOOTH, NEAR THE LOBBY OF THE theater. Five circuits of the interior of the building had yielded exactly nothing. He was beginning to think that the amateurs weren't going to take a shot.

He watched the debate for a moment, which appeared to be in a round robin stage, with candidates giving short one-line answers to questions. Debate for the MTV generation. This round seemed to be about creating jobs.

Eleanor Black said, "When we all work together to provide an environment that is conducive to business, then corporations will *want* to locate here. Right now, we are actually driving business away with our corporate and tax policy. If we moderate our existing policy, the rewards will be substantial for the people of California."

John smiled. That line would drive Mom over the edge. She leaned as far to the left as was possible without falling over, and Eleanor had been getting more and more centrist over the years. Something that ticked off their mother to no end. John turned to the next in line, the popular Latino politician.

Michael Sanchez said, "When we permanently remove the environmental regulations that are shackling our state's best companies, they will be free to create more jobs and turn our economy around."

John shook his head. Harley would go nuts when he heard this guy.

Richard Steel said, "You stole my line, Mr. Sanchez. You must've been listening to my speeches." Chuckle. "Listen, as a former high-level employee of Pfester Pharmaceuticals, I can guarantee that they will *not* move their headquarters and facilities to another state..." Steel gestured toward Sanchez "...even if I have to *shackle* them to the state. What's more, if elected, I will do whatever it takes to make sure that Pfester's new Science and Engineering Division will go up right here in Los Angeles County."

Two-Bits gestured toward Steel and Sanchez and said, "Are you kidding me? You racist motherfuckers!"

John almost laughed at the swearing, picturing the censors scrambling to bleep out the rap star's F-bombs.

Two-Bits continued, "You talk about business being shackled when the only people I've ever seen shackled are my black brothers. When us brothers stop being slaves to the Man and rise up...and take charge of this great country, *that's* when the economy will get better. Not when you give tax breaks to your butt-buddies. Peace out." Two-Bits flipped them both the bird, then flashed them a gang sign and stood there with his arms folded.

Sanchez stuttered, attempting a response, while Steel's smile looked pasted on his face. John muttered under his breath, "Three ring freaking circus."

"The Mountain" Schwarzkov piped in, "You are funny man, Two-Bits. With da profanities and tings of dat nature. But you would have to be two hundred years old to see black slaves. And you don't look that old." Schwarzkov gave a big grin. "People, I tell you dis now. America is strong and beautiful. If you give *Caleefornia* a chance, it will surprise you. 'Da Mountain' can take care of dese problems and many more, if you hand me your vote."

John nearly laughed out loud at the rhetoric being spewed onstage. *Someone was trying to kill Eleanor instead of these guys?* John turned away from the stage and looked at the gleeful, rabid expressions and the furious scribbling of the reporters, which somehow called to mind an image of vultures waiting for animals to die, and turned his back on the lot, only to find Sierra watching him from the doorway.

"It's kind of pitiful to watch, huh?"

"Which side?" John said. "The candidates or the reporters?"

"I was thinking...both."

John nodded.

Sierra asked, "Did you find what you came here for?"

"Not yet."

"Well, let me know if I can help." She turned toward

the press box and said, "I'm afraid I've got to get back to the jackals."

He watched her go, appreciating the similarities in their viewpoints—jackals and vultures. Turning back to the stage, he tuned out the proceedings and keyed his headset radio. "Harley, you got anything out there?"

"Not a thing, mate. No suspicious activity and nary a sign of the skinny dude."

"Maybe we're missing something. Or maybe that's good news. You think Hillary and Amber might have scared him off yesterday?"

"Anything's possible. But if I was a killer, even an amateur like this guy, I don't think a couple of teenagers would scare me off. 'Course, I'd have to make sure I took care of the witnesses."

John flinched. "Don't joke about that, Harley."

"Sorry, mate. Wasn't joking."

John looked at his watch. *Shit.* "We're running out of time. The debate is almost over. It's going to be now or never for this guy."

"I know. And I've got the outside covered. But I'll bet you a hundred dollars this guy makes a mistake, so keep a sharp eye. If anything happens out here, I'll let you know. Out."

John decided to do another circuit of the theater, starting backstage.

ON THE ROOFTOP, HARLEY WHISPERED, "HELLO. WHAT HAVE WE here? A predator?"

He trained the scope on an enormous black man who was circling through the parking lot. Suspicious as a dingo circling a sheep. Harley tried to get a look at the man's face, but the big man never turned fully 'round.

"Dingo? Or trucker?"

The blokes who drove the trucks with the TV equipment seemed to share a similar body shape with the black man, but something about the way he moved didn't seem quite right. He had a gimp leg, but Harley was pretty sure that wasn't it.

The bloke was even larger than most of the truckers.

Then Harley had it. The man moved with power, even with the bum leg. The truckers had a lot of flab under them, while this bloke had muscle. More like a football player or something. Definitely worth a look-see.

Harley tensed as the man stopped near the front of Eleanor's limo, on the driver's side. He put his finger on the trigger as the man bent down.

Harley snorted. It was an awkward sight, a four hundred pound man bending over—doing what? He couldn't make out anything behind the bulk, but the guy was acting like he was tying his shoelaces. Harley chuckled. *Not bloody likely.*

He looked for Eleanor's security guy, the one who was watching the car, but saw he wasn't paying close enough attention to the big guy. Probably bought the whole shoelace gag. *Idiot.*

Harley took his finger off the trigger, but continued to watch.

BARRY FINGERED THE PACK OF SMOKES HIDING IN HIS POCKET, tapping a steady drumbeat. He checked his watch, then fidgeted some more, wishing they allowed smoking inside the theater. Eleanor Black was still alive, the debate was almost over, and Barry was starting to see his life flash before his eyes. He kept getting mental pictures of Sasha and Lexi peeling his skin off one inch at a time.

The first problem he'd taken care of, finding the right cable. It had taken half an hour to find the cable for Black's microphone, but he'd finally found it. The darn thing was actually labeled with a piece of tape with Black's name on it. Go figure.

Then he'd managed to connect the electric thingy to the cable. His buddy Sparky had kindly showed him how to rig it, as well as how it worked—basically, just click the remote trigger and hundreds of volts of electric current would pass through Eleanor Black's body, quickly turning it into crispy fried chicken.

Which would probably give him nightmares for a month, but what could he do? That same current was also supposed to melt the device into an unrecognizable mush. And he'd even managed to do all these things without a single person seeing him mess around with the cables.

But the real problem was that Eleanor Black never touched her microphone. Not when she was making a point, not to adjust it. Nothing.

And it was pretty dang hard to electrocute somebody who wouldn't cooperate.

Barry watched the backstage monitor like he was watching a horserace, his gaze pinned to the screen, hoping for a come from behind finish. He had a great spot, in the middle of a crowd of people, and next to an amazingly hot woman with a black dress that had a slit going all the way up her thigh.

From past experience, he figured the best way to keep people from remembering your face was to stand next to the hottest woman around. Nobody ever remembered the douche bag standing in a babe's shadow. Plus, with the sway of the crowd, it was possible to cop a feel every now and again. And, wow, did she have a nice, tight body. She'd turned around a couple of times, even looking his way, but hadn't been sure who had been responsible.

Friggin women never paid him much attention! His skeletally thin frame and buggy eyes were courtesy of a thyroid condition he'd had since childhood, one that had caused him numerous painful memories over the years. Kids were cruel little animals. And women were even worse. One woman he'd asked out had laughed and told her friends that he looked like the Grim Reaper, only with eyeballs.

Barry jumped as his thoughts turned from a painful memory to a painful future—Sasha and Lexi skinning off another inch of flesh.

But what could he do? He couldn't make Black grab hold of her microphone. Thank God Nails was taking care of Plan B.

As the hot woman shifted her body, Barry grabbed hold of her and gave a little squeeze. But then he saw that she'd been shifting toward him, and with an angry swing of her palm, she batted his hand away. Then she gave him a shove, knocking him out of the crowd.

"Don't touch me, you little pervert."

He raised his hands in a gesture of innocence and tried to show her an angelic expression, but was pretty sure she wasn't buying it. He turned to the right, looking for another monitor to watch, and saw a man standing there talking on his radio.

"I've got him. Death-on-a-stick is five-foot ten inches, wearing a black suit..."

Barry started. *That guy is talking about me! Son of a...*

The man moved toward him. Frantic, Barry turned to the left and saw the back doors, then bolted through them.

twelve

JOHN launched himself through the doorway and into the back parking lot of the theater. He brushed past teamsters, electricians, and limo drivers, and was slowed by the crowd, but the beanpole had picked up speed and turned down the alley.

John keyed his radio. "Harley. Let me know which way he goes, then grab your car."

"He's headed south down the alley, and now he's turning east at the corner."

John hit the alley and went south. "Got it. Now get your car. I'll talk you in."

"I'm on my way down. But listen, John, we've got another situation. I spotted someone messing around near your sister's car. Nothing definitive, but certainly suspicious."

"Well, stick with me. I'm positive this is Hillary's bad guy. Call Eleanor's security guys and tell them to check out *every* inch of the car before she leaves!"

John leapt over a homeless man sleeping near the mouth of the alley, got a whiff of a rank aroma, and turned east, heading into a rundown residential area. He caught a glimpse of the beanpole turning another corner. "He's headed south again."

HARLEY RAN DOWN FOUR FLIGHTS OF STAIRS, ONLY SLIGHTLY OUT OF breath, and moved toward his car—unfortunately one block in the opposite direction. He dialed the main number for Parkway Security while he double-timed it up the street.

"Hello, Parkway?" Now he was huffing a bit. It was harder to run *and* talk. "I got an anonymous tip for ya. Check out

Mayor Black's limo by the driver's side front fender."

Harley clicked his remote to unlock the doors of his Suburban and climbed inside, still breathing hard. "What? No, this is not a prank. The heavy breathing is because I'm running. What do you mean, why? Listen up. I saw someone messing around with the car. Tampering with it."

He flicked a switch under the dash, disabling the self-destruct mechanism—handy for car thieves and what have you—then hit another switch, this one turning off the environmentally-friendly natural gas engine, and turning on the souped-up gas-hog V8. He hated doing it, but he needed the power.

He listened for a moment, his jaw dropping at each comment from the secretary / dispatcher from the company. "Shit. Are you hearing me, sheila? You've got to check out the car, now. Before Eleanor Black gets inside. It's a matter of life and death."

Harley drove off, bearing south, then turned east. After passing the alleyway, he took the first right, heading south once more, and kept his eyes peeled for John. The dispatcher was still blathering away on the phone, talking about wanting his identification and other crap. Harley snorted. *Like I'd ever want my name in the papers.*

"Look, I can't really talk right now. I'm in the middle of something."

Harley scanned each side of the road, taking note of the cars on blocks and the general disarray of the neighborhood, and only half paying attention to the sheila on the phone. But his immediate problem was that she wasn't taking him serious enough. There had to be some way of lighting a fire under her behind. Then he got it.

"At the theater, I saw this bloke put something on the car. It had...uh...flashy lights and wires and things...and a digital clock. I'm pretty sure it was a bomb. Ya got me? I'm talking about a bomb, right? Okay. But the bloke who put it there, he saw me and now he's chasing me. So I'll call you back later to give you my info. All right, honey? You'll have them check it out? Great."

Harley threw the phone across the car. Good help was impossible to find these days. But the more he thought about the bomb story, the more he realized it was a real possibility. He looked around, scanning bushes and driveways for signs of life. *Where the hell is John?*

"Go one block west on Magnolia, Harley, then south down the first alley. The beanpole just hopped a dark brown fence about halfway down on the east side. I'm going over."

John jumped over the six-foot privacy fence and stopped dead. *You've got to be kidding me.*

Filling the yard and surrounding him were dozens of agitated Rottweilers, most with their teeth bared.

Some were growling low, while others seemed to be sizing him up, maybe wondering how tender his flesh might be. Everywhere he looked in the sea of dark fur, he saw moist noses and shining black eyes staring up at him.

And big teeth.

Thankfully, he hadn't landed on top of one, so he hoped that would cut him a little slack with the canine carnivores. A couple of them sniffed his crotch—something he never cared for, and a breach of etiquette to his mind—but he kept stock-still, figuring it was probably best not to antagonize the beasts in their own territory. And since being a statue seemed to be working, he decided to continue on with his statuesque inaction until a better course presented itself.

The growling slowly died away, with the Rottweilers seemingly more content to jump around and sniff than attack, so he carefully turned his head to spy out the surrounding area. Behind him, the fence was about six feet away. Probably not too far if he moved fast enough. To his left he saw row after of row of small cages, barely large enough to fit one dog each. But the cages were empty, like all the dogs had been let out for playtime, or for exercise in a prison yard.

And there was the beanpole. He stood, quivering, toward the far end of the yard. He'd almost made it to the other side, but the dogs seemed to be holding him back, penning him in.

John almost laughed. The Rottweiler breed was a stocky, muscular type, and they were menacing the weakest of the bunch—the beanpole—completing John's mental image of a prison. The only things missing were the orange jumpsuits.

He smiled and edged toward the skinny dude. But as soon as he started to move, the sea of heads swiveled in his direction and a chorus of growls rose around him.

He froze, and the growling subsided to a subtle, rumbling sound—low, but still distinct. In his earpiece, he heard Harley asking for his location. John thought about it, then tried to slowly bring his hand up to the radio, but a dog closed its teeth over his wrist. *Great.*

The dog didn't chomp down, but it didn't let go either. And the other dogs seemed to be getting agitated again. Some dogs circled him, and another bumped against his leg, like a shark checking to see if something is edible.

Harley's voice buzzed in his ear for the second time, now sounding a bit worried.

John looked around and sighed. Of all the stupid things. If he could just call Harley over here, Harley could easily grab the beanpole, then extract him from this mess. John heard a faint whimper from his quarry. Was the guy losing it? "Just relax. If you don't provoke them, they'll probably leave you alone."

"Probably?" The beanpole's voice was squeaky, like he was deathly afraid.

John said, "Hey. They're only dogs. Just don't move."

"Ha. You'd like that, wouldn't you? All your cop buddies, they're probably surrounding the neighborhood right now."

"Naw, it's not like that." John tried to place the guy's accent—Jersey, most likely—but figured it was better not to spook the guy. Try to calm him down. Even do a little fishing, though it wasn't likely to help. "I'm not a cop. I was hired by Ms. Black. She's not too happy with what you did to her car yesterday."

"It wasn't me," he squeaked.

"Yeah, right. I bet there are half a dozen bug-eyed skeletal dudes hanging around Ms. Black." John paused for a bit. Since the dude's voice was downright shaky, the dogs should make a good leverage point. "You know, since you're back again, I ought to let these dogs rip you apart. What the hell did Eleanor Black ever do to you?"

The guy's buggy eyes squinted in disbelief. "Nothing. I never met the lady." His head shifted from side to side, like he was trying to watch all the dogs at the same time. "Don't leave me with these things!"

John was pretty sure he was telling the truth, which made him dumber than a bag of hammers.

The beanpole clamped a hand over his mouth. "You rat bastard. You're trying to get some friggin information out of me."

The hand movement attracted some attention and the dogs' heads pivoted in his direction—one of them biting the beanpole on his rear end. He yelped and raised a little black thing in his hand.

"You get me out of here *and* let me go…and I won't push this button. Ms. Black will live to debate another day."

John looked at the device and poised himself to spring. The damn thing looked like a remote. "You push that button and I'll kill you myself. The dogs can have what's left."

"No, wait! Take it easy, cowboy. I'm offering you a trade."

John shrugged. "I can't let you go, Beanpole."

"But I've got to get out of here!"

The guy looked ready to pass out, and John would've laughed except the beanpole's hand was still on the button and Eleanor's life was still on the line. "I'll tell you what I will do. If you disarm that trigger, I'll distract the beasts and bring them all over to me. While they're over here, you'll have a clean shot at hopping that fence behind you, and a small head start before I come after you. That's my best offer."

Another dog nipped the beanpole's thigh, and he yelped again. *"Deal!"*

He popped off the back of the remote and pulled the battery out.

John's shoulders sagged as a moment of pure relief washed

over him. "All right. Now toss it away and then I'll distract the doggies."

The guy noticed that the dogs around him were riveted to the waving remote in his hands and started to laugh. "You like this? Hey, doggies. You wanna fetch? Wanna fetch? *Go get it!*"

John saw the remote coming right at him, with a dozen growling dogs following right after, and instinctively covered his privates. Things were getting ugly, and he was ready to jump for the fence, when a high-pitched, girlish scream cut through the night.

John turned back and saw the skinny dude running for the opposite fence, squealing the whole way.

All the dogs in the yard stopped, saw the fleeing 'bunny,' and chased the live prey to the fence. The skinny dude leapt over, to freedom, and the dogs crushed up against the fence.

John thought about going over the boards nearest him, but figured that would give the beanpole too much of a head start. The dogs were packed in tight as sardines, frothing at the mouth and searching for the missing bunny—noses pointing everywhere but back at John.

Here goes nothing, he thought, and ran toward them. As he approached the seething mass of bodies, he jumped, vaulting off the backs of the dogs and over the six foot fence.

He hit the ground with a thud and saw the skinny dude running down the street.

John took off after him, keying his radio along the way. "Harley. I'm heading north on the street that runs parallel to the alley, one block to the east."

The skinny dude was closer now, and slowing a bit, when John heard an engine roar behind him. He turned and saw an old, brown Chevy bearing down on him, only five feet away. He leapt into the air, noticing first the Chevy emblem, then spinning as the vehicle clipped his legs.

His gaze snapped to the dirty windshield and the grinning, corpulent, black man sitting inside. That view was quickly obscured by a spider web of cracks as John smashed into the windshield. Then there was more spinning, followed by the asphalt getting closer and closer, and an incredibly intense pain as he hit the ground.

Through a thick haze, John watched the car stop and pick up the skinny dude before peeling away. Then John blacked out.

"CAN YOU HEAR ME, JOHN? ARE YOU ALL RIGHT?"

John opened his eyes and tried to focus. He turned his head to the left and felt a sharp, shooting pain. "Ahh...ouch."

"You with me?"

John turned to his right and found Harley with an unusual expression on his face—worry. *Shit*. Things must be pretty bad if his partner was worried. "Yeah, I'm here." He tested a couple of tender areas. "I don't think anything's broken, but I feel like I just went thirteen rounds."

Harley let out a long breath and chuckled. "Crikey. Never pick a fight with two tons of Detroit steel, eh mate? I'm pretty sure I taught you better than that."

John squinted. "I'm glad your sense of humor is back."

"You gotta admit. The car won by a knockout." Harley grabbed hold of John and raised him to his feet. "But I *am* glad you're all right. You had me worried there."

"Me, too. But I don't think the car was going that fast." John shook his head. "The damned driver was working with the beanpole, and he caught me napping. I wasn't looking for anyone else."

"Did you get a license plate? Or a look at the driver?"

"Before I passed out I got a partial plate when the car stopped to pick up the skinny dude. But the driver...it was pretty fast. All I can tell you is that the guy was huge. At least three hundred and fifty pounds."

"Was he black?"

"Yeah. And the dude smirked when he hit me."

"The same guy who was messing around near your sister's limo, I expect."

John felt his whole body turn rigid. "You warned the security company?"

"'Course I did." Harley squinted. "But those blokes are idiots."

"I got a remote trigger off the skinny dude. But if they've got another one, and if they put a bomb on her car..."

John whipped out his cell phone. The LCD was cracked, but it was still operable. He hit the memory speed-dial for his sister's cell, then waited impatiently through a couple of rings before he got an answer.

"Yeah. What's up, Bro."

John felt his muscles relax. "Thank God you're all right. Did your security guys find anything?"

"What are you talking about? At the house?"

"No. Security checked your car before you left the theater, right?"

Harley chimed in, "Front, driver's side fender."

John repeated it to his sister.

Eleanor said, "I don't know anything about this. Hang on a second."

John waited and heard his sister ask the guard riding shotgun. The guard said that dispatch had received a call, but that it must have been a prank because he'd watched the car during the whole debate and hadn't seen a thing.

John cringed as he felt a rock drop in his stomach.

"Eleanor! Listen to me. Harley and I were keeping watch at the debate. They were messing with your car, Eleanor. Tell the driver to pull over. Tell him right now!"

John listened as Eleanor yelled at the driver to pull off the freeway. But, two seconds later, John heard a loud bang followed by tire squeals. *No, No, NO!*

He clutched the cell phone, cracking the plastic. Then he heard some yelling and a horrible, huge crunch of metal.

And then silence.

thirteen

JOHN paced the floor of Mercy Hospital, doing his best to wear a hole in it, and tried to calm himself down. How could he have let this happen? He pounded his fist into the wall, upsetting the nurses for the umpteenth time.

"Take it easy, mate. You're scaring the pretty ladies," Harley said. "How is she?"

John turned and found Harley slipping through the door, looking slightly worse for wear, like he'd been rolling around in the mud. John gave him a big hug, startling the prickly Aussie, and followed up with a rueful smile. Harley had never been much of a touchy-feely guy. "She's stable right now. But she's in a coma."

"Aw, that's the shits, ain't it? Is there anything I can do?" Harley flushed and looked at the floor. "Sorry, mate, don't mean to sound so lame. I guess my people skills leave something to be desired."

John shrugged. "Don't worry about it. So do mine."

"Yeah, right. Compared to me you're good at this people crap. Probably why the business has been doing loads better since you took over."

"Hey, I appreciate what you're doing. I really do. But you're not going to make me feel better so let it alone, all right?" John slumped into a couch, his mind firmly stuck thinking about Eleanor, feeling guilty about what happened.

"But that's where you're wrong. Even though I don't have people skills, I do have other talents." Harley reached into his coat pocket and pulled out a baggy filled with black, broken pieces of plastic. "Don't you want to ask why I'm all covered in mud?"

John shook his head, perking up a bit. "You're kidding

me. How'd you find the remote trigger with those demented Rottweilers standing guard?"

Harley held up a torn sleeve. "You know me, mate, I've got a way with animals. Once I made the leader of the pack my best pal, the rest wanted to be friends, too. But the bad part is, they'd already chewed the thing like it was their favorite rag doll. I'm taking it to my buddy down in Copville to see if he can get a print off of it, but I'm not real hopeful. I think our best bet is with one of his blue brothers from the bomb squad. They'll take a look, and with any luck, turn up something useful."

John held the baggy up to the light and frowned, looking at lots of little pieces covered in doggy saliva. "I don't know, it's pretty damaged. How about the license plate?"

Harley sighed. "I wish I had good news for ya. We matched the partial, but the title turned out to be from a junked car. The plate was probably stolen from a junkyard."

John hit the wall again, but pulled the punch at the last second, mindful of scaring the nurses again. "Wishful thinking, but I was hoping they were stupid enough to use their own car. The cops find anything at the scene?"

Harley snorted. "They barely looked. Multiple eyewitnesses, mostly the security goons that were following the limo, told the police that it was an accident. That the tire just blew out. Unfortunately, the security guys are covering their arses pretty well, claiming they checked out the car thoroughly and that it's impossible there was any tampering with the car. With no evidence of a bomb, or any other device, your story has been discounted as coming from a grieving relative."

"What? That's it?"

"No, of course not. They're still going to investigate. Your mother is a senator and Eleanor is the mayor, so they won't close the case. But since they think they know the answer, they won't break their necks looking, either. The only way that might change is if your mum applies some leverage or an eyewitness comes forward. Your mother is so hard to figure that heck, the old Barracuda might not want to make a big deal out of it. Who knows? As for an eyewitness, the driver and security guard didn't make it, and Eleanor's not capable of talking, so the chance of that is slimmer than the skinny dude's khakis."

John took a deep breath, trying to think things through and get proactive, but his mind wasn't working too well. Still, it was good to be working on a plan. He dreaded telling Hillary about what had happened to her mom, and kept picturing the look on her face years ago when she'd found out her father had died. Even worse, now he was worried about her safety. "These guys are trying to make it look like an accident, so they'll have to try for Hillary and Amber."

"And you, too. You're all loose ends."

"Yeah. But they probably don't know who I am, yet. And even if they did, no one knows about my place in the canyon. I'm worried about Hillary. And Eleanor. Since she's still alive, they might try again."

Harley shook his head. "If it was just guarding the two of them, we'd be fine. But we need to quit playing defense and start a major offensive effort. Find the bastards who did this. That's too many points for us to cover effectively."

John paced the same path he had for the last few hours. "You're right. I'll pick up Hillary and Amber and stash them at my place for a day or two. You search the crash site and drop off the trigger at the precinct. Then we'll meet up at Gil's place and squeeze till we get a list of suspects out of him. And take care of the funding problem with his child support at the same time."

John looked over his shoulder when he heard a burst of crowd noise from the opposite end of the hallway. Dozens of flashbulbs went off as his mom strode through the doorway, answering a couple of questions over her shoulder, but putting distance between herself and the reporters.

Harley said, "Ah, Barbara Black ventures from her lair. You know, I think that's the first time I've ever seen the Barracuda refuse to suckle at publicity's monstrous teat. Maybe all is not lost."

"Come on, leave her be. Her daughter's in a coma."

Harley had the grace to look embarrassed. "Sorry, mate."

"Before you leave, talk to the security detail that's watching Eleanor. Let them know what'll happen to them if anyone else hurts Eleanor. Put the fear of God into them."

Harley gave a malevolent grin. "God? I'll make sure they fear *me*."

John shivered. As Harley slunk out the door, with the same dangerous elegance as a panther, John marveled at the way a sixty-year-old man could still exude the same killer vibe he'd had back with Special Forces. *Good thing he's on my side.*

John heard the telltale click of high heels on linoleum and turned to his mother. She was almost unrecognizable. Of course, they only saw each other a couple of times a year, but that wasn't it. Her visage was devoid of her usual, poised expression—the poker face she wore twenty-four hours a day as a politician and a parent—and instead was filled with emotion and pain. He reached out and gave the old Barracuda a warm hug, but she quickly disengaged and gave him a peck on the cheek.

"My God. What happened to my baby?"

Through the doorway at the end of the hall, John saw cameras taking their picture. He covered his mouth with his hand and spoke in a low voice. "Someone tried to kill her. I'm not sure why."

"Oh, the police told me that nonsense, but they assured me it was just that. So tell me what's really going on."

John sighed, dredging up memories of old fights. "Mom. I know we disagree about politics and morality, and everything else for that matter, but I would never say it if I wasn't sure."

Barbara focused her laser-like gaze on him and John couldn't help but cringe. "Damn it, of course you're telling the truth. When it comes to the truth, you've got diarrhea of the mouth."

John blinked in surprise at his mother's cursing. She must be even more worried than she seemed.

She continued, "How on earth would you know anything about this? When I don't?"

John took a deep breath. "There was an attempt yesterday. Hillary saw it, and called me for help. I was chasing the bastard tonight, when a car ran me down."

He gestured toward the bloody bandage on the back of his head, for some reason hoping for a little sympathy, but his mother barely glanced at it. Instead, the lasers focused directly on his eyes.

"So you failed to protect your sister? Is that what you're saying?"

John winced. Mother was a master of manipulation and guilt—even Presidents had crumbled under her baleful glare—but this time he didn't need her help to feel bad. "Yeah. I screwed up."

His mom's political mask slipped back into place and made it hard for him to read her expression.

He continued, "But I won't screw up again. I need to know where Hillary is. She might be in danger."

"Oh my God." Barbara's facade remained intact, but her hand clutched at her chest. "She's spending the night at her friend Amber's house, which is three doors down from Eleanor's place, and on the same side of the street. You pick her up and take care of her, John."

"I will."

Barbara's hand clenched into a fist. "Have that associate of yours, that Harley person, do some digging. But don't say a word to the press until we talk again. I have to find a way to salvage this politically. For Eleanor's sake."

John shook his head. "I don't think she's worried about her political career right now."

"Of course not, that's why Mummy's here. Now go on, I'll stay with Eleanor. Call me with any news."

Barbara turned back toward the doorway filled with reporters, her expression two parts sorrow and one part stoic strength, and solemnly walked toward them. She tilted her head slightly to the left, keeping her best side toward the cameras.

John sighed as he watched her approach the publicity machine that was the elixir of life for his mother and all other politicians. The feeling of dismissal irked him, as always, but that was just part of her personality. He took one look at the swarming reporters pawing at his mother and ducked through the side door.

Nails turned off the shower and grabbed a towel off the rack. He winced as he stepped out of the tub, his knee killing him like it always did. The hot water hadn't done a thing to get rid of his foul mood.

He grunted. *A coma. Can you believe that shit?* The tube had said that Black had lived through the crash, which seemed impossible since the car had rolled several times. But even worse, there was now another witness. First the two teenagers and now an unknown security guard. Nails felt his eye start to twitch, as it sometimes did when he got agitated. Barry was a useless hunk of human being. He couldn't get anything right.

He heard a voice in the living room and opened the door a crack, with the undersized towel barely covering his midsection. Barry was lying there on the couch, moaning, "No, Lassie. *No!* Bad dog."

Another of the dude's freaky dreams. Except this time the stupid cracker was pitching a tent in his shorts, like he needed to get laid or something. *Shit, what could make you get a hard-on in a nightmare?*

Nails shook his head. Never mind, it was better not to know.

Feeling a bit of envy, he closed the door and removed his towel. Then he grabbed a sliver of glass from the mirror and held it by his goodies. *Not bad.* They seemed to have sprouted a little bit. Although the purplish color didn't look too good.

He put the sliver back in its place. It was about time to stop taking these crazy, experimental meds and schedule knee replacement surgery, *if* the bastards paid him for the Black job. They might try to weasel out of it since she was technically still alive.

He heard a scream from the living room and put his towel back on, then squeezed through the doorway, getting a splinter in his belly in the process. Barry had moved to a sitting position on the couch and his hand was covered in blood. *You gotta be kidding me.* "If you got that blood on my couch I'll have to hurt you."

Barry started yammering, running off at the mouth, "It must have been those dogs, Nails. I'm so sorry. I don't know what happened. I was having this dream about screwing those teenagers from the Black house."

Nails grimaced. "I don't want to hear about it."

"And that Lassie look-alike, the one from Odie's place, came up and started peeing all over us. At first I wasn't sure what to do, but the girls squealed, 'Ooh, a golden shower' and didn't seem too upset about it."

Nails eye twitched rapidly as he tried to erase the image in his brain. "That's disgusting. And I don't want to hear it so shut up."

"I thought I'd go with the flow, so to speak, but then Black's hand reached up from under the earth and started clawing at me. It held me down, scolding me for screwing her daughter, while the Rottweilers started tearing at my flesh. Then I woke up all wet. I wasn't sure if it was dog pee or what."

Nails gave him a slap upside the head, knocking Barry back into the couch and finally shutting him up. *Sick cracker.* "If I had dreams like that, I'd do something about it. Get stoned out of my mind. Or maybe a lobotomy. Whatever it took."

Barry rubbed his jaw, giving Nails a pitiful look, and then pulled his pants down and tried to look at his backside. It was dripping red. "I think I'm gonna be sick. Is that my blood?"

Nails grunted.

Barry said, "I knew I got nipped, but that dog must have gotten a huge, friggin piece of me when I was jumping the fence. I gotta get to the hospital."

As Barry started to get up, Nails shoved him back down. "No way, no how. We got enough problems with witnesses without you showing your ugly mug at the hospital. Besides, we've got to see Mr. S in an hour."

Barry looked at the darkened windows and then his watch,

his eyes narrowing. "It's only four in the morning. Why's he wanna meet now?"

Nails shrugged. "Because he's smarter than you are."

"But if there ain't any witnesses..." Barry started trembling. "Black ain't exactly dead. Are you sure it won't be the Russians waiting for us instead of Mr. Steel?"

"Don't be stupid," Nails growled. "He's not going to whack us in his office right before the election."

Barry let out a deep breath and grinned. "Yeah, what was I thinking? That's the one place we don't have to worry about. You don't get elected with bloodstains on your carpet. Imagine the headlines."

"Yeah, imagine." Nails reached in a drawer and grabbed a travel sewing kit with a Holiday Inn logo on the case. "We can get some antibiotics when we stop by Pfester. They got some pretty good stuff there."

"What are you talking about?"

As the look of confusion spread across Barry's face, Nails held up the needle. "Don't worry about it. When I was playing football, I saw the trainers stitching up people all the time. I think I can handle it."

Barry's jaw dropped. "You gotta be friggin kidding me."

SIERRA OPENED THE DOOR TO HER APARTMENT OFF CAHUENGA, AND slipped into the safety and security of home. She carried her son to his room and tucked him in, kissing him on the forehead.

She watched him for a moment, loving the way Bobby looked when he was sleeping, which was nothing like Gil, thank God, but instead was a look of pure innocence. *He must have gotten that from my side of the family.*

These days, Bobby was almost too heavy to carry, though the walk from Grandma's was short, only one apartment over. Sierra tiptoed into her bedroom, trying her best to keep quiet, and started thinking about the last several hours.

The night had been a blur. It started with the debate, which had been spirited—and laced with profanity—unlike any other debate she could remember. She smiled, thinking of a couple of choice phrases from Two-Bits. That was some pretty good television. Or rather, fabulous ratings and *not* very good television, for those who could tell the difference.

Then she'd seen John there—using her press pass, of course—working on something mysterious. He'd vanished abruptly, and her story sense was already working overtime when the call came from her producer to rush down to Mercy Hospital.

Sierra fanned herself, wishing for better air conditioning, then grabbed a light tank top and matching cotton panties from the dresser drawer and started to change for bed. Not that she'd get much sleep before Bobby woke up.

Senator Black had been less than forthcoming about the nature of Eleanor Black's accident. Which was typical. The Barracuda never let anything out to the public till she was darn good and ready.

But was it an accident? The police said yes, but John's demeanor at the hospital said no. He was grief-stricken, that was obvious, but he was also focused, like when they were having lunch and he was listening to the details about Gil.

He'd clearly been on the job tonight, and his head had been bandaged. It could have been a coincidence, but she was pretty darned sure it was related to Eleanor's crash. She sighed, wishing she could investigate and find out what was going on. But she'd promised John to let him tell it when he was ready, so of course she would wait. But it was agony.

She took off her little gold necklace and placed it in her jewelry box on top of the bureau, then looked down at her perfumes and frowned. The little amber bottle of *Shades of Venice* was off kilter. She could remember putting the fragrance on, now almost twenty-four hours ago, and setting it back in its normal place.

She quickly glanced at the rest of the bureau. At first, everything else looked all right, but then she noticed a tube of lipstick sitting on its side, with a weird black cap on the end. She picked up the lipstick, pulled off the cap, and found herself staring at the business end of a lipstick-sized video camera.

Damn it, Gil! She threw the camera on the floor and stomped on it ten or twenty times, pretending the electronic device was Gil's face. "You've got money to pay for little spy toys for your sick and twisted perversions, and you don't have enough money to pay for Bobby! What the hell is the matter with you?"

She cringed, thinking of the video he'd just gotten of her changing, and stomped on it a few more times, just for good measure.

fourteen

RICHARD Steel sat in his office, mesmerized. He had the sound turned up, and the blinds closed, even though the sun hadn't quite risen yet. Fascinated, he watched himself on TV, giving an interview for the morning show *Rise and Shine, Los Angeles*, and thought, *Damn, I'm good. I could sell monkey shit as a facial tonic!*

He chortled, enjoying his witticism, and muted the sound. *See. Don't worry, Dick. Everything's going to work out.* Per both his Zen master and his shrink's instructions, he sat back and envisioned the road to success, as he did every day to keep his feet firmly on the path. With crystal clarity he could remember the day he'd sold a red Corvette convertible to an old granny with a bad hip. It was the day he'd taken the first step and had enough cajones to quit his job at Big Mike's auto dealership, ready to move onto bigger and better scams.

His keen nose, which he liked to believe could sniff out money from a quarter mile away, had led to two years of mail-order law school for a fancy, if somewhat phony, degree. But the degree was merely a way to get to where the real money was—politics.

There were hiccups along the way, of course, like his short-lived internship for the pudgy congressman from District 22, which had ended poorly. After an unfortunate incident, where he'd tried to blackmail the congressman, he'd found out just how tough it was to pry money away from a politician. Evidently, the expression "From their cold, dead hands" began with a politician.

Despite the incident, he bore a grudging respect for the asswipe who'd fired him, finally realizing that the congressman would do whatever it took to stay in power. An admirable trait, and one shared by many of the politicians he'd met. And what's more, they were sneaky bastards, capable of anything.

But so was he.

After a brief, wonderful taste of the miraculous corruption of politics, he was hooked. So he took his second step. Public office had seemed a bit lofty at the time, too much of a long-term goal for his taste. He wanted in as quickly as possible, and the lucky break was having an uncle working at Pfester Pharmaceuticals. That got him a job in the PR department. After a boatload of ass-kissing and backstabbing, he'd earned a promotion to Executive in Charge of Congressional Relations.

Lobbying was his dream job. Exchanging money, hookers, or even promises in order to get legislation passed that was beneficial to Pfester. And they paid him for it. He'd been successful working with the state and local boys, as well as the Washington jerks, as though the job of lobbying had been created especially for him.

But after a while, the thrill of the bribe grew thin, and he grew tired of giving kickbacks to others for their votes. Like everyone in Hollywood, what he really wanted to do was direct. He wanted others to be kissing his ass for a change.

So he'd set his sights on being leader of the sixth largest economy in the world—California. And when the current governor was caught with his pants down, groping like a madman, Steel knew the time was ripe. He'd been laying the groundwork, a little whisper campaign, that it would be good for a company like Pfester to have their own man in the top reaches of government. And that the right person was Richard Steel. Or as he liked to call himself, Tricky Dick.

Thinking ahead, he'd also spent the last year cultivating his relationship with the Russians, Sasha and Lexi, two of the board members at Pfester. Not only were they into his plan, they were also into organized crime, with ties to all the big unions in California. A lot of muscle to help get those extra votes. Steel had a grandfather from Moscow, so he'd gotten along well with the Russians from the start.

But then the bomb dropped—the recall election got way

out of hand. Even with the backing of a Fortune 500 company, and some ex-KGB / Mafia guys who were good at covert voting campaigns, he wasn't sure he would win.

A couple of solid politicians posed the biggest problem, but there was also an assortment of popular TV stars, wrestlers, and rappers in the running. Candidates were cropping up faster than illegal aliens were crossing the border. And California had already proven that it was willing to elect anybody who was famous.

That's when he'd come up with the plan. It was really just a practical matter. There were people who stood in the way of progress. Well, his progress anyway.

He'd already learned from the pudgy congressman that you did whatever you had to, if you wanted the power. So he'd contacted the Russians, they'd had a sit-down and gone over all their options.

What they wanted was a hit man. Maybe even more than one. They wanted somebody to take care of the extraneous candidates. Someone who could take care of things, but could also be used as a fall guy if things got ugly.

They'd gone over the possibilities and come up with what they'd hoped was a good team. Guys who had connections to them, but weren't identified with either Steel or the Russians.

And more important, they had leverage points. Barry's gambling debt had him into the Russians for six figures, and Nails, a four hundred pound beast of a man, needed industrial strength painkillers in the worst way. Which happened to be a specialty of Pfester. Nails took part in scientific "studies" there, needing the potent medication to keep walking. It was perfect. For a carrot, they could offer him enough money for a knee replacement, and for a stick, they could withhold the pain meds.

It had seemed like a brilliant plan. But the meatheads couldn't keep up with the production schedule. They were already two politicians behind, with less than ten days to go before the election. They needed to get back on schedule.

Steel thought about the problem for a moment, watching

the muted television as he went over his options. His concentration was broken when the stooges in the television audience applauded his line of B.S. He cracked a smile. *Hook, line and sinker.*

Then he frowned. He was lucky he got any airtime at all with the coverage of Black's 'accident.' He hoped it didn't turn her into a martyr or something, winning with a ton of sympathy votes.

A couple of picture frames fell off the wall and he jumped, thinking it was another of California's famous earthquakes, before he heard large thumps on the side door of his office. Nails had arrived.

Steel unlocked the door to the back stairs and let the goons inside. They looked sullen, like naughty schoolchildren. How to deal with them? Maybe friendly, with the Russian threat looming large. "Come in. Have a seat, boys."

Nails dropped into a chair, threatening to squash the thing, but Barry remained standing with a grimace on his face.

"If it's all the same to you, Mr. S, I think I'll stand."

Was this insubordination? "Excuse me? Did I hear you correctly?"

Nails grunted. "Dogs ripped him up pretty good. His ass feels like it's on fire."

"Then I guess he'd better stand." Steel nodded to himself. "I'm not pleased with how things have been going. And what's worse, Sasha and Lexi aren't thrilled, either."

Barry blanched. "But Black is out of the picture. Plus, it looks like an accident. Come on. Work with us here."

"I'd like to, Barry. I really would. But at this rate, I'm going to lose the election. And now there are witnesses. You understand why I'm concerned?"

"Of course, Mr. Steel. Nails and I...well, we're both very sorry about what's been going on. But we'll take care of things. We'll make things right."

Steel smiled. There, that was better. They were all on the same page now, the help properly motivated. He opened his mouth to speak, but stopped when Nails' eye started twitching—which was disconcerting, to say the least. Steel did his best to ignore it, knowing it was a bone of contention for the beast.

"Look, gentlemen. We're running out of time, and we've still got Sanchez, Arnold, and Two-Bits on the list." Steel grimaced, remembering that Two-Bits had called him a racist on primetime. Which was idiotic, since he'd kill all races equally.

"You're going to have to split up for the next one. Nails, I want you to take care of Two-Bits. I like the drive-by shooting idea. I like it a lot."

There was a grunt from Nails that he took for assent. "Barry, you need to take care of the witnesses. According to Black's schedule, tomorrow morning she and her daughter were supposed to be visiting her husband's grave. The anniversary of his death, or something like that, so I bet the daughter still goes. And with any luck her friend will be there, too."

"You gotta be kidding me. You want me to kill the girls?"

Steel focused his gaze on Barry. "Is that a problem?"

Barry shuffled his feet for a moment before replying. "No, sir."

"Good. I'll work out the details for Sanchez. Since he's a buddy of mine, you won't have to kill him. Instead, you're going to get some video on him. He's a huge horndog, and I know a girl that's into some twisted stuff..." He paused. "Do either one of you have a video camera?"

"I got one," Nails said.

"Do you know how to use it?"

Nails grunted.

"Well, make sure you keep it with you. When I get this set up, I may have to call you guys on short notice."

"No problem."

"And when you make the video, don't get any of that missionary position shit. You get some really disgusting stuff on film. Nothing normal! It's got to be something that he'd never want to hit the airwaves."

"You got it, boss."

"Good. Now go take care of business. And don't let anyone see you leaving the building."

Nails heaved himself from the chair and rumbled through the side door. As he went down the stairs, sounding like a herd of elephants, Barry paused in the doorway.

"We still get payment for the Black job, right?"

What nerve. Steel laughed. "Is she dead?"

More shuffling feet. "Practically. She's out of the picture anyway. Enough so you got us moving onto another target."

"But she can still cause me some problems. I'll tell you what. I'm feeling generous today, so I'll notify the Russians that you guys get half for putting her in a coma. If you want to finish her off next week, we'll give you the rest."

Barry's gaze narrowed, apparently unhappy about the payment, but he kept walking through the door without saying another word. As Steel locked it behind them, he thought he heard Barry mutter something about unions and friggin teamsters.

fifteen

JOHN parked his car one block from Gil's place and glanced around, looking for Harley, but he was nowhere to be found. The sky was just starting to lighten and John briefly wondered if the ever punctual Harley had gotten hung up at the crash site. But before long his thoughts had returned to his sister, as they had every few minutes since the accident, worrying about whether she would pull through.

He felt a presence coming up on his blind side, and snapped his head back against the headrest. A hand streaked through the open window of the car, where his head had been, and John used its momentum to push it into the steering wheel. He yanked on the arm, pulling its owner halfway into the car.

At the sight of the graying head beside him, John groaned and released his partner. "I'm not in the mood, Harley."

A snort. "No one ever is, mate. You think the bad guys will give you a break 'cause you're not in the mood?"

"Even so, for the time being, let's keep the training to minimum. All right?"

Harley nodded, and opened the door for John, who stepped out and onto the sidewalk. They started walking toward Gil's house, watching both sides of the street for activity. "Did you find anything at the site?" John asked.

"Sure, lots of things. A used condom, cigarette butts, about twenty beer cans, and a dozen rusty nails. The typical stuff you'd find on the side of an L.A. freeway."

"That's it?"

"Well, so far. I didn't have time to finish my grid search before our session with the councilman. I'll go back after we're done with Gil." Harley gave him a sidelong glance. "So why are you late this morning?"

"Don't get me started. Picking up the girls was rougher than I thought it would be. Hillary's doing as well as can be expected, but her friend Amber is a handful."

"Her parents didn't want her to leave?"

"No, not even close. Her parents could care less where she sleeps at night. That's part of the problem. I'm going to have put a lock on my bedroom door if I don't want her sneaking in there."

Harley snorted and wheezed, his version of quiet laughter. "It's hard to fathom a young shiela like that going for an old man like you."

"No kidding."

They started up the steps and onto the front porch, John checking over his shoulder on the way.

Harley said, "I've cased the house. Wonderboy is not home. And lucky for you, no dogs."

John shook his head, but ignored the bait and positioned himself to shield Harley from the street. His partner pulled a lockpick set from his coat pocket and got to work on the door.

John said, "He's not supposed to be here yet. According to Sierra, Gil always does his workout from six to eight a.m. So that gives us about an hour and a half till he gets home."

"Great. We'll scare the bejeezus out of him, inflict a little injury if he needs it, and then grab some breakfast."

Harley opened the front door and slid inside, gun at the ready. John followed, moving past the tacky, ultramodern furniture and minimalist décor and toward the hallway on the right. Harley went left.

They did a quick check, verifying that no one was there, then got down to business. John sat down at the laptop computer to dig through Gil's files while Harley did a thorough and more destructive search on the dwelling.

AN HOUR LATER, THE PLACE MOSTLY TORN APART, HARLEY SAT DOWN next to John. "I've got nothing. Either he doesn't have much to hide, or I'm losing my touch."

"Well, you do qualify for a senior discount. Maybe you are losing it."

Harley glared at him. John hid a grin behind his hand and said, "He's a politician. He's got plenty to hide, but he keeps it all on his computer. I've got enough stuff here to get him twenty years. Payoffs, illegal business deals, and hours of secret video of Sierra. Some kind of spy-cam thing. He's a pretty sick bastard."

Harley's glare softened. "Now we're cooking with gas."

"Damn straight." John turned back to the screen, reading through another email, and making notes. "I've got a little bit more to go."

Harley took a seat by the window. Watching and waiting for Gil.

GIL PARKED HIS BEAMER IN THE GARAGE, GIDDY FROM THE endorphin high he'd gotten exercising, and headed inside. Singing the Police song, "Every Breath You Take," he was also feeling pretty amped about the day ahead. There would probably be some good video of Sierra with that new lipstick cam he'd installed. And there was an excellent chance that the land developer he was working with would offer him a hefty bribe this morning. Sweet!

He got about two steps into the hallway before he noticed that the whole place had been trashed. Trashed! Books taken off the shelves, sofas upended, and every cupboard emptied onto the floor. He couldn't believe it.

And there, sleeping at his desk, was the bastard who'd done it all. Sleeping! It was even more unbelievable. Like after he'd finished vandalizing the place, he'd passed out in a drunken stupor.

Gil thought about it for a moment, endorphins pumping madly through his veins, and decided to beat the living hell out of the intruder before calling the police. He grabbed a fireplace poker, raised it over his head, and began sneaking up on the guy. He'd taken two steps when he felt a something cold pressed against his neck.

"Take it easy, mate. Don't want to hurt you unnecessarily."

Was that a gun? Gil slowly turned his head and found himself looking down the barrel of a handgun with something weird attached to the end of it. A freaking silencer. He backed away from the gun until he noticed that it was a senior citizen holding the weapon. A senior citizen! *This is like a bad dream.*

Gil thought about rushing the guy, but quickly thought better of it. The guy did have gray hair, but other than that he didn't look like any senior citizen Gil had ever seen. He looked dangerous.

From behind Gil, a voice said, "I want you to relax, Gil. Don't do anything stupid."

They know my name! Gil whirled around and saw that the sleeping guy at the desk had been faking it all along. He was wide awake. And what's more, the sleeping guy had been searching through Gil's computer files. His computer files!

Gil nervously shifted to his left and looked past the sleeper's shoulder at the LCD monitor. He cringed, wondering why on earth he'd kept that stuff on there. Way too incriminating. Way too disgusting. But where could you keep stuff like that? He shook his head. In a freaking safe, of course.

He shifted back to his right foot, and then back to his left, petrified. What could he do? He shifted a few more times, kind of like he was dancing in place, and tried to think. Hey! If the laptop was destroyed, there wouldn't be anything to worry about.

"Quit jumping around. You going to take it easy or not?" the sleeper asked.

"Oh, sure. You don't have to worry about me."

As soon as he said it, he dashed toward the desk and the sleeper. The guy took a step back into a defensive position, which was perfect. Gil smashed the poker into the laptop, then flung it across the room. He had just enough time to hear the crash, as it banged into the wall, before he felt a sharp pain in the back of his head.

I think they hit me. Then he blacked out.

GIL CRACKED HIS EYES OPEN AND WINCED. WHY DID HIS HEAD HURT so much? He tried to lift his hands, but they wouldn't move. Looking down he noticed that they were duct-taped to the arms of the chair. *What the hell?*

He looked up and noticed his computer was back in its place, screen cracked but still on. Filled with images of Sierra, as well as files relating his meetings with developers and lobbyists. He groaned, then snapped his head to the right. With a flash of pain from the movement, he saw the senior and the sleeper watching him.

"That was pretty stupid, Gil," the sleeper said. "Even if you dropped your laptop from the top of your roof, the information on the hard drive would still be there. All you did was mess up your screen."

"I'm a city councilman. I've got friends in high places."

The sleeper gave a small laugh. "Right now, we're the only friends you've got."

Some movement caught his eye, and Gil turned to the senior citizen, who was smiling, flipping through some gruesome photos. He snorted and stopped at one particular picture, holding it up so Gil could get a good look.

It was a picture of a man, covered in blood, who had been tied to a chair. And the senior was there, with his arm around him, like it was a family picture instead of the grisly thing that it really was. Gil whimpered.

"Quit scaring him. Gil's going to cooperate. Aren't you?"

"Oh, yes." Gil nodded. "One hundred percent. You don't have to worry about me."

The sleeper frowned. "That's what you said when you ran at me with the poker."

"Oh…I'm real sorry about that, guys. I think it was the endorphins or something. But I'm all better now. Honest."

The sleeper looked him in the eye and nodded, apparently satisfied. "First, tell me about Eleanor Black. Your dealings with her, other people and their dealings with her, as well as any enemies she might have. After we've exhausted that particular subject, we'll start talking about Sierra. And your responsibilities as a father to your child."

Gil's mouth opened. What was he talking about? *And who freaking cares?* Gil turned to the senior citizen, who stared back at him with a malevolent grin, while idly fingering a hunting knife.

Gil gulped and reassessed his priorities. *Don't think. Just talk. Tell 'em whatever they want to know.*

And with that, he started babbling, sometimes blubbering.

sixteen

THE RINGING phone tugged at Sierra until she finally woke. She yanked the receiver off the hook, stopping the infernal racket, and gave a quick glance toward the clock. *Three hours sleep! So unfair.*

She looked at the caller ID and felt her heart skip a beat. She smiled and answered, "Hello."

"Hi. It's John. It's not too early, is it?"

"No, of course not." She paused to yawn and rub the sleep from her eyes. "Sorry. It was a long night."

There was a moment of hesitation before he said, "Yeah. I know what you mean."

All at once she remembered the events of last night and mentally cursed herself for being insensitive. The words started pouring out of her, "I'm so sorry, John. Here I am talking about me after you've just experienced one of the worst nights of your life. The accident was so horrible and then I saw you there with your mother and I know how hard *that* must have been. And you know it wasn't an accident, even though the police say it was…"

She took a deep breath, wishing she had more self-control when it came to her emotions, and started tapping her heels together. "I'm really sorry, John. If there's anything I can do…"

"Thanks, I appreciate that. I really do. But I'm calling about something else."

Sierra stopped clicking her heels and listened.

"I've got someone here who wants to talk to you."

She heard some rustling before she heard a familiar voice, "It's me, Sierra."

Gil. She glanced at the smashed lipstick camera in the corner. *Scumbag.* But why was he on John's phone?

"I just called to apologize for my actions this last year."

She nearly dropped the phone. She tightened her grip and said, "Okay."

"No, I mean it, Sierra. I've been a complete jerk. An ass really. And starting today I'm going to be a new man. I've even given John a check for all the back child support I owe you. From now on, that's the first check I'll write every month."

Sierra's mouth opened wide. John was a miracle worker.

"And I'm not going to skip out on my weekends with Bobby anymore. I'm going to start being a better father from now on. Anyway, I'm not much for showing my emotions, so that's all I've got to say right now. I'll say the rest in a letter or something. Please forgive me."

She again heard some rustling as John got back on the line.

"Do you believe him?" John said.

She smiled. "I do. And I can't even begin to explain how relieved I am. How on earth did you do that?"

"Trade secret."

"Well, you just impressed the hell out of me. I owe you big time, and I don't mean your fee. If there's anything I can ever do to help you out, let me know."

"Thanks, I appreciate it. Listen, I'll bring you this check a little later. But if Gil ever gets out of line again, you let *me* know."

Sierra hung up the phone and decided to take a long, hot bath—to soak, and to think about her new hero.

JOHN SLID HIS CELL PHONE INTO HIS POCKET AND LEANED TOWARD GIL. "Good news, she believes you're serious. But more important, does Harley believe it?"

Gil's eyes rolled back.

Harley took a step toward him, twirling his knife in his hand. "Unfortunately..."

"What?" Gil blurted out. "But I do mean it! I'll be a good boy!"

Harley snorted. "You didn't let me finish, mate. Unfortunately, I do believe you."

Gil spluttered, "But...but how's that unfortunate?"

Harley put his knife in a sheath behind his back and clamped a hand around the back of Gil's neck. He held Gil in place and leaned into him. "Because I really wanted to do some damage. Now I don't get to have any fun."

Gil stared at him, eyes popping from his skull, and John almost laughed. But he held it back.

Harley said, "Crikey! Now I'm in a foul mood. I feel sorry for the next poor fella who cuts me off in traffic."

"Come on. Let's go." John picked up the laptop and headed toward the door. Over his shoulder, he said, "Be good, Gil. You don't want to wake up one night and see Harley at the foot of your bed playing with his knife."

John closed the front door and headed down the steps. "You didn't have to be so rough with him. He would've caved without it."

Harley shrugged. "I didn't do any permanent damage. Besides, we had to be sure he was telling the truth about Eleanor."

"He was. And we can cross Gil off our list of suspects. But his answers surprised me. He seemed confident that none of the other councilmen were gunning for Eleanor."

Harley snorted. "Nor the commercial developers, either."

"If anything, Gil seemed more amused by the fact that Eleanor wouldn't take a bribe. Like he thought Eleanor was naïve, so he didn't find it offensive."

"Twit. You're sure he's in a position to know?"

"You saw his computer files. He's taken and given more bribes than I would have thought possible for a low-level politician."

"So where's that leave us? We've got nothing so far from Eleanor's mayoral dealings and nothing in her personal life."

"If there's nothing from her past, then we've got to be talking about her future." They stopped at John's car. "I hate to say it, but someone doesn't want her to be governor."

Harley sighed. "There are over a hundred candidates. Most of 'em whack jobs. Even if we limit our suspect list to candidates, that's a heck of a long list."

"Yeah. I know." John opened his car door and slid inside. "I'm thinking we need some extra help on this."

Harley cocked his head.

John said, "Gil's ex, Sierra, works the political beat."

"You want to trust a reporter?"

"She's got a good reputation and we just made her a happy camper. I think it'll be all right. Plus, she'll have access to files on all the candidates. Hopefully we can narrow the list down to a dozen crazies and the top ten candidates who might be elected if Eleanor's out."

"Sounds like a lot of grunt work."

"Then we better get started. I'll make some calls from my house while I'm checking on the girls. You finish up at the crash site and touch base with your buddy on the bomb squad. I'll talk to you in a few hours."

NAILS SHUFFLED AFTER BARRY, WINDING HIS WAY THROUGH THE towers of wrecked cars and keeping his gaze glued to the dirt path in front of him, on the lookout for one of Sparky's bombs. With a grimace, he popped another of the blue pills, trying to remember how many he'd taken this morning but coming up empty. He was pretty sure the doc had said no more than eight pills a day, but then again, sometimes the docs weren't realistic.

Barry said, "Come on, keep up. Sparky's got a ten a.m. start time so he's gotta take off any minute now. We don't want to miss him."

Nails grunted and shuffled faster, wishing his gimpy knee would quit slowing him down.

Barry spat on the ground. "Can you believe Mr. Steel is only paying us half for the Black job? Rat bastard! And after the crap I went through running the gauntlet of vicious dogs, trying to stay one step ahead of that deranged security guard." Barry shuddered. "That dude was freaking me out. I'm telling ya, the man kept on coming. It was like he was the Terminator or something. I get my rear end chewed off and he's got twenty of those creatures between him and me and somehow he gets through it without a scratch. Then he comes after me again."

Nails withheld a chuckle. "I ran him over with four thousand pounds of Detroit steel. I'm pretty sure you don't have to worry about him any more."

Barry sighed. "I don't know, man. The way he bounced over the car...it was like he had a force field protecting him or something."

Nails stopped dead, wondering if the blue pills had him hearing things. "A force field?"

"It wouldn't surprise me if he was standing guard at the hospital right now, keeping us from finishing Black off and getting the rest of our money."

Nails gritted his teeth. *Idiot.*

"And Mr. S only wants to pay us half! Heck, we should be getting friggin hazard pay. I'm telling you, Nails, we gotta do what the Teamsters do. Organize and demand better wages."

"You didn't say shit to Mr. Steel."

"Well, yeah. But that's because I was on my own. The strength of a union is in its collective power. That means that together we have power. We just have to get some of the others on our side."

Nails shook his head. "You talk to any of the guys working with our Russian employers and you'll be dead within the hour. Try not to be such a stupid white dude."

When he saw Barry stop and open his mouth to protest, Nails decided he'd heard enough and raised his hand to knock Barry upside his head. But before he could, there was a flash of light and a loud *CRUMMMP*. The earth shook as bits of burnt plastic pelted him, and Nails turned and saw smoke coming from the trunk of a dead Ford Crown Vic at the end of the row. *Crazy cracker is blowing stuff up again!*

There was a hard clunk as something hit the little Honda to his right. The head of what looked to be a crispy, blackened Barbie rolled off the Honda and onto Nails' shoe.

Another explosion! Nails felt faint. He leaned against the car, denting the fender as he put his full weight on it. Just as he was losing consciousness, his head rocked with a blow.

"Hey, snap out of it. It was just Sparky."

Nails shook it off and leveled a glare at Barry. "You ever slap me again and I'll skin the flesh from your left arm."

Barry looked bewildered. "But you looked like you were gonna pass out."

"I've never passed out in my life."

"You did last time we were here."

Nails pulled a utility knife from his pants pocket.

Barry backed up, hands in the air. "Hey, man. Whatever you say. Let's just pick up the guns from Sparky. Then you do your thing with Two-Bits and I'll take care of the girls."

"Hey, Denny," a voice called. "Barry."

Nails turned as the wild-eyed hillbilly came running up to them, a video camera in his good hand. Grinning, Sparky reached down with his stubby hand and picked up the doll's head.

"Oh, that was a beautiful one. Did you guys see it?"

Wheezing, Nails said, "Bits and pieces."

Sparky stood stock still before barking in laughter. "Hey, Denny Nalen made a funny." Sparky slapped his shoulder. "Good one, Nails."

Barry chimed in, "I just about crapped my pants when I heard that explosion. How about a little warning next time?"

Nails hitched his breath while his eyes darted around. "You got more bombs around here?"

"Well, sure. I can't make my little video without bombs. I'm making a reel, a sample of my work, to try to land a gig directing movies. So in my spare time I'm making a little mini-flick called *Bondage Barbie vs. the Crab People.* Kind of an old fashioned B-movie."

Barry nodded his appreciation. "Catchy. But hey, Sparky, I know you've got a ten o'clock call time at the set, so why don't we get down to business."

With a wild, toothless grin, Sparky ambled over to a rusted out El Camino and reached behind the seats. He pulled out a large canvas bag and set it in the dirt. Raising an eyebrow, he shoved the Barbie head into the bag and slid out a hefty gun wrapped in cloth.

"This one's for Nails, an over-under twelve gauge for close-up work. And a nice semi-automatic deer rifle for you, Barry. Obviously, if you're using the scope I'd take it off semi and switch it to single shot, or you'll never hit anything with it."

Nails grunted, appreciating the freak all over again. It was amazing how many guns he could get at such short notice. Nails leaned in, waiting for the next toy to come out of the bag. But when Sparky reached into his bag of tricks and pulled out a couple of bombs, Nails found himself backing away and starting to swoon.

Barry turned toward him. "Take it easy, big guy. Deep breaths."

"Shut up, string bean." Nails focused on his breathing, trying to act cool, but knowing he was failing. "Are those things loaded, Sparky?"

"No, no. Of course not. Well…they do have the trigger and primer cord rigged to go. That's just to make it easier for you guys to set 'em off. So right now they definitely can make a little bang. But you have to load the gasoline at the site. You don't want to be driving around with the fuel rigged to the device."

"I don't *want* to be driving around with it, ever."

Barry said, "Don't worry, big guy. We're taking separate cars from here. My cousin has a couple of decent wreckers for us. And I'm taking the bombs with me, all right?"

Nails grunted, trying to be cool. "Yeah, whatever."

"Barry, I need these guns back in twenty-four hours, you understand? They were hard to get. And they'll be missed from the movie set if I don't get them back."

"No problem whatsoever."

"Good. How'd the pipe shooter work out?"

Barry smiled. "Pretty impressive. It was a good design."

Sparky rubbed his finger nubs on the back of his neck and reddened. "Aw, thanks. You mean it?"

"Abso-friggin-lutely. It was a beauty."

"Wait a second. *Was* a beauty?"

Nails raised his head at the tone in Sparky's voice, his instincts telling him something was wrong.

Sparky said, "You mean it didn't survive the crash? I was expecting it to be dinged up, but I was hoping I could use at least some of the parts to make another one."

Barry shrugged. "I don't know if it survived or not."

Sparky's mouth dropped open. "Please don't tell me you left it there."

Nails felt his stomach lurch. "What's the problem?"

The hillbilly bit on a knuckle. "It doesn't look like part of the car. If it didn't get thrown clear, the cops will find it and trace it back to me."

Nails heard a groan, then realized the sound came from his own mouth. *Another loose end.* He focused his gaze on the skinny twerp beside him. "Don't worry, Sparky. You've got my word that Barry will get it back. Or he'll die trying. Right, partner?"

Barry swallowed. "Uh...right."

seventeen

JOHN maneuvered his way down the narrow, tree-lined road and came to an abrupt stop. He was already anxious to make sure that Hillary was safe, and there, at the edge of the dirt driveway, where it started to widen as it met up with the concrete pad near his house and garage, sat his rusty Jeep. It should have been in the garage, but there it was, the front tires flattened by wooden stakes protruding from the ground.

John gave a quick glance toward the house and felt a stab of fear, wondering if the killers had somehow found the girls here and if Hillary had tried to escape in his old Jeep.

He pulled a Beretta from a special bracket under his front seat and moved toward the side door of his house, listening at the doorway. Nothing but silence. *Shit.*

He pushed the door open, stopping before it got to the part where it squeaked, and slid inside. John frowned as he moved through the kitchen, noticing dirty pans and dishes in the sink. He leaned against the swinging door that led to the living room and crept inside.

There were clothes strewn all over the place. He listened again, but it was still silent. He thought he caught a flash of movement through the blinds and glanced toward the sliding door that led to the rear wraparound deck. It was cracked open.

John took a deep breath and slipped through the doorway.

He stopped and immediately reddened—and the squeals that erupted sent him scurrying back into the house. "Sorry."

Hillary stormed inside, tying a bathrobe around her body.

"That is not cool, Uncle John. Why'd you point a gun at me? And why'd you sneak up on us?"

"What do you mean, why? I was concerned."

Amber came in, closing her robe a bit more slowly. "Maybe he wanted a peek."

John found himself reddening even more. "I'd like to know *why* you were lying around in the nude? In my house?"

Amber gave him an amused look. "Nobody wants tan lines, John. And your deck is ultra-private, or at least it used to be. There's not a soul around for miles."

He thumbed the safety on his gun and tucked it behind his back. "And why is my Jeep sitting in the drive with two flat tires?"

Amber shrugged. "We were bored."

His gaze narrowed when he heard her answer.

Hillary looked down at her feet. "I'm sorry, Uncle John. It's my fault. Amber didn't believe that you had booby traps surrounding the house, so she kind of talked me into going out."

"Going out?" John shook his head, feeling out of his league. *Teenagers.* "The whole reason you're *here* is so you won't be out *there* with the killers!" He fired a glare toward Amber. "Because if they find you, tan lines will be the least of your worries."

Hillary nodded, looking contrite, while Amber merely smiled. John sighed. "This isn't a game, Amber. There's a good chance that people are going to try and kill you."

Her smile grew even bigger. "That's what you say. But no one's tried yet. Maybe you just want me to stay here with you for a couple of days."

John gritted his teeth and grabbed Hillary by the arm, pulling her aside. He whispered to her, "I need your help for this to work. I can't stay here every second if I want to catch the people who tried to kill your mom. And since they might try again, or they might try for you, it's important that I keep focused on finding them."

"I know."

"And this place is safe. I told you Harley had rigged the entire perimeter with traps and I meant it. The chances of them finding you here are practically nil. And Harley is nothing if not lethal. The odds of them making it through the traps are slim to none. You just have to stay here."

Hillary nodded. "I will."

"Good girl." John gestured toward Amber. "And I also want you to take care of Lolita, there. So instead of letting her talk you into things, I want you to be the leader. Just like your mom's a leader."

At the mention of her mother, Hillary's eyes started to tear up and John reached out to hold onto her, wishing he knew the right thing to say. But dealing with teenagers wasn't his forte. With their raging hormones they might as well be an alien species, as far as John was concerned.

They stayed like that for a couple of minutes before she asked, "What if Mom's not all right?"

John froze, then stroked her hair, buying time to come up with a suitable answer. "She will be. Your mom's a fighter. And the doctors agree with me. I keep in constant contact and they've only been saying good things this morning. There's no permanent brain damage and her condition has stabilized."

The look of horror on Hillary's face told him he'd given her too much information.

"Brain damage?"

John spluttered, "I said *no* brain damage. None."

"I just don't know how much more I can take, Uncle John. The bad guys are out there, running free, while I have to stay locked inside. Like a prisoner."

"A prisoner? Come on, Hillary."

John wiped a tear from her eye.

She sniffled a bit. "I'm exaggerating, I know. But tomorrow it will be eight years since Dad died. Mom and I always go. Always. But she's in the hospital and you don't want us to leave the house."

John let out a breath. "You're right, you've got to go. Harley and I will take you tomorrow morning to both the hospital and the cemetery. Somehow, we'll make it work."

She gave him another hug. "Thank you so much!" She hesitated. "Are you sure Harley has to come? He's kind of scary."

John relaxed, feeling back in his element. "A harmless sixty-year-old man with white hair has you scared?"

"He's not exactly harmless, is he?"

John shook his head. "No, he's not."

"Sometimes I can see it in his eyes. That's what scares me."

"Don't worry. That part of him is reserved for the bad guys."

John leaned forward and gave her a kiss on her forehead. "Okay, I've got to go, but I'll be back tonight. You and Amber be good. And *don't* try to cross the perimeter."

As he started toward the door, Amber winked and called out, "Bye, John, see ya later. Call me."

He snorted, then realized he sounded like Harley, and turned the door handle.

Hillary piped in, "Oh, yeah. I forgot to tell you that grandma called like six times, trying to get hold of you."

John tensed. "Is it about your mom?"

"She said it wasn't, but she was acting pretty weird. And her messages were getting more and more intense. She's pretty unhappy that she doesn't have your cell number."

Cringing, John said, "You didn't give it to her, did you?"

"No. And she's furious about that, too. Why don't you want her to have it?"

He shrugged. "It's easier that way. When we don't talk, it keeps our relationship on a better note. Cuts down on the amount of time we spend arguing with each other. Look, you know my cell number if you need me. If my mom needs something, she can pass it on through you or leave a message on the machine."

John shut the door, wondering what could possibly have his mom calling six times in the last few hours. It couldn't be good.

WITH A SIX IRON, RICHARD STEEL HIT THE BALL WITH ALL HIS MIGHT, whacking it like a piñata and picturing Two-Bits' face the whole time. *Damn rapper.* The ball drove two hundred yards before dropping onto the fairway.

He waited for a congratulatory comment from the peon who'd been prattling on for the last hour, but the man remained silent. With a curl of his lip, Steel removed his tee and stepped away. *Now that Eleanor Black is out of the picture, the bastards are supposed to be sucking up without a moment's hesitation.*

His golfing partner was a political colleague he'd 'done business with' before, from his Pfester days, and Steel had found the man to be remarkably amenable to monetary persuasion. All well and good, but that was in the past. Now it was time for Councilman Gil to reverse course, like all good minor politicians, and start leeching onto the Governor-to-be. Only the man didn't seem to be up to the task.

Gil took a swing and promptly dinked his ball into the lake.

My god. "While it is a good idea to lose, Gil, you still have to make a game of it. This is the first round I've been able to squeeze in since the campaign started. And I only got this one because the media isn't paying a bit of attention to anything but the Black accident."

Gil winced. "I'm sorry, Dick, it's been one of those days. And your shot was fantastic, by the way. Fantastic! I think I'm out of my league."

He took a swing at his second ball, this time dropping it fifteen yards shy of Steel's.

Excellent. Steel took a seat in the golf cart, waiting for Gil to chauffer him to their respective balls. The councilman sat in the driver's seat and started nattering on about a group of commercial real estate developers—his partners—and the perks they were prepared to give him, along a with a sizable donation, of course.

But as the pitch went on, Gil stumbled a few times, and Steel began to pay closer attention. Usually, the man was capable of performing the intricacies of politics. But right now Gil's mind was definitely somewhere else.

And then it hit him. The small, fresh lacerations about the face and arms, the shell-shocked expression—Gil looked just like he'd suffered a threat to his well-being, a la the Russians when they were leaning on someone.

Steel smiled. Here he'd been looking to pull in some cash and find a twisted girl to set up Sanchez, and an opportunity had been handed to him.

He poured on the charm and flashed the big guns—his pearly whites. "You know, Gil. It never hurts to have powerful people in your corner. They can help take care of your problems."

Gil turned a wary gaze in his direction. "Yeah?"

"Oh, most definitely. We have resources that others just don't have. Why don't you tell me what happened today?"

Gil shook his head. "I don't know, Dick. The guys were scary, especially the senior citizen."

Steel smothered a laugh, picturing a geriatric brandishing his walker at Gil. Turning serious, he said, "I know some scary people as well. Terrifying people."

"Yeah, you do. But these guys seemed to be well connected, too. They're looking into the Black accident."

A dour expression crept across Steel's face. "They weren't police?"

"Oh, please, I'm a Los Angeles City Councilman. Why would the police frighten me? No, they weren't cops 'cause they smiled when I told them who they were dealing with. It didn't phase them at all."

Steel put on a neutral facial expression, keeping his concern from showing. "Why don't you tell me the whole story? Start with how they found you."

"That's the worst of it." Gil took a swipe at his ball, launching it into a sand trap to the right of the green. "My ex-wife is a psycho she-devil. I think she actually sicced them on me."

JOHN WALKED THROUGH THE OFFICES OF THE CHANNEL SIX NEWS team, following the instructions Sierra had given him to find her office, and pretended to ignore the people who recognized him. Walking through the media whorehouse was only slightly better than catching one of Eleanor's fundraisers, but it was hard to figure out a better way to get info on the different candidates. Of course, his mom had access to a lot of information as well, but asking her for anything made him feel like a bit of his soul was being leeched away.

His cell phone starting spewing out "Achy Breaky Heart," and he quickly turned off the ringer and said, "What'd you find out, Harley?"

"Nothing good, mate. My buddy at the bomb squad came up zeroes."

John refrained from punching the wall. There hadn't been many leads to follow in the first place, but so far none of them were panning out. "Nothing?"

"Well, he agreed that it was a remote trigger, but that all the pieces were common items you could find at any electronics store. No signature quality that he could identify."

Harley's voice was drowned out by the sound of a semi truck.

"Sorry, mate, I'm still working Eleanor's crash site, trying to find the actual device. At the speed she was going, along with the multiple rolls of the vehicle, the potential trajectories leave a lot of ground to cover."

John flinched, picturing the rolling car. He stopped at a doorway and read the nameplate—*Sierra Rodriguez*. "All right, Harley. Keep me posted."

"Hold on, there is one bit of nice news. I did a dry run at the hospital to test the blokes who are guarding your sister. And they were paying serious attention. In fact, the cops were pretty impressive, so you probably don't have to worry about anyone getting past 'em for a while yet."

John let out a breath. "That's good to hear. At least there's one less thing to worry about. The girls, on the other hand, are driving me out my mind. They've already tried to leave the house."

Harley snorted. "Typical sheilas. Sometimes it's like they don't want you to protect 'em."

"Seems like it."

The door opened and Sierra jumped back when she nearly ran into him.

John smiled. "I gotta go, Harley. Keep tomorrow morning open for some sniper duty."

He hung up and slid the phone into his pocket. Sierra's expression was a bit comical.

"Sniper duty?"

"Don't ask."

John could see the curiosity eating away at her, as it would for any reporter, but she kept quiet. Which he found pretty admirable. "Would you mind if we talk inside your office?"

"Of course not. Come on in."

As Sierra sat behind her desk, John took a quick look around the room. Huge, seemingly haphazard piles of papers and videos surrounded her, making the office look like a storm had swept through just minutes before.

"It's chaotic, I know. But I'm hardly ever here. My home doesn't look anything like this."

"No it doesn't. Your place looks very nice."

Sierra frowned as John set Gil's laptop onto a relatively clean spot on the desk.

"I'm really sorry to have to break this to you, but Gil took some spy cam videos of you and your place. You can access them on the main screen if you want, they're called the 'S Files.'"

"I knew it! That scumbag."

Sierra let out a stream of curses in Spanish, which John didn't understand, then rattled off something about the Wicked Witch of the East and flying monkeys, which John didn't comprehend either, before she came to an abrupt halt.

She reddened and covered her mouth with her hand. "Oh my God, that means you've seen video of me naked."

John turned away. "You have my word that as soon as I saw what they were, I closed the files. But I thought you should have them in case you want to press charges."

Sierra put her hand on top of his. "I appreciate that. Thank you for getting my privacy back. And for taking care of Gil."

John leaned forward and gave her an envelope with Gil's child support payment inside. "My pleasure."

Sierra smiled. "Interesting choice of words."

He opened his mouth to protest when Sierra continued, "So tell me why you're here. On the phone you said you wanted my help."

John shook off his lingering embarrassment. "I do. I need your help with something that means life or death for my family. But it's necessary that you keep it a secret for the time being. At least until I get further along with my investigation."

Sierra nodded. "Is this about your sister?"

"Yes."

"I'm in. Whatever you need, you have it. How can I help?"

John let out a breath that he hadn't realized he was holding. "Thank you. And I promise you'll get the exclusive story as soon as possible."

Like a schoolgirl, Sierra jumped up and down and gave John a big squeeze, brushing her lips against his cheek. "Ahhh, now that right there makes you my hero. Don't get me wrong, I was already impressed, what with Gil's turnaround and what you do for kids. But now...well, this has got to be the biggest story of the year. And I get to be part of it."

"I appreciate your enthusiasm." John tried to keep his mind on business, ignoring how close she was. "Hopefully, it will carry you through the boring part coming up. I need in-depth information on all the candidates. Whatever you've got on paper and whatever insights you can share with me."

Sierra's jaw dropped. "You think one of them tried to kill Eleanor?"

John nodded. "Yes."

Sierra shook her head. "God, I wish I could do this story."

eighteen

"CAN this be real?" John asked. "In this stack alone, I've got candidates that are pimps, circus midgets, used car dealers, and a loser from a reality TV show. Someone who got ousted on the first day, according to your file. Do any of these people think they have a chance?"

Sierra smiled. "Only the delusional ones. Most of them want attention or a story to tell their friends over drinks."

John put down his pile of folders next to the other stacks. "Well it's driving me crazy. There's no way to check everyone out before the election. And my fear is that the killers will be harder to catch once the election is over." He sat back in his chair, rubbing his temples. "You know, I'm actually starting to appreciate the normal political process. At least then there are teams of people vetting each candidate before they ever get nominated."

"John Black appreciating the political process?"

"Don't tell anyone I said that."

"No problem."

John's phone started ringing—a Kenny G tune this time. He took a peek and groaned.

Sierra said, "How do you make your phone ring with a different tune each time?"

"I have no idea. It's my partner's idea of a joke. Even when I change it to vibrate mode, the thing still rings. I think the only way to make it stop is to answer it or chuck it against the wall."

He held the phone over his head and aimed for the wall, but poked the answer button instead. "Hello, Mother. How are you this evening?"

"Oh don't give me that crap, John. Being polite doesn't suit you any better now than when you were a wretched teenager. And speaking of wretched teens, do you know how hard it was to convince Hillary to give me this number?"

John frowned. "Hey. She's just doing what I told her."

There was a pause. "Nevertheless, I've been trying to reach you all day."

"Is Eleanor okay?"

"No change. They think she has a good chance of pulling out of it. But they don't know for sure."

He nodded to himself.

"Look, John. I need to talk to you. It's urgent."

"All right, shoot."

"In person. Immediately."

John noted the steely tone in her voice. In the past, when she'd used it on him, it had meant she wanted him to do something he would find offensive. Like attend a political rally, standing two paces behind her and smiling for the cameras until his cheek muscles cramped from the extended workout.

After a moment of hesitation he said, "All right, Mother. Pick me up in an hour at the corner of Melrose and Vine. And if you can, bring any files you have on the candidates that are running against Eleanor."

"I was planning on it," she said, and he could hear the surprise in her voice. "I've already talked to Eleanor's campaign manager."

She hung up and it was his turn to feel surprised. *Why was she planning on it?*

Sierra interrupted his thoughts. "The Barracuda is known to have files on everyone. They should be able to help us whittle down the number of suspects."

He looked at the mounds of paper on the floor. "Yes, they will. But we have to get further along before I leave. Let's start prioritizing by separating this into three stacks. The first, our highest priority, will have the candidates who stand to gain by Eleanor's absence in the race. People who might win if she's not in the game. Then we'll divide the other two stacks into the delusional and the sane candidates. Hopefully, the sane ones have enough sense to know they're out of the running and that there would be no point in killing Eleanor. So they'll be our lowest priority."

Sierra said, "That'll just leave the crazies."

"I know. And this is a Hollywood election, so it's probably a vain hope that there aren't that many nutjobs."

She gave a rueful smile. "I think you're right."

NAILS SHIFTED THE WRECK INTO DRIVE AND PREPARED TO FOLLOW Two-Bits and his crew down the street. After a fairly successful merge into traffic—with just a few scrapes along the fender of the car that had been parked in front of him—he popped another little blue pill and turned up the boom box on the seat next to him. Damn beater car didn't have a working stereo so he'd brought along some Two-Bit tunes to keep him company while he looked for the best place to pop a cap in the ex-gangbanger.

Nails grunted, picturing Barry flailing about, trying to find the girls. *Stupid cracker really screwed the pooch this time.* Hopefully, he wasn't messing up anything else tonight. Nails was starting to worry about how poorly the jobs were going. That maybe the Russians might decide that he and Barry were a liability instead of an asset.

He shook his head, clearing it of the fear that was starting to spread. It was probably best not to go there. And with Barry out of the way on this job, it should go down without a hitch. It would look like a real murder, of course, but gang related instead of political. Two-Bits' old homeys were called the Eastside Bloods, and so long as Nails was wearing a blue bandana—Crip colors—when he shot Two-Bits, the rival gang would be fingered for the deed.

Nails moved his head to the beat of the song, digging the groove. Shit, he almost hated to pull the trigger on such a musical genius. It hadn't been that hard to take out a TV actor like Odie, but then again all that had taken was a quick football move to push him up and over the balcony. It felt like rushing the quarterback, only more satisfying.

He watched as Two-Bits and his posse pulled into the parking lot for one of the fancier strip clubs by the airport. A gentlemen's club. *Yeah, right.* Nails pulled the shotgun onto his lap and flicked off the safety. He started to turn down the boom box, but stopped to hear the rapper's gentle, yet throbbing, refrain.

Sometimes killing a COP—will take you straight to the TOP— 'cause it's the RIGHT move—the BEST groove—the ONE move you GOTTA do...

Nails grunted, appreciating the poetic skills Two-Bits displayed. Definitely nasty lyrics, but still way cool. And while he might just be a poetic genius, the brother was definitely not governor material. Yet somehow this guy was near the top of the governor's race. Nails chuckled at the idea. What the hell was the matter with California?

He drove past the club and did a U-turn, looking for the best angle across the passenger seat. He pulled the blue bandana over his dome and waited for Two-Bits and his party to approach the main doors of the club. The timing would have to be perfect if he didn't want the posse protecting his target.

He was ready to accelerate when he noticed that his right forearm was bleeding all over the shotgun. *Shit.* That made the third time he'd bled for no reason in the last couple of days. *Must be those damn pills.*

He looked up and noticed that the group was almost to the door. He stomped on the accelerator, putting more into it than he wanted, then slowed to a crawl as he approached Two-Bits. His crew, apparently alerted by the sound of the junker's acceleration, watched the advancing car with an unusual intensity, hands in their jackets.

Nails noticed the scrutiny but decided he'd already committed himself. He raised the shotgun toward Two-Bits, inspiring quick action by the posse. Four handguns whipped out and started pointing toward Nails.

He fired twice into the crowd, scattering shot into most of them and dropping the guy next to Two-Bits, then attempted to hunch down and crouch sideways behind the metal in the car door. His bulk interfered with the movement, and in panic mode he shoved backwards with all of his might as Two-Bits and his gang peppered the car with twenty rounds. The seatback broke away, allowing him to get lower and protect himself.

He hit the accelerator pedal and took off, the car tires squealing like a stuck pig.

John waited a few seconds after the limousine stopped, dreading the upcoming reunion, before opening the door and sliding into its luxurious interior. He took the rear-facing seat, opposite his mother, as the car pulled away.

Barbara Black pushed the button to close the privacy window. "You're a hard man to get hold of, John. Thank you for deigning to meet with me."

He squinted, noticing the scotch in her right hand and her harsh tone of voice. *Now this should be a real interesting conversation.* But all he said was, "My pleasure."

"Oh, don't toy with me. We haven't enjoyed each other's company since you discovered that 'politician' was a dirty word."

John tensed, wondering what had her so upset. "I'm sorry, Mother." He looked on the seat next to him and found two large file boxes. "Is this complete? Are there files on all the candidates?"

Barbara smiled. "I'm nothing, if not thorough. Everything we need is in there."

"What does that mean?"

"It means I have what you asked for. Although you didn't say why you wanted them."

"And you never said why you'd already put them together for me." John pulled out a file on Two-Bits, original name Clarence Marion Washington, and thumbed through it. "I have to admit that I'm a bit worried."

His mother took a large gulp of scotch. *"You're* worried?"

John put the folder down. "Yes, I am. You've all but written me out of your life. Over politics. Hell, I've only seen you a few times in the last couple of years. Yet here we are, talking twice in two days. And this time you say it's urgent. Well, if it's important, let's get down to it."

"Don't rush me, John." Barbara looked out the window, fingering her empty tumbler. "You were always difficult to talk to."

"That's because I'm not a politician. I say what I mean instead of dancing around the subject."

Barbara turned back toward John, narrowing her gaze. "Yes. Too true."

He waited for her to say more, trying to stay patient, but wishing he was still working on the suspect list instead of playing word games. *There has to be a way to move this along.* "If you really need to know, the reason I want the files is to help Eleanor. I'm fairly confident that our killers work for one of the candidates. That means there is probably more danger in the next week, for Eleanor and for Hillary, and that it all stops the second the election is over. Which will make it much harder to catch them. So I want to cross-reference your files with some that I got from a reporter friend. Is that all right?"

Her lip curled. "A reporter?"

"She's trustworthy."

He watched the machinery churn in her brain as she thought things over. When he was younger he used to wish she'd put her mind to a better purpose. But she excelled at turning things to her advantage, finding the best angle. She was brilliant, really. And that's what made him nervous now.

She turned toward him. "Do you remember the '88 campaign when my opponent dug up some nasty dirt on me?"

"Buchanon, right?"

"Yes, that's the bastard. Do you remember how I defeated him?"

"Yeah. You set a trap for him."

Barbara's eyes glinted. "That's right. Using me as bait. And once he was hooked, using info from the stolen files we'd leaked to him, I caught him dead to rights on live television."

He nodded. "That's right. You know, that was pretty fun for a debate. You had him on the ropes in no time."

"But it wouldn't have worked if I hadn't set myself as the lure."

John frowned. Where the heck was she going with this? "What's your point?"

"I want you to be the bait this time. To catch the bastard who hurt my daughter."

He put the files down and leaned forward. "What'd you have in mind?"

She filled her glass and took another sip. "Most people aren't aware of this, but in 1872 they were having problems with elections in California. Too many cowboy types, I guess, who were interfering with the electoral process."

"1872? I'm not following you."

"There were a few people killing their political rivals in order to win."

"All right. It's a familiar story, but what does this have to do with us?"

"Back then the murderous candidate would win because nobody else could get on the ballot in time. If they weren't caught doing the deed, they'd win by default. So they came up with a new election law, Section 87-12B. One that allows a close relative of the deceased or incapacitated candidate to take their place on the ballot."

John felt his chest tighten. "What kind of relative?"

"A father, a son...or a brother."

Shit.

His mother continued, "They hadn't heard of equal rights yet, so women weren't allowed."

"And you're saying that this statute is still on the books? Since the eighteen hundreds?"

She smiled her famous barracuda smile. "I've had my legal team working on it all day. As soon as the doctor said Eleanor wasn't likely to be in any shape to finish the race this week. The statute has never been removed. It hasn't been used since 1888, but it's still valid. I can have you on the ballot tomorrow."

"Wait a second. Just wait a damn second, here. This is a

flat out crazy idea. First of all, I'm not a politician so I could never pull it off. In fact, I've been quoted on national television calling politicians blood-sucking vampires. So I wouldn't make good bait because no one would believe I could win. The killers wouldn't need to come after me."

She focused her laser-like glare on him. "I know you're not a politician. But we've done some private polling this afternoon. And with the short time frame before the election, you being an outsider might work in your favor."

"You've actually polled people about me running for governor? Then you're fucking serious?"

"I'm dead serious, John. And don't swear. Half the people voting for 'Black' would think they were voting for Eleanor. Of the ones who understand the ballot change, some would love your anti-establishment bullshit. And the rest would vote for you out of sympathy for your sister. Our numbers show that you would have a solid chance to win."

"That's even worse. Why in the hell would I want to win?"

She burst into tears.

For a moment, he couldn't help but feel sorry for her, until he remembered this was his mother doing the crying. He'd never once seen her shed real tears.

On the other hand, crocodile tears, shed at the appropriate TV moments, had served her quite well over the years. He tried to ignore them.

Between tears she said, "Why? For Eleanor. This is all for Eleanor."

John looked at the floor, wondering if the emotion was real, and felt his normal protective reaction kick in. "But how would this help Eleanor?"

The waterworks slowed and her hard expression returned. "Because you wouldn't be doing this merely to catch the attacker. That's important, but the chances are miniscule that Eleanor will recover in time to win this on her own. And she needs this election. It's her springboard into higher politics, what she has always dreamed of."

"And how does my winning her dream job help her out?"

"It's simple, John. I want you to win it for her so you can appoint her your lieutenant governor when she's recovered. Then, at the appropriate time, you resign and let her have the governorship."

"But lieutenant governor is an elected position."

With a glint in her eye, his mother said, "Not if he resigns midterm."

"And you've got something on him?" John gritted his teeth. "Never mind. Don't tell me."

She dabbed her eyes with a tissue. "I know you don't want to do this. But Eleanor needs you."

"Look, being the bait doesn't bother me in the slightest. I'd do anything for Eleanor and Hillary. But if that doesn't work, it'll be difficult to track the bad guys if the media is always on top of me."

"I know. But your partner can follow the outside leads while you work them from the inside. It might help to take two different approaches."

He nodded, dreading the idea and not quite accepting it, but knowing his mother had every angle covered. "Yeah...it might."

She smiled her infamous smile. "Great. It's settled then. Sign these papers and I'll take care of them in the morning."

John looked out the window for a couple of minutes, thinking it over, while the Barracuda's gaze bored a hole in his head. His thoughts drifted from the impossible choice before him to the helpless feeling he'd had when he'd first seen Eleanor lying in the hospital.

He took the pen she was offering and started signing away. "If you would have told me yesterday that Eleanor would be in a coma, Hillary would be a target, and that I would be running for office...I would have said you were crazy."

"Well, it wouldn't be the first time." She took another sip of scotch. "In fact, I remember a time when you were eighteen, and we were having a heck of an argument about corruption in politics. You told me that the day you ran for office would be the day hell froze over. You remember that?"

John shivered. "Yeah, of course." He tossed the pen onto the seat next to her and handed her the Declaration of Candidacy. "But who knew that day was today?"

nineteen

"AAARGHH! Get it over with, you pasty pinhead!"

Barry dug around for another minute, doing his best to ignore Nails' screams, but it was like the darned thing didn't want to come out. He took a slug of Pepto and made another stab with the tweezers, but the slippery bullet eluded him.

Nails lashed out and knocked over a lamp—a naked hula girl with a grass shade over the bulb. "Shit! That was my favorite. Got it at the Pro Bowl in Hawaii."

"Hey, man. I'm doing my best. I'm no friggin doctor, all right?"

Nails grunted.

Barry fished out the last slug and placed the foul thing on the coffee table. "Got it."

Nails started to rise off the ratty couch before Barry said, "Whoa, we still got to patch you up. You're bleeding like a stuck pig."

Nails turned back onto his belly and grabbed Barry's wrist with a vice-like grip. "I thought you said the damage didn't look too bad."

"It isn't," Barry yelped. "Your fat is so thick it was like those twenty-twos were hitting a dirt bunker."

Nails released the wrist. "Then what's the problem?"

Barry massaged his numb joint. "Man, I don't know. I'm not medically inclined. But if I was to guess, I'd say there's something wrong with your skin. It's like it's made of paper."

Nails glanced down at his scabby arm. "It's those damn painkillers they gave me at Pfester. They're experimental."

"No foolin'? That's messed up."

"That's not even half of it. You don't want to know what kind of side effects these magic blue pills have."

"I'm sure I don't." Barry frowned as Nails popped another blue one. "You think maybe you should stop taking 'em?"

"So now you're giving medical advice after all?" Nails shook his head. "You wouldn't last two seconds living with the pain I have every damn day." He stared at the scabs on his arm again, then grimaced. "But if the docs over there can't fix this skin thing, I might have to do some experimenting of my own and inflict a little 'experimental' damage on those stupid quacks."

Barry looked at the mess on Nails' back, actually feeling a little sorry for the big guy. "You got any ideas? There's no way regular bandages will take care of this."

"Not yet."

"Well, you better come up with something before you bleed to death."

The look on Nails' face made Barry tense up, wondering if he would have to bolt. Like somehow this mess was *his* fault. But this time it wasn't. He snapped his fingers as his thoughts came together. "Hey, that's right...I didn't screw this one up. You're the one who missed Two-Bits."

Nails started to rise from the couch.

"Not that it matters," Barry said quickly. "I mean we're not keeping score, right?"

He let out a breath as the behemoth settled back onto the couch. When the phone rang, he jumped up to answer it.

"Leave it go," Nails said. "I don't want to talk to Steel right now. And I definitely don't want to talk to the Russians."

Barry leaned against a pile of pizza boxes, several steps away from Nails. "Yeah, sure. Whatever you say."

Nails' voice came over the machine's speaker, saying "Speak your mind, bro."

After a short beep, Steel's voice said, "Another screw-up. How delightful."

Barry cringed, fearing the worst. Then again, if the worst was coming, it wouldn't be a phone call.

"But I'll tell you what," Steel continued. "Consider yourself lucky. All will be forgiven if you're successful with the other thing tonight. You know, the video camera thing. Bring the camera, and some brains this time, to Bungalow 12 at the Beverly Hills Hotel. Call me when you get there. You have one hour. No more chances. If you're late, or you screw this up in any way, you'll be hearing from Sasha and Lexi."

There was a sharp click, followed by a nasty sounding dial tone. Maybe it was the tinny quality of the speaker, but Barry was pretty sure he'd never heard a phone sound so ominous.

He turned to Nails and said, "You got your camera battery fully charged? We better not blow it this time."

"Yeah. No problem. The real trick will be getting me patched up and making it over to Beverly Hills in time."

Barry looked at his back and blanched. "You got some kind of solution to fix you up? I think stitches would just tear right through you."

"Go down to the garage and bring my red tool box and the tire patching kit."

Barry's jaw dropped. "You gotta be friggin kidding."

JOHN HEADED OVER TO HIS SOFA AND PLOPPED DOWN WITH A THUNK, not even bothering with the lights. It was after midnight, but there was enough moonlight to see that his place looked like a natural disaster had swept through. Hurricanes Amber and Hillary. He half wondered if all teenagers trashed the places they lived in, or if these girls did it because they were rich and used to having maids pick up after them.

Life was sure as hell simpler yesterday.

Today things had been going so fast and furious that it had been easy to keep from worrying about Eleanor in the hospital. But now that it was quiet he found he couldn't stop thinking about her. He put his head in his hands and tried to shake it off. *I can't get sidetracked!*

John smacked his forehead a couple of times, hoping it would clear his mind, and tried to bring his thoughts back to the case. He pulled out his notes and did a rundown on the suspects. Marveling at the short list, he made a mental note to thank Sierra tomorrow. Her help had been instrumental in cross-referencing his mother's files with the news agency's files. Together, they'd managed to narrow it down to a top-ten list of suspects.

But what a list. John sighed. Six crazies, including one nut job who thought the top candidates were all aliens trying to take over California. The most likely suspects, however, had all been debating with Eleanor the night she was attacked.

Two-Bits, rapper extraordinaire, was known to have killed other rival gang-bangers back in his gangsta days—and he'd seemed the best possibility until word had spread through the news agency he'd been shot at tonight. Of course, it could've been a fake to deflect suspicion away from him, but that seemed unnecessary since the police didn't even appear to be concerned at this point. And one of his homeys was seriously injured, which also didn't seem to fit.

Arnold "The Mountain" Schwarzkov was a possibility, but John had a hard time believing that a "Pro" wrestler was capable of real violence. For some reason, all that fake TV stuff made John doubt Schwarzkov's ability to commit actual violence. But he knew that was his own prejudice and he'd have to put it aside. For one thing, in his experience anyone could be capable of violence. And lots of the wrestlers seemed to be steroidally challenged. 'Roid rage was definitely a violent phenomenon. Plus, the big black guy that had tried to run him over had the physique of an overweight wrestler.

Michael Sanchez was the least likely of the top tier candidates. For one, he was a consummate politician—and politicians tended to use money as a means to gain power, not murder. Also, he was popular with the Hispanic vote. Every year the Latino population grew bigger, so even if he lost this year, the chance that he'd make it next time was even better.

John shook his head. If Two-Bits wasn't at the top of his list, then it had to be Richard Steel. No record of violence, but an uncanny and quick rise to the top of the sordid lobbying profession. You didn't rise that fast keeping your nose clean.

And Steel obviously didn't have much of a conscience if he could lobby for Pfester Chemicals and Pharmaceuticals. They'd been sued numerous times for bypassing pollution laws and wreaking havoc on the poor souls who happened to live near their dumping grounds. But the real kicker was Russian organized crime. The group was well known for killing their rivals and rumor had it Steel was connected to them.

When his eyes blurred, John threw his notes in the folder and headed for his bedroom. *I'll work on it tomorrow. After the press conference.* He groaned. "Press conference. Unbelievable."

He kept on mumbling, even cursing to himself as he brushed his teeth, then undressed and slid into bed. "Damned governor's race."

He started to pull the covers up when he noticed some movement beside him. He saw a hand reaching toward him and let instinct take over. With his left hand, he grabbed the slender wrist and pushed it down into the bed, then used his right hand to grab the other wrist. He pushed down with his body but stopped when he noticed that the person wasn't struggling beneath him.

In fact, she was docile, and naked, and blonde.

"Ooh, kind of kinky, John. But I'm up for it."

At the sound of Amber's voice, John shot out of bed. "What the hell are you doing in here?"

Amber smiled. "Nothing yet. So far it's all you."

John reddened and pulled on his boxers. "Get out."

Amber's smile turned to a pout. "You don't mean it."

John looked her in the eye. "Yes. I do."

In the span of a few seconds her pouting turned to indignation and anger, followed by cool calculation turning to sadness. Tears started to form. "But...why?"

He tried to ignore the tears. "Because you're fifteen."

Her chest shuddered as a big sob burst out. "I'm sixteen!"

"Whatever. Sixteen. Either way you're way too young for me."

Amber turned into the pillow and bawled.

John looked up at the ceiling. *This can't be happening.* But her tears were starting to affect him. Like always.

"Amber..."

Sob. "Lots of men like younger women."

"Yeah, but…"

Sob. "What's the matter with me?"

"Nothing."

Sob. "It's 'cause I haven't had my boobs done, isn't it?"

"God, no."

Shudder. Sob. "But it's not my fault. Daddy won't pay for them until the stock market improves."

John fought the instinct to reach out and comfort her, knowing it would only make things worse. *There has to be a way out of this.*

"Look, Amber. It's not you. It's…me."

There was a hitch in the tears as she gave a hopeful glance toward him. "What do you mean?"

"I, uh, got some news tonight that changes things."

"What?"

"I'm going to be taking my sister's place on the ballot."

Amber turned away and started crying all over again. John sat on the edge of the bed. "What's the matter, now?"

Sob. "I'm not stupid, you know. Hillary told me all about you and that you're not like the rest of the family. You're a rebel." Sob. "There's no way you're running for governor."

John pulled the sheet up to Amber's chin and immediately relaxed. "You're right. I wouldn't be running if my sister hadn't been injured. But she is. And I feel responsible. And now the two of you are in danger. I'll do whatever it takes to make things right."

Amber turned toward him, managing to knock the sheet down to her waist. "You're doing this for me?"

John gulped. Maybe this wasn't the right tactic. But he'd already committed to the strategy. "I'm doing it for all of you. Running for governor means that I can't do whatever I want. I have to make sure I'm scandal free, if you know what I mean."

Amber nodded. "All right, John. I understand." She slipped from the bed and grabbed some clothes off the floor, covering herself in a slight bit of modesty.

"Thanks," John said.

Amber smiled. "That's the first time I've ever been thanked for *not* getting busy. You're something else, John."

She blew him a kiss on her way out the door.

NAILS HID BEHIND THE CURTAIN IN THE HOTEL BUNGALOW AND flicked a switch on the side of the ultra-long shotgun microphone, checking to make sure the camera was picking it up. But there was no symbol or anything to show that it was receiving audio. So he hit the record button, aimed the parabolic dish toward his mouth, and spoke into the mike. "Check one. Check two. Check three. Sibilance. Sibilance."

"Yo, Nails, you gotta check out the bathroom in this place. They gotta thing in there that looks like a toilet only it shoots water up your bumhole. It's the craziest thing you ever saw."

Barry kept spouting off about the toiletries and whatnot, but Nails ignored him and hit the stop button. Then he rewound and played it back. It was all there, down to Barry's idiot remarks. Some of it sounded distorted but he was probably too close. The mike was meant for more distant work.

He rewound it again. *No sense in leaving my voice on the tape.*

Barry's voice got louder as he left the bathroom and the pitch started to pierce Nails' concentration. "Dude, shut up. I don't want to hear about the complimentary shaving cream."

"But this just proves my point about how rich guys get everything and us worker bees get squat. I'm telling you, we gotta unionize. I mean, they don't even have to wipe their own ass. They got a machine to do it for 'em."

Nails gave him a light rap on the skull, knocking Barry onto the couch. "For the last time, we're not organizing the Russian mafia. And if you want to live through tomorrow we got to do this job right, so shut up and connect the mike to the stand. Sanchez and the bimbo will be here any minute."

Barry pouted, but finally shut up and got to business. Nails switched off the lights and cracked open the living room window, then settled into a comfortable chair to wait.

Barry finished messing with the microphone stand and peered out into the night. "Where they gonna be?"

Nails pointed to the bungalow across the walkway. "She's going to lead him into the bedroom over there. The window on the right side."

"Won't they turn the lights off?"

"Shhh. Keep it to a whisper. If Sanchez comes down that walkway, we don't want him to hear you spouting off."

Barry whispered, "But what about the lights?"

"Don't worry about it. I've got night vision on the camera if it's necessary, but I hear Sanchez likes to see what he does to the ladies. The only part we have to worry about is the chick. She's supposed to make sure the curtains are open enough that we can get a clean shot with the camera and that the window is cracked open so we can get a sound byte. If necessary, she's supposed to maneuver her way past the window so she can be seen through the curtain. Lead him by the Johnson if she has to. Steel said she's a soap actress so she knows how to find the camera, get her close-up and all that."

Barry perked up. "There she is."

Nails grunted and hit the record button. "You got the microphone aimed right?"

"Hey, I'm not a retard. All you gotta do is point the thing right at them."

Nails scratched at his back where the tire patches were stuck to the skin. They were starting to itch badly.

Barry said, "Wow, that's Terri Johnston from *As the Days Go By*. She's a hot babe. Why's she doing this job?"

"How should I know? It's probably a favor, or maybe she thinks it's a way to get a better part on another show."

Barry laughed. "You scratch my back, I'll scratch yours, huh?"

Nails scratched at the tire patch. On the video screen, the couple was starting to go at it like a couple of dogs. He tried to tune out Barry and watch the show, but the skinny dude wouldn't shut up.

"Heck, this room is probably a favor. I betcha Steel didn't

have to cough up one penny to get this primo cottage. Or Sanchez for that other one."

Nails cringed and turned away from the screen. *What the hell? Sick crackers!*

"Jeez, that's friggin sick. What is that? Ouch! He shouldn't do that to her."

Nails covered his eyes. "No. He shouldn't. No man should."

Barry squirmed in his seat. "It's a crying shame that that guy could be governor."

"It ain't right. That's for sure."

"You know, maybe we're doing the world a favor. Maybe we're like a divine influenza or something."

Nails turned to stare at the stupid ass sitting next to him.

Barry said, "Hey, man, don't do that. It's bad enough I gotta be watching this sex stuff in the same room as another guy. But if you look at me at the same time, it's gonna get weird, you know?"

Nails turned away and glanced at the screen, then recoiled and quickly looked at the ground. *Shit.* There was nowhere to look. Stupid, sick crackers were everywhere. With a sigh, he closed his eyes and scratched at his rubber patch.

twenty

JOHN held out his arm to hold Amber and Hillary back, then keyed his lapel mike and said, "We're almost out the front door of the hospital. Are we all clear?"

Harley's voice came over John's earpiece. "No worries. Everything looks good outside. When you reach your vehicle, give me a minute to leave my perch and catch up."

"What are you talking about?" John squinted into the early morning sun and led the girls outside. He kept his gaze roving. "It'll be better if you've got your own wheels at the cemetery."

"I know. My car is already parked there. I took public transport to get here 'cause I've got something to show you."

John grinned, then opened the back door on his Suburban so the girls could slide in. "You found something at the crash site?"

Harley snorted. "Just wait for a tick. I'm on my way."

John started the engine, but kept it in park. He checked the rearview mirror to see how Hillary was doing. *Not bad, under the circumstances.* She was leaning against Amber's shoulder and shedding a few quiet tears.

John shook his head. Amber actually seemed to be helping Hillary. Comforting her. The first real sign why Hillary wanted to be friends with the girl.

He fought back a couple of tears himself, wishing he could deal with this as well as Hillary. When he'd seen Eleanor this morning—with the myriad of tubes sticking out of her and the clicking, whirring machines producing a nasty symphony—he'd just about lost it.

The passenger door opened and Harley dove in. "Go."

John shifted into drive and pulled away. "What'd you get?"

Harley reached into his duffel bag and pulled out what looked like a smashed pan pipe.

John frowned. "What is it?"

"Solid gold, mate. It's the would-be murder weapon."

John took the twisted piece of metal and looked it over. Lots of little, tiny pipes. Essentially a dozen gun barrels.

"A little to the right, mate."

John looked up in time to see that he'd drifted over the center line. He brought the car gently back to his side of the road, but still received an obscene gesture and a lean on the horn from a passing car. In his rearview mirror he noticed both Amber and Hillary return the gesture.

John tossed the pipes back to Harley. "Okay, I give. How's it work?"

"They use these things in the movie industry when they need to make a flat tire happen on cue. This little beauty fires nails with a force strong enough to pierce the tire."

"Son-of-a...and you found rusty nails at the scene."

"Yeah. This is what the hefty fella was putting on Eleanor's car. If those damned security agents had pulled their heads out of their arses for two seconds, this whole thing wouldn't have happened."

"I take it there were no prints."

"A partial. I dropped it off with my buddy at the precinct, but it doesn't look good. Plus, the partial is from a different bloke than the skinny dude. If they were off the same guy it would be easier for the computer to narrow it down."

"That doesn't sound like solid gold, Harley."

"Ah. Well, this is the good bit. There aren't that many pipe shooters laying about. And the only guys that can use 'em have to be licensed pyrotechnic experts. With a little legwork and a bit of luck, we'll find out who supplied the unit."

"Not bad," John said. "Unfortunately, the leg work is going to be all you."

Harley gestured toward the girls and whispered, "You

think they need babysitting every second? Or maybe just the frisky blonde?"

"Funny," John said. He hesitated, wondering how Harley would take the news about the governor's race.

One of the biggest things they had in common was a mutual distaste for the political process. When he'd first met Harley, his biggest clients had been politicians until extreme disgust had driven him away. It was one of the reasons he and Harley had always been great partners.

Of course, Harley was always willing to go a little farther than he was. Sometimes to a pretty dark place. There'd been a couple of occasions when John had reined in Harley's more violent side.

In Harley's mind, the ones that seemed untouchable—the politicians and big corporations—needed oversight and punishment more than the rest of the world. Something he didn't mind dishing out when he had the time. And for the most part, John had enjoyed the outing of a gay-bashing congressman or the mysterious document leaks detailing exactly where certain companies had been dumping illegal waste.

John shook his head. Harley's methods had worked in their favor more than once. But would he see the value in John's running for office, or would it make their partnership uncomfortable?

"Still thinking about the blonde, eh mate?"

"No, you filthy old man. I'm trying to think of a way to tell you something."

"Well, don't beat around the bush."

"I had a conversation with my mother last night."

Harley squinted. "What'd the Barracuda want this time?"

"She actually had a pretty good idea."

"She's not an idiot. Her smarts are what make her so dangerous."

"It's a way for me to work on the candidates from the inside."

Harley cocked his head to the side. "How's that possible?"

John hesitated.

"Spit it out, mate."

Amber leaned forward and put her hand on John's shoulder. "He's running for governor."

John reddened, hearing the words out loud for the first time. A moment later a snort burst out of Harley with the force of a gunshot, immediately followed by wheezing and snorting together.

Amber said, "Hey, it's not funny. He's got a press conference this afternoon and a debate tonight."

When he heard the words 'press conference,' Harley started wheezing harder, and when he heard the word 'debate,' he began snorting uncontrollably.

John gripped the steering wheel and said, "Glad you haven't lost your sense of humor, Harley."

BARRY SLAPPED AT THE ANTS CRAWLING ON HIS ARM AND SQUIRMED TO a new position in the brush. In New York, the biggest problem was roaches the size of Nails' thumb. But out here in California, you didn't have to stray too far off the beaten path to find yourself hip deep in a pile of creepy crawlies. Maybe if they paved over this place the bugs wouldn't have anywhere to go.

Ten minutes before, he'd stuffed a couple of cigarettes into the anthill, hoping to gas 'em or something, but it just made the little buggers angry. Now the place was covered.

He slung the rifle over his shoulder and crawled through the bushes, looking for a good vantage point over the grave of one Frank Black. After he'd put about thirty feet between him and the anthill he found a tree to lean against.

This assignment blows!

All the waiting was starting to drive him batty. Yesterday he'd spent most of the day camped out at the hospital, figuring the girl would have to show up to see her mommy, but he hadn't seen squat. Like maybe the girl was deliberately hiding out, trying to stay out of his sight.

Wouldn't surprise me.

His luck was crap right now. He hadn't had a horse

race come through in weeks. The jobs were going crazy, what with Nails blowing the Two-Bits job. Even when it went perfect, like last night with Sanchez, things got pretty weird. It should have been the best porn he'd ever seen, a live show starring a famous soap actress, but the friggin thing had turned into this bizarre sex act with whips and animals.

Barry shuddered. He'd never look at a hamster the same way again.

He took a peek with the scope, but found the funeral plot deserted. The girl had to visit her dad's grave today, right? And hopefully, her friend as well.

Barry knocked back a shot of Pepto and lit another smoke, then tried to rub the sleepiness out of his eyes. The friggin dream last night had starred the psycho who'd chased him through the dog pen, only this time the psycho had been chasing him through the pits of hell, surrounded by rabid, carnivorous Lassies.

And to top it all off, he couldn't find the right gravesite this morning. Two whole hours wasted trying to follow the map. All the streets looked the same, but he couldn't ask for help because he didn't want to call attention to himself.

He was starting to wonder if it was one of those psychological things—that he couldn't find the grave because he didn't really want to. God knew he didn't want to waste the hot girls, but he didn't feel like he had much of a choice. Law of the jungle and all that.

He caught himself nodding off and woke with a start.

I gotta do something to stay awake here.

He looked at the bag next to him and wondered if he was brave enough to mess with the bomb inside. He smiled. Screwing with *that* would definitely keep him awake.

"TELL ME AGAIN WHY WE'VE BEEN DRIVING AROUND IN CIRCLES FOR the last ten minutes," Amber said.

John rubbed his forehead and sighed. "I told you, we have to give Harley time to get into position. He'll be watching our backs to make sure you're still alive at the end of this trip."

Harley's voice piped in over the headset. "I'm in position. There are two potential problem areas, the foothills to the west and the bushes to the north. Try to keep the trees between you and those two areas as much as possible."

"Got it. Thanks for the help."

"Anytime, governor."

John held back a reply, then got out of the car and opened the door for Hillary. He caught a snatch of conversation as the girls stepped out.

Amber said, "I think that old dude is scary. He gives me the creeps."

"Shut up," Hillary said. "You do *not* want him to hear you. Harley's the last person you want to piss off."

Amber stood still and glanced around. "Do you think he can hear us?"

John cut in, "He hears more than you want him to."

Amber hung back a few paces as John put his arm around Hillary and walked toward the grave. He leaned in and whispered, "You know Harley would never harm either one of you."

She whispered back, "I know. I'm just trying to keep her quiet. She's been getting on my nerves. Too much time together, I guess."

"I can see that."

John turned toward the north and scanned the tree line.

"I tried to stop her, Uncle John. I told her you wouldn't be interested, but she wouldn't listen."

John stopped. "You knew she was in my room?"

"Yeah, but I knew you'd do the right thing. And somehow you kept her from getting too upset. She's only been turned down once before, and she tortured the hell out of the poor guy who did it. By the time she was through, he'd have done anything she asked."

Hillary stopped and knelt down, placing a bouquet of flowers at the base of the headstone.

BARRY RUBBED HIS EYES AND CHECKED THE SCOPE AGAIN. WAS HE dreaming? How did that psycho security guy end up with the girls?

He'd had a clean shot on the daughter when the guy who was comforting her had turned to stare right at him. He'd about crapped his pants. Somehow, the Terminator had risen straight out of his dreams and stared him in the eye. Barry couldn't help it. He'd frozen.

And now the darned trees were in the way. He had a shot on one of the girls, but he needed to get all three of them in the open if this was going to work.

His heart raced, beating fast enough to be distracting. Could he even make three shots in a row from this distance? The first one would have to be the security guard. There was no way he wanted that guy chasing after him, coming straight out of his nightmare.

His heart felt like it was stuck in his throat. What he needed was a better shot.

Back to the ants.

He grabbed his bag and rifle and started crawling back toward the anthill. It seemed like the guy was searching up here, so he kept his pace slow and steady, hoping the affair down below would be a tearjerker and last a long time.

JOHN KEPT A FEW PACES BACK FROM HILLARY AND AMBER, GIVING his niece as much time as she needed, and wishing he could help her out. His own memories were stirring—the ones he kept tucked deep inside. Memories of his dad dying when he was a teenager. The memory of his girlfriend being killed shortly afterward.

The part of his memory he hated.

He saw a flash of sunlight in the bushes on the north side, just past the lush green carpet. "Harley. Are you on the north?"

There was a small bit of static before his reply, "No, I'm in the grassy foothills to the west."

"Check out the north side, thirty feet up the hill at twelve o'clock,"

Harley's voice shouted in his ear, *"Get down!"*

John dove toward the girls as bits of stone exploded from the headstone in front of them.

twenty-one

BARRY took three quick shots, destroying the heck out of some tombstone, then jumped as the bushes around him seemed to disintegrate.

Someone's shooting at me!

The tree to his right spat bits of bark in his direction and then the tree to his left did the same. He froze, sitting squarely behind a thick tree trunk that stood between the other two.

This friggin tree saved my life!

He realized his mouth was hanging open and shut it. The thick tree hiding his skinny body was a good thing, but how much longer could he expect a piece of wood to protect him? Barry started to shake and reached into his pocket for the pink elixir.

Empty.

He pounded the ground beside him. *It's not my fault. The guy ducked BEFORE I started shooting. How is that friggin possible?* He replayed the events in his head—the psycho had seemed to look right at him just before ducking behind the headstone. It had been unnerving and he'd taken a couple of seconds to get up the nerve to shoot. Naturally the shots had missed the relentless cyborg and now the Terminator would be ticked off and coming for him.

But wait a second. The bushes had started to disintegrate at almost the same time.

His mouth dropped open again. Two of 'em. It had to be.

JOHN KEPT HIS ARMS AROUND THE GIRLS, KEEPING THEIR HEADS below the level of the tombstone. "Harley, do you have a clean shot?"

The radio crackled. "No. He's behind a tree, but I've got him pinned."

John looked to the foothills where Harley was positioned. "I'm closer, and you've got the scope. So cover me till I hit the tree line, then come get the girls."

"Got it."

John looked at Hillary and Amber. "Stay put and keep your heads down. I'm going after the shooter."

The girls screamed in unison, *"What?"*

"Harley will be here in thirty seconds to pick you up and keep you safe. Just stay down until he gets here."

John keyed his mike. "Hit it."

At the sound of gunfire from the hills, he hurdled the headstone and rushed toward the trees.

BARRY SCRUNCHED UP AGAINST THE TREE AS THE FOLIAGE EXPLODED around him. Sharp, stabbing pains came from his shins. *I'm hit!*

There was a pause in the gunfire and he pulled up his pant leg and frowned. No blood, but tons of little welts where red ants were crawling on him. Frantic, he started slapping at the little buggers, amazed that such tiny creatures could cause so much pain.

The shooting started up again and he had to wonder why they were shooting when he was completely protected by the tree trunks. *Oh, God, the Terminator's coming!*

He looked all around, trying not to panic. He had to get out of there. But with the bullets flying there was nowhere to go.

He looked at the bag at his feet. The thing was covered with those biting buggers, but it beat dying, so he put his hand into the seething mass and pulled out the bomb and remote trigger.

The bullets came to an abrupt halt. Barry clenched his buttocks as tight as he could, figuring the Terminator was right on top of him. He pictured metallic limbs reaching for his throat as he flicked the arming trigger and waited for the red light to go on.

Nothing.

Where's the friggin light?

No light meant it wasn't armed. He flicked it off and on ten more times in rapid succession, working himself into a lather, before the red light blinked on. "Hah! Got it."

Barry's elation died when he felt a gun barrel pressing against the back of his neck.

"Drop it."

Barry half turned and found the man from his nightmares staring him straight in the eye. In panic mode, he started to drop the remote.

Holy crap. Don't do what the man says!

He clenched the trigger in his hand before realizing that was a bad idea as well. He loosened his grip a little, trying to hold the remote firmly, yet not squeezing too hard.

"Drop it, asshole," the Terminator said. "Or I drop *you*."

Barry tried to slow his breathing. He wiggled his hand toward his foe. "Come on, ya gotta see what I'm holding here. In fact, I think we've been through this before."

The man sighed and looked around. "But no dogs this time."

Barry flinched. "Yeah, but now we're sitting right on *top* of the friggin bomb."

The man raised an eyebrow. "Friggin? Is that a word?"

Barry squeezed his eyes shut for a second. Even with a bomb in his hands people were giving him crap. It was like eighth grade all over again. *Unbelievable.*

He gestured toward the bag on the ground. "Hey, genius. Maybe it's hard to tell what that device is the way it's covered in ants, but with that bomb I'll have no problem turning those little guys into crispy critters. Or you either, for that matter. All it takes is pushing this little button here."

Barry slapped at a couple more ants, then danced to his feet, waltzing a few steps backward. The Terminator matched his steps, maintaining a steady distance between them. "What are you doing?" Barry yelped. "Get back!"

"Not going to happen, Beanpole. I'm not giving you another head start."

Barry held up the trigger. "Then you're toast."

The man grinned. "So long as I take you with me, that'll be fine."

Just like my dream! Barry started shaking. "What kind of security guard are you? Aren't you taking this a little personal?"

"It got personal when you shot nails out of those pipes into Eleanor Black's car."

Barry's eyes bugged out. *How does he know about that?*

He took another step back, with the Terminator pacing him.

"And it got more personal when you tried to shoot a fifteen-year-old girl who was visiting her father's grave."

Barry shrugged and tried to look nonchalant. "At least I missed, right?" He took a step to the left, keeping the bomb between the two of them.

The man smiled. "Your incompetence is limitless."

"Hey. Shut up."

"Your boss has got to be pretty pissed off. Probably calling someone, as we speak, to have you taken out."

Barry raised the trigger and mimed pushing the button. "I said shut up."

"Even your partner can't take care of business. A gun at point-blank range and somehow Two-Bits is still alive, still fighting the power."

"Shut up. Shut up. Shut up!" *Why won't he shut the hell up?* Barry shook his head. *It's like the Terminator's trying to keep me talking.* Barry whipped his head to the left, then back to the right. *His partner must be sneaking up on me! Holy crap. I gotta get out now!*

Barry racked his brain and came up empty. All he could think about was a second Terminator coming for him. *But he's not here yet, so I still got time!*

He took another step to the left and noticed his nemesis

also circled to his left. The guy was trying to keep close to him, but was also trying to keep away from the bomb.

So he wasn't invincible. The Terminator *was* scared of the bomb.

Barry smirked. "Okay. Here's what I'm gonna do. In three seconds I blow this puppy to pieces. If you're coming after me...well, you can try it, I guess. But more than likely there'll be bits of you spread all over the place, fertilizing these nice bushes."

The man tensed, but didn't move toward him.

Barry cackled and started backing away. "One..."

"Tell your boss I'll be seeing him tonight."

Barry frowned and started running. *What does that mean?* He checked over his shoulder to see if the guy was coming for him. But he wasn't even moving.

He should be moving! Why isn't he moving?

Barry felt a tree branch sting his cheek as he hurried away from the humanoid robot. He tried to calculate if he was far enough away, but he'd flunked math three times and the running seemed to be pulling oxygen away from his brain.

He turned back and noticed the guy was finally looking lively, diving for shelter behind the same tree that had protected Barry from the bullets minutes earlier.

CRAP! No more friggin calculating! Barry pulled the trigger.

A CONCUSSIVE BLAST ROARED OVER THE ROLLING GREEN HILLS. Harley looked at the orange fireball in his rearview mirror and slammed on the brakes, pulling the wheel hard to the right. The girls' screams subsided as the Suburban came to a stop by the cemetery's entrance.

Thoughts raced through his head—*Shit. John! Stop. No time. Worry later. Think. Act. Now!*

Harley turned to the girls. "Can either of you drive?"

"Amber's got her license."

He tossed them his cell phone and hopped out of John's car. "Drive north until you hear from me."

"Where?"

"Anywhere. Just stay where there's people. If someone is following you, call 911 and head for the nearest police station."

Harley slammed their door shut and jumped into his own Suburban. He grabbed a first aid kit from under the seat. By the time he had the engine started, Amber and Hillary had driven through the black iron gates, out of the cemetery.

Not bad for a couple of young sheilas.

He watched for five seconds, making sure no one was tailing the girls, and started driving back up the hill.

He hopped out, then ran up the lush green knoll, past the headstones, and into the scrub at the edge of the property, following the same trail John had taken a few minutes earlier. When he got to the blast site, he stopped cold.

The diameter of the blast reached thirty feet, but behind one sturdy tree trunk was a thin line of greenery that hadn't been blackened. And lying right in that green shadow was John. Out cold, but otherwise looking pretty healthy.

Good job, kid.

Harley snorted, then threw John over his shoulder and headed down the hill.

JOHN WOKE WITH A START AND RAISED HIMSELF TO A SITTING POSITION. He looked out the back window and saw traffic moving at a snail's pace along the 101 Freeway. The sound that had wakened him, a long horn blast from the car next to them, stopped after Harley stared at the man for a couple of seconds.

John almost laughed. A quick glare from Harley was enough to stop just about anyone.

And he would've laughed if his head didn't feel like it had been split down the side. But even worse was the smell. Burnt gasoline and some sort of chemical had seemingly etched its way into his nasal passages. He hoped it wasn't permanent.

"Are the girls okay?"

Harley looked in his rearview mirror and said, "As much as teens ever are."

"Where are they?"

"Two car lengths in front of us."

John felt around his body and found no real damage, other than the ringing in his ears. "Tell me the blast got the skinny dude."

"Sorry, mate. While the slimy bastard couldn't kill a meal to save his life, he's got a bit of a wily streak in him. He was gone by the time I reached you."

John sighed and leaned back in the seat. "That's twice he got away. I must be losing it."

"Hey, you don't win every sortie. You did the best that was possible. The girls survived an assassination attempt, and you survived a detonation from ten feet away. Not a bad job by my way of looking at it." Harley snorted. "Damned tree saved your life. I'm always telling people if you take care of the environment..."

"The environment will take care of you. Yeah, yeah. You're like a broken record sometimes."

Harley's lip twitched into a smile. "And I thought no one listened to my eco speeches."

"Not if they don't have to," John said. "But I have to admit, that first half-second when the heat washed over me, I started to have serious doubts about my plan."

"Things turned out all right."

"Yeah. I guess so. Except the bastards are still out there." John massaged his temple and stared at the traffic. "I'm not thinking too clearly. What are we doing next?"

"Well, I've got the boring job. Tracking down licensed pyro guys with those pipe shooters." Harley paused. "*You've* got the exciting job."

John frowned. "What are you talking about?"

Harley grinned. "Your press conference, mate. Don't tell me you blacked it from your memory. We've got just enough time to get you cleaned up and back to the Barracuda."

Son of a... John closed his eyes and rubbed his temples. "Which is worse? The skinny dude getting away, him trying to turn me into extra crispy KFC, or being grilled by the press about running for office?"

Harley snorted.

twenty-two

STEEL sat back in his chair and kicked his feet up on the desk, trying to ooze confidence from his pores. He gazed at the large, imposing Russians sitting across from him and showed them his Cheshire Cat smile. "Sasha, Lexi...you've got to relax. Things are going well."

Sasha leaned forward and pounded his fist onto the desk, smashing Steel's Lobbyist of the Month award. "Things are *not* well. We force ourselves to kill Frankie this morning."

Steel's smile slipped for a moment. *Who the hell is Frankie?* He dug deep, looking for an angle to soothe the Russians. He'd probably better go with smile #3, the Redford, which worked in practically any situation.

He dialed it up and said, "I'm sorry to hear about Frankie, an associate I presume. But our plan is working beautifully. I've jumped two slots in the latest poll. When Sanchez takes a look at the tape we sent him he'll drop out of the race. And there's a good chance I'll rise straight to the top. So what's the problem?"

Sasha started spluttering, ready to blow a gasket.

Lexi put a restraining hand on Sasha's shoulder and said, "What my brother means to say is that we are having big morale problems in our businesses."

"Morale problems?"

"Image is king of our business. Without it, the wolves come preying."

Steel's smile faltered again. "Wolves?"

"Yes. At sign of weakness."

Steel racked his brain, trying to follow the conversation. Maybe it was some kind of cultural thing, but he couldn't figure out what had their tighty-whities in a bunch. *Time to grease the wheels a bit.* "But you guys are anything but weak. You're on the board of directors for one of the biggest pharmaceutical companies in the world. And after I'm elected you'll be partners with the Governor of California."

Sasha relaxed, seeming almost human.

Lexi nodded and said, "Yes. All is true. And that part is good. But these things you speak of are in legitimate business arena. Our main business is very different."

Sasha thumped the table with his fists, "And these idiots are making us look bad."

Steel said, "Are we talking about Barry and Nails?"

Lexi said, "Yes. These...how you say...nincompoops...are messing with our cruise. If you take my meaning?"

Steel smiled a softer #2 this time. "Okay, I'm following you now. Barry and Nails' mistakes are making you look bad, right? But no one is supposed to know what they're doing."

Sasha shrugged. "*Nyet. Nyet.* Of course we tell no one."

Lexi waved his hands. "No, definitely not. But is more like a rumor. Then one thing leads to another, and our other employees start to make like wolves sniffing for weakness."

Sasha moved his finger across his throat in a slitting motion. "So we had to kill our best driver, Frankie."

Lexi continued, "This goes on much longer and we have to kill whole lot of them and start fresh. And that would hamper our many business goals."

"Hey, just a couple more days, all right?" Steel said. "That's the plan we agreed on. *After* our boys kill one or two more, the police will finally be looking for the assassins. And that's when you can deliver them to the cops. Dead, of course. Hell, make an example out of Nails and Barry first. That way you can solve your employee problems at the same time."

Sasha growled, "They are trying at my patience."

Steel reached inside and pulled out his #6 smile, the best buddy smile. "They try my patience as well. But we're almost there. Can't you taste it? All we need is for Sanchez to drop out of the race and..."

The door to his office burst open, shaking dust from the

ceiling as Sanchez boiled through the door, his fists quaking like those of a crack addict with no money.

"Speak of the devil," Steel said.

Sanchez hurled a DVD at Steel, who ducked as the disc sailed past and smashed into the wall. "You slimy piece of worm-ridden filth! You scum-sucking pimple!"

Steel rose to his feet and brushed imaginary lint from his lapel. "Take it easy, Sanchez. I know why you're upset, and if I were in your position I'd feel the same way. Believe me, my heart aches for you."

Sanchez squinted in disgust and his whole body tensed to spring. Sasha and Lexi rose up on either side of the politician and clamped onto his shoulders.

"Get your hands off me!"

"They will, Sanchez, as soon as you calm down. Say hello to Sasha and Lexi Khrushchev."

Sanchez's eyes opened wide as he turned to face Lexi. "Sasha *Khrushchev?*"

Lexi gestured toward his brother. "He is Sasha. I am Lexi. You have heard of us?"

The color drained from Sanchez's face as he stopped struggling. "Of course."

Steel turned his chuckle into a cough, out of politeness for his vanquished foe. "We received a copy of the video, too."

Sanchez glared at him.

Sasha picked his teeth then said, "Is very disgusting what you did with hamster. I almost lost my breakfast, if you take my meaning."

Sanchez muttered in Spanish what was probably a string of profanities.

Steel thought the odds were about fifty-fifty that Sanchez might try to attack him, even with the Russian presence. He sighed. This day was turning into one of those days where all he did was put out one fire after another. "Let me assure you that the bastards who did this have no connection with me or any of my staff. There's no call for this kind of behavior in politics."

Sanchez seethed and tensed again before Lexi squeezed his

shoulder. Sanchez grimaced, then slumped. He took a couple of deep breaths and put on his usual political face. "Maybe we can help each other. Right, Dick?"

"You know, I bet we can." Steel mused at the irony that Russian organized crime was helping to restore civility to politics. He smiled, this time giving his best Bill Clinton—the one that charmed all the ladies, yet also made heads of state know that he understood their concerns. "I share your pain, Sanchez. These are horrible times."

"Yeah, horrible," Sanchez echoed.

"So it's settled, then. We'll work together. I'll help you and you'll help me."

"What do you mean?"

"The copy of the note we got with the video said you would have to exit the race. Which is awful. But it also said you would have to endorse my candidacy when you step down. And that has to feel like a red hot poker shoved up your ass. Why these blackmailing bastards want me for governor, I'll never know. But I do know that it must be difficult for you."

Sanchez glared. "You have no idea."

"I'm sure you're right. But I am prepared to do the same for you, Sanchez. After my governorship is over, I promise to endorse *you* as the next governor. I think it's the right thing to do."

Steel extended his hand toward Sanchez, hoping the bastard would know it was the best opportunity available.

Sasha piped in, "Is win-win situation."

Lexi added, "One hand washes the other."

Steel waited with his hand extended, savoring the thrill of the victory, and watched Sanchez's eyes while the man thought over his options. If Steel was a good judge of people, and he liked to think that he was, hatred was reflected in those eyes, followed by a grudging respect. And when Sanchez reached out and shook his hand, Steel smiled. And this time he didn't even have to dial one up. It was all natural.

But the joy left when the phone intercom buzzed and his assistant yelled out, "Code two on Channel Six News. Turn it on. *Now!*"

Steel grabbed the remote and switched on the television. "What next?"

He recognized Gil's ex as the TV reporter on the tube. *Oh, great. She's a nasty piece of work.*

She raised her hand mike up to her face and said, "Once again, we have reason to believe that a newcomer has been added to the mix in the race for governor of California. With less than a week to go, John Black, the younger brother of recently hospitalized candidate Eleanor Black, is going to announce his candidacy at a press conference that starts in five minutes. We'll be there, live, to bring you this unprecedented event. And immediately following the announcement we'll bring you more details about the newest candidate, as well as information regarding the obscure 'Wild West' law that got him on the ballot. This is Sierra Rodriguez from Channel Six News."

Steel started gnawing at his fingernail. At first glance, the candidacy didn't seem like a problem. After hearing Gil's story about John Black's investigation into his sister's "accident," Steel had culled together an extensive file on John. And the file had showed an extremely anti-political, even anti-social, malcontent. Someone who'd be hard pressed to run an effective campaign.

So why was he running?

There had to be more to it. He knew John Black was investigating the assassination attempts on his sister, and that he'd chased Barry through some kind of doggy day care. But why would that make him get into the race at this late juncture? *Unless...*

Steel noticed Sanchez was watching him instead of the television. He hastily removed his fingernail from the vicinity of his mouth.

Sanchez chuckled. "Not everything comes up roses, eh Dick?"

Steel stumbled, then dialed up his #12 smile, the one that froze on his face when he didn't know what to say. It wasn't his best expression, but he knew it looked better than the deer in the headlights look most politicians got when caught with their pants down.

For Steel, or all of them for that matter, the expression represented just one particular thought: *Shit!*

SIERRA FIDGETED WITH HER MICROPHONE AND SAT DOWN IN THE MIDST of the other reporters, tapping her heels in excitement. *I'm not in Kansas anymore, am I, Toto?* She checked over her shoulder to make sure that Blake, her cameraman, had lined up a good shot. And of course he had. She didn't really need to double check, but her exhilaration was getting the best of her.

Her first scoop! Courtesy of John, and soon to be followed by her first exclusive interview of any note. She craned her neck and spotted John coming toward the podium, looking positively yummy in a three-piece gray suit. When he frowned and loosened his tie, she smiled, thinking he must be dreadfully uncomfortable out of his customary jeans.

But he was wearing the suit anyway. The clothing, the run for office, spending time with the press—all things that he couldn't stand. Yet he was doing them. And all for his sister and niece. *A real class act.*

She shook her head. It was getting harder and harder to stay detached and objective around John.

The Deputy Mayor, the one who'd taken over for Eleanor since her accident, stepped up to the podium. "Ladies and gentlemen, may I present Barbara Black, senator of the state of California, and her son, John Black."

A whir of clicks and buzzes rose to a crescendo as photographers snapped the senator's picture as she stepped up to the podium. John stayed a step behind her and to the right.

"Today is a momentous day," the senator said. "My daughter, Eleanor Roosevelt Black, has worked very hard for the people of California. Both as mayor of Los Angeles, and during her campaign for governor. Her priorities have always been the people's priorities. Unfortunately, the woman who can and should be elected governor of this great state is lying in a hospital, slowly recovering from a horrendous accident. And while Eleanor's prognosis is good, it would not be fair to expect Californians to vote for someone who is incapacitated, even if it is only for a brief period of time.

"For those of you who know my son, John Kennedy Black, you know a man who has more morals than all the congressmen put together. Indeed, it is that very moral fiber that makes him the strong man he is today. And for those of you familiar with some of John's more infamous quotes—I won't bother to repeat them here, I'm sure you'll hear all about them without help from me—you might be surprised that John is even running for office.

"But anyone who knows John's character knows why he's here. John has always worked hardest trying to help others, and that's what he'll do for you when you elect him governor of California."

A few scattered claps arose from the peanut gallery.

Barbara stepped back and made room for John, who slowly approached the podium. He looked out at the sea of microphones and cameras and gave a wry grin. "Hi, I'm John Black, and I'm running for governor."

Sierra almost burst out laughing. Her first thought was that John was speaking at an Alcoholics Anonymous meeting instead of a press conference. But then she realized that wasn't quite accurate. It wasn't like either kind of meeting. There was none of the usual stuff of politicians—no big smile, no fake attempt at charm. In fact, no phoniness of any kind. Just a natural, easy way of talking.

John continued, "Which is kind of funny, since I don't really want to be governor."

There were gasps from some of the reporters present. Sierra smiled.

"The person who should be here is my sister, Eleanor. To my knowledge, she's the only good person in politics today. And she is the woman who will be your governor. A *great* governor.

"But we need to get from here to there. And the problem is that Eleanor is in the hospital. So my mother and her band of merry lawyers came up with this legal maneuver to get me on the ballot. What you want, and what you need, is Eleanor. But what you have is me.

"Why should you vote for me? Two reasons. The first is that I'll only be a temporary placeholder until my sister gets well. That's good for everyone in California. Second, I'm a straight shooter. If any of you have been paying attention, you know that's a rare species in politics. Practically extinct. Hell, politicians are mostly scumbags."

There were a few chortles from the gallery.

"That's why I've never run for office before. And why I'll never run again. When I'm elected, and while I'm waiting for Eleanor to recover, I will bring both barrels to bear on the corruption that fills this state. I will not allow the politicians and the corporations to trample all over the rest of us.

"So here I am. And here's my platform. *'No bullshit!'*"

More gasps, and this time Sierra gasped along with them.

"That's it. Plain and simple. Keep the greedy bigwigs from stomping on the little guy and then turn things over to the only good politician I've ever known."

John looked over his shoulder. "Sorry. No offense, Mother."

Barbara gave a half-smile. "None taken."

"So vote for me if you'd like to see a little sense knocked into our leaders in the state capitol. Better late than never, right? Or you can vote for me if you want to see Eleanor Black in office. Either way, you win."

Sierra turned to see how the rest of the group was taking John's unique pitch. The reporters were eating it up. Loving the new angle to an already interesting election. Grins all around. Excited hands scribbling away.

"Any questions?" John asked.

Dozens of hands shot up like a bunch of schoolchildren in dire need of a bathroom break.

John shrugged. "All right then. Fire away."

twenty-three

"YOU say that kind of thing to torment me, don't you?"

John turned to his mother and replied, "Playing the victim doesn't really suit you, Mother."

Barbara turned toward the limo driver and said, "Would you be a dear and close the privacy glass?" With the dark window raised, she knocked back a tumbler of scotch and aimed a fierce glare in John's direction. "Would you allow me just *one* moment of self pity? I can see the remnants of my political future flashing before my eyes."

John rubbed his temples, attempting to erase the last hour from his memory. Thirty minutes of playing "Who's got the dumbest question?" with the reporters, followed by a half hour puff piece with Sierra for the evening news. He'd never had a migraine before, but he was sure it couldn't feel any worse than he felt now.

His mother gave a harsh laugh.

"No *bullshit*?" Barbara said. "That's not a platform. It's a piss poor sense of judgment is what it is."

"There you go, Mother. Now you're sounding like your old self. I was beginning to get worried."

"Don't be a smartass. I'm not the one who just cursed on live television. You probably lost the senior citizens with that one."

"You already said that the seniors were a lock to vote for Eleanor and that they'd confuse me with her when they mark their ballots. So the seniors aren't the issue here. What's the problem?"

"You, John. The problem is you."

He held his tongue.

She continued, "You're a live grenade. Ready to go off at

any second. You didn't follow the speech my staff prepared for you. And you ridiculed that reporter from Channel Four."

John muttered darkly, "It was an inane question. How was I supposed to answer it?"

"Not by questioning his credentials! And not by suggesting someone had let him in by accident."

John chuckled at the one bright spot of the afternoon. At a grumble from his mother he decided to offer his apologies. "You're right. I should tone things down a bit."

The Barracuda smiled. "And follow the script? You'll deliver the speeches as written?"

"No. Of course not. I could never pull off those canned speeches. I'm only good at talking straight, you know that. And you said yourself the focus groups liked the idea of a straight talking, no bullshit kind of candidate. Someone real."

His mother sighed. "I know, I know. But I'm afraid you might be a little more real than they meant."

"I thought your advisors said this campaign could work."

"They've been wrong before. And speaking of wrong, would you at least read these position papers before tonight's debate? You want to sound intelligent, don't you?"

John looked at the top file on the stack as she handed them over. "I'm pretty sure I can sound intelligent on urban crime or taxes without your…eloquent input."

"Oh, for God's sake, they're Eleanor's papers. Not mine. You still respect her opinion, even if you don't care for mine. Just look at the damn things. If you agree with them, you can use them for your debate."

"All right."

"Thank you. And here's your schedule for the next couple of days. I'll finalize the rest of the week as we get confirmations for your speaking engagements."

John glanced at the schedule. "Mother, I want to help Eleanor with this election. I do. And I know that means I have to give speeches." He shuddered. "But this isn't possible."

"Don't worry, dear. You'll get used to speaking in public. I bet you're a natural, like the rest of our family."

John felt chills run up his spine. "Bite your tongue. The last thing I want is to be a natural at any of this. My main goal is to find Eleanor's attacker before he strikes at the girls or Eleanor again. Winning the election is secondary."

His mother tried to interrupt, but he held out his hand. "That was our agreement."

"Of course, John. But the election is a *close* second."

John shook his head. "For every one of these events, I'll be a target. That means we have to limit the opportunities to ones we can cover effectively. Plus, every event is another couple of hours taken from our search."

His mother poured another scotch. "Now you're just being difficult. Can't you have Harley working on the investigation while you're giving speeches?"

"No. Someone has to watch my back when I'm out in public. Harley will have to be covering me instead of looking for the killers."

"But you didn't have Harley there for the press conference."

"Today was a gimme since no one knew I was running. Now that it's out in the open I'll have to be ready for an assault at any public function, starting with the debate tonight. So my partner will be there. By the way, Harley will have to check out the venues first and okay them."

The Barracuda glared. "Out of the question. The Aussie hit man doesn't get to veto the venue."

"It's not negotiable."

"Don't be naïve. Everything's negotiable."

As THEIR CAR PULLED TO A STOP, NAILS TURNED HIS GAZE TOWARD the street outside of the Russians' restaurant. *Rich bastards.*

Maybe Barry was right about the whole union idea.

The spooky Russians owned the entire city block, which included the restaurant they worked out of, as well as an art gallery and an older, multi-storied office building—all connected to each other. Steel's offices were at the far end of the block—which probably made it easier for them to keep tabs on him—with the gallery in the middle and the fancy restaurant on the other side, with one of those nice valet services with skinny Russians parking your car for you.

For some reason, it always gave Nails a thrill to see white boys parking cars.

He glanced down the length of the building, looking for cops or Feebs, 'cause you never know who might be scrutinizing the Mafioso Russkies' activities. But it looked like no one was watching the place.

So why am I nervous?

A valet opened his door and he started levering himself from the front seat of the microbus they'd picked up from the junkyard.

"Get a move on, Barry. We don't want to piss off Sasha and Lexi any more than we already have."

"Just a sec."

Nails swiveled toward Barry, who was sucking down Pepto like he was dying of thirst. *Stupid cracker.*

"Now, Barry!"

"Hold your friggin horses. I'm coming."

Nails thought about busting Barry behind the ear but decided against it. Just one more week with the Pepto-swilling, skinny ass, bug-eyed freak and the election would be over. *Take it in stride.*

He popped a couple a bluesies, dry, and noticed the back of his hand was bleeding again. *Shit.* Everything was bleeding lately. If he could ever get a moment away from the job, he'd have to pay a visit to the doc at Pfester for some better pills.

Barry gave the keys to the valet and headed for the restaurant. "I hope to God Sasha ain't here. We gotta be two of his least favorite people right about now. With any luck, we can see Steel without even having to meet up with the Russians."

Nails grunted. *No shit.*

Working for the Russians had plenty of ups and downs. Lexi was mostly all right, more of a businessman than his brother. But even under the best of circumstances Sasha was difficult to work for. On the upside, the pay was pretty damn good, although Barry seemed to disagree.

But the downside—if you screwed up, you knew you'd get your ticket punched.

Which was the main problem right now. And why he was feeling nervous. He knew they'd screwed the pooch on a couple of these jobs, but somehow Sasha had never come looking for them. It didn't make sense.

He'd been thinking that maybe they'd gone soft, that they were trying to work the "legitimate" business angles. The politics and stuff. But then he'd heard that Frankie had been whacked this morning. Found in the trunk of his car with his toupee rammed halfway down his throat, like he'd choked on a Pekinese.

So they weren't going soft, but they weren't killing Barry or himself.

Yet.

He got anxious when his mind added the "yet," but it had to be added. In fact, the more he thought about it, the more he was certain that *yet* was right around the corner. There was no way to know what the dudes were waiting for, but the moment had to be coming soon.

Maybe right now.

Shit.

Barry opened the door and said to the maître d', "Lexi back there?"

Nails checked over his shoulder. No one was sneaking up on them, but he still felt uneasy. The maître d' waved them to the back, and after wandering the halls for a couple of minutes, they finally found Lexi going over some papers.

"Boys, is good to be seeing you."

Nails let Barry enter first, figuring if it was a setup it was better to let the cracker take the first shot. The skinny twit made a small enough target as it was. Nails peeked in the room and noticed that Sasha was missing. *Finally. Lady luck is looking our way.* He stayed in the hallway and tried to keep an eye out.

Barry said, "Hey, Lexi. You want a progress report before we see Mr. S?"

Or maybe Lady Luck is giving us the finger. Because instead of answering, Lexi just stared. His hands were out of sight under the desk, which was never a good sign.

As the pregnant pause became unbearable, Barry started squirming, and Nails figured Lexi was debating whether or not to kill them—making up his mind right then and there.

Barry held up his lunch sack, his hand trembling. "This is the bomb that Steel requested. We're supposed to give it to him. But maybe you want it instead?"

Nails noticed that Barry's other hand was in his coat pocket, like he had his finger on the trigger. *Sweet move.* For the first time, Nails felt some respect for the skinny dude.

Lexi stared at the sack, then brought his hands out from behind the desk and clapped them together. Barry and Nails both heaved a big sigh and relaxed.

"No, boys. Nyet. I do not wish to see device. In point of fact, I do not wish you to see Sasha either. He is not…happy…with you boys. You would do yourselves a service to make visit with Steel very short. If you can get in and out within half hour, you will be missing Sasha altogether. This is good for everyone. Yes?"

Nails and Barry nodded in unison. "Yes. Absolutely."

"Okay. Good. Here is key for back stairway to Steel's office. Off you go."

Lexi herded them toward the doorway with the underground passage to Steel's office.

Barry said, "But I've got some good news. I've tied up one of the loose ends that everyone was worried about."

"No," Lexi said. "Tell me nothing. As long as you keep Steel happy, I will be happy as well. Okay? Yes. Okay."

Nails started down the stairs, with Barry in tow. As he hit the lights, the doorway up above closed. He fought a moment of dread. The damp, earthy smell always reminded him of a crypt. He went down one flight, his knee killing him, and started down the long hallway that led to Steel's private stairs.

As they eased away from the stairwell, Barry whispered, "I think we almost got deep-sixed back there."

Nails shushed him.

"What do you mean, shhh? This is friggin important."

Nails put his finger to his lips and pointed at the walls around them. "Later."

Barry looked around and said, "What?"

"These guys are ex-KGB."

"Yeah, I've heard that. So?"

Nails squinted, but kept moving along. "So they might have bugs and shit watching us right now. Listening to us."

Barry whipped his head around, peering at the walls.

Nails started up the stairway and groaned. *Three flights this time.* Barry kept silent, but started hopping around, peering into the nooks and crannies of the stairwell.

Nails stopped. "Settle down. It's not a great idea to be jumping around with that bomb in your hand."

Barry calmed and started walking gingerly up the stairs. Nails followed, huffing and wheezing, until they reached the door. They could hear Steel yelling at someone, and Nails had to pound on the door a couple of times before it opened.

Steel waved them in, then put a phone up to his ear and resumed his tirade against the poor sap on the line. "You're telling me that some law from the fucking Gold Rush days can't be overturned? Is that what I pay you five hundred dollars an hour to tell me?"

Nails sat down on a rickety chair and caught his breath, enjoying the fact that even the rich boys had problems.

Steel listened for a moment before screaming, "No! No! NO! The least you can do is pull some strings and get him booted off the debate tonight. Can you do that? Good, that's a start. I'll work on Barnes from the election commission to get Black's candidacy overturned. Barnes owes me one."

Steel slammed down the phone and turned toward Barry and Nails.

Barry said, "Things ain't going well, huh?"

Steel stabbed a finger at Barry. "Don't you start. Sit down."

Barry jumped toward a chair and said, "Hey. Sorry, boss. Just making conversation."

Steel sat on the edge of his desk and said, "Give me some good news for a change."

"Oh, yeah. No problem, boss." Barry placed the brown paper bag on his desk. "Here's the bomb you asked for, with instructions inside."

"Good. But not that good."

Nails cringed when he saw Steel smile. It was a predatory, used-car salesmen type of smile. A shark's smile.

Steel continued, "Where's the *good* news?"

Nails said, "I've got a great idea for taking out Two-Bits. I got it while we were watching Sanchez doing his sick sexual tricks."

Steel's smile changed to a happier smile. "Yeah?"

"Yeah. We go set up for it while he's at the debate with you tonight. All his posse will be hanging out there, so we'll have the whole house to ourselves. Plenty of time to set things up before he gets there. Whips, bondage, leather. We'll make it look like he died getting it on. Tomorrow morning the headlines will be insane."

"Nice. I like it. Excellent job, Nails."

Barry spoke up. "Oh, hey. I got good news, too. I took out that security guard who was on our tail."

Steel frowned. "What are you saying? When?"

"At the cemetery this morning. You should have seen him. He was like this relentless machine coming after me, but I turned him into barbecue with one of these bad boys."

Barry pointed to the bomb on the desk.

Steel glowered. "*This* morning?"

"Yeah. I took out the Terminator with one big boom. It was beautiful. Like a dream come true."

"Is that right?" Steel grabbed a remote control from the desk. "Did you see his body?"

Barry hesitated. "Yeah, sure."

"I think I realize why you guys aren't successful at your current job. Rule number one is to make sure there's a body." Steel clicked on the television and pointed at the screen. "This is my new opponent, Eleanor Black's brother. Got on the ballot this morning on a technicality."

Confused, Barry watched a shot of the anchor on TV. "What? Is that guy a new target or something?"

The shot switched to the press conference, and Barry leapt out of his chair.

"Holy crap! That's the guy. That's the guy I killed!"

"That's Eleanor's brother, you putz. And he looks pretty healthy to me."

Barry started to wilt. "You can't mean it...he's still alive?"

A look of panic filled Barry's eyes as he turned away from Steel's glare. "Holy crap."

Nails couldn't help it. He started to laugh.

twenty-four

JOHN stepped out onto his deck and closed the sliding door, trying to drown out the cyclone of activity that his mother always had swirling around her. He'd taken the place out here in the canyon because it was its own world. An idiot-free zone. A politics-free zone. But now idiots and politicians had invaded his sanctuary with the force of an atom bomb.

The sound of Yanni emanated from his cell, and he almost threw the phone into the creek below the house. Instead, he stabbed the answer button and tried to keep the irritation out of his voice. "What is it, Harley?"

"Good news. On my second visit to a Hollywood movie set, I struck gold with the pipe shooter. Oh, yeah, and I also got Tom Cruise's autograph."

John heard a wheezing sort of laugh over the phone and realized the Aussie jokester had struck again. "What did you find out?"

"The pipe shooter we've got isn't a brand name. It's a knock-off."

"So it's like one of those fake Rolex watches they sell off the street. That'll make it even harder to find. The guys who sell those are like cockroaches. You kill one, and there are twenty more to take their place."

"Nah, it's not like that in the film biz. These guys all know each other. And they know who's doing what. There are only two guys from the list that have an imitation pipe shooter. So I've knocked fifteen off the list without even breaking a sweat."

John grinned. "Maybe you should do the legwork more often."

"Wouldn't dream of it. Legwork is your thing. I just shake and break 'em."

"Well, maybe you'll get lucky with the next guy. Maybe he'll refuse to answer your questions."

John heard some more of the wheezing laughter on the other end.

"I've got to get back to work, Harley. Let me know what you find out."

John put his phone back in his pocket and took a deep breath, enjoying the smell of the eucalyptus trees. Then he turned, opened the door, and entered the lion's den.

The noise hit him like a sledgehammer. His mother was grilling somebody on her cell phone, tearing a new hole in the guy from the sound of it. Hillary was smooth-talking on the land line, apparently getting a head start on the hellish political life she was being groomed for. The television was tuned to one of the twenty-four-hour news channels, and since there were no current celebrity scandals happening, John's addition to the California election was a hot topic.

Great...I've always wanted to have my face on the boob tube twenty-four hours a day. Now I'm officially a boob.

Amber tugged at his arm to get his attention. She was typing up a manifesto for the campaign—translating his mother's bad handwriting into something easier for everyone to read.

John tried to ignore her, but Amber pressed her bosom up against him, forcing him to turn her way. "Hey, Amber."

She leaned in and whispered in his ear. "I don't want to complain or anything, but I am *not* a secretary. I barely know how to type."

"I've got nothing to do with this. Talk to my mother."

Amber's voice rose to a whine. "But don't you have people to do this kind of thing?"

His mother hung up her phone and aimed a glare at Amber. "Oh, do shut up and get on with it."

Amber cringed, and John couldn't help but feel a little sorry for her. This was probably Amber's first real work, and his mother was a harsh taskmaster.

"If John could stand to have any of my staff working with him, we'd all be in better shape," Barbara continued.

John shrugged. "But I can't."

The Barracuda turned her gaze toward him. "Reminds me of the time your fourth grade teacher told me you didn't play well with others."

"Let's not make this about me. If just one member of your staff had any morals at all, this wouldn't be a problem."

"You don't even try to get along. What was it you called my chief of staff?"

"I don't know. Smarmy? Bottom feeder? Soul-sucking demon?"

"But that's his profession, for Christ's sake. Smarmy is in the job description."

John leaned back on his couch. "And yet you truly wonder why I don't like politics."

"Oh, do be a dear and shut up. Things are bad enough without having a Dudley Do-Right, 'moral high ground,' freak for a son. Let's operate in the real world for a moment, shall we?"

"Dudley Do-Right?"

The Barracuda shot him a look. "I've got bad news from two different fronts. Although maybe from the same source."

John sat up. "What's the problem?"

"You've been taken out of the debate. A ridiculous excuse about the stage only having enough room for four. And you'd be number five."

"That sounds bogus. Definitely someone else behind that. What else?"

"Someone is bringing a lawsuit against your being on the ballot and Barnes, the election commissioner, is thinking about suspending your name until the courts can decide. Since there is less than a week to go, that would effectively end your campaign before it even began."

"So where's the bad news?" John smiled, then noticed his mother's displeasure. "Sorry. Force of habit. It's always fun pushing your buttons. But think about it. If these two problems are connected, our killer is tipping his hand. The initial reaction to my candidacy should be laughter, not fear, because normally I wouldn't have a chance. I'm the anti-candidate. And there are no polls showing that I might actually take this thing. Yet. So the only person who would take such drastic steps, and so quickly, is someone who has more to fear than the election. Someone who knows I'm after a killer."

The Barracuda laughed. "I like it. The trap is already springing."

"Yeah. So do your thing, Mother, and find out who's behind these 'problems.' My gut is telling me Steel."

"We'll know soon enough."

John leaned back again, settling into the couch.

His mother said, "Don't get too comfortable. You still have to go over the debate notes."

"But I'm off the debate."

The Barracuda barked a laugh. "You think I can be beaten that easily? This is me. You'll be back on before the cameras go live."

BARRY SHIFTED INTO THIRD GEAR, GRINDING THE TRANSMISSION. "Where we headed?" he asked Nails.

"Sex shop on Sunset. Turn right at the corner."

"Oh, you talking about Smitty's? They got some cool stuff there. And a peep show booth in the back." He felt Nails' stare. "What? Like you never been to one of those. Gimme a break."

"I don't need that kind of shit to make my love life work."

"Yeah, whatever." Barry lit up and opened a window. "What are we gonna get there?"

"What else? Sex paraphernalia."

"Well...yeah...but I guess I mean...how are we gonna do this? How do we take him out?"

"Cuff him to the bedposts spread-eagled, then asphyxiate him."

Barry's stomach heaved. *Oh my God!* He poked his head out the window of the microbus and said, "That's disgusting."

"Some people are into that kind of thing."

Barry stomped on the brake pedal and pulled over, parking in a red zone. "You can count me out of that part. There's no way I'm killing somebody by sticking stuff inside their rear end. I'm no homo!"

Nails coughed like he had bugs flying down his windpipe. "What are you talking about?"

"Holy crap! *Ass fixing*? That's just plain cruel. And it sounds like a homosexual deal to me. If you don't mind, I think I'll leave that to the kind of guy who pats other people's behinds while pretending to be a straight pro-football player."

Nails' hand clamped down on Barry's neck like a vise, pinching off his air supply. A transvestite walked past the van and pretended to ignore the dispute.

"First of all," Nails said, "what you're feeling right now is asphyxiation. It comes from a lack of oxygen to the brain. The ass is not involved."

Barry spluttered, gasping for air.

"And second, all football players pat each other on the behind. It doesn't mean I'm queer."

Barry nodded, his face reddening.

Abruptly, Nails let him go and slumped in his seat, looking thoughtful. Barry took a moment to squeeze some badly needed air into his lungs.

Nails said, "You know, maybe I overreacted a bit."

Barry shrugged, wondering if Nails was putting him on. "If you say so."

"I do. I don't know, maybe it's the drugs or something." Nails shifted in his seat, causing the car to rock. "Doesn't matter. Forget about it. We've got more important things to figure out. Life or death things."

Barry rubbed his neck, feeling nervous. *What's he talking about?*

"Normally, I can't stand to be in the same car as you. I think you're about the dumbest white boy I've ever met, and that's saying something. But that move back there in Lexi's office, that was genius. Pure, cool, genius."

Barry found himself grinning. "Hey, thanks."

"And I owe you one. You saved our butts back there. The Russians were going to kill us."

"But why would they want to do that? The jobs are working out okay. I know we're not fast, but at least they're getting done."

"You heard what happened to Frankie. *That's* what they do if you're a problem."

"And we're problems?" Barry asked.

"Straight up."

"Then why aren't we dead already?"

"That, my white friend, is the million dollar question," Nails said. "But I think I figured a way to find out."

HARLEY EXITED THE 210 FREEWAY AT SUN VALLEY AND TURNED into a neighborhood of rundown houses that were built in the sixties. He double-checked the address of the ratty bungalow and matched it to the paper in his hand. *Charles "Sparky" Henderson.*

Hard to believe this guy makes a grand a day. This place is a dump.

He thought for a moment, trying to figure out the best way to get Sparky to admit the pipe shooter was his.

The guy Harley had met at the movie set, the patent holder of the pipe shooter, had told him that he'd worked with Sparky in the past, but that things had gotten messy when Sparky claimed to be the real inventor of the pipe shooter.

Harley shrugged. It was probably as good an angle as any. He knocked on the door, doing his best to act old and non-threatening.

After a minute with no answer, he walked down the side of the house, peeking in the windows as he went along. Toward the back of the house, in a rear bedroom, was a large television with some kind of B-movie playing on the screen. The picture froze, displaying an image of a Barbie doll that had been transformed into an S&M style dominatrix.

Harley heard a cackle from inside as a wild-haired man worked away at a computer, moving the image of the Bondage

Barbie back and forth, one frame at a time. As the guy worked a trackball, Harley noticed he had a few fingers missing and figured this must be the pyromaniac he was looking for.

The image on the screen started moving forward and the doll raced ahead, in what must have been a remote-controlled toy convertible. It roared past a miniature road sign that warned of an upcoming minefield. Two seconds later, Barbie and her convertible were blown into a million pieces. The guy with the missing digits howled with laughter. Harley shook his head. Definitely the pyro guy.

The film cut to a wider panoramic shot, and Harley took in the setting for the movie. Like so many B-movies, it was set in some kind of post apocalyptic future, with sand and jagged metal pieces filling the screen.

As Harley walked back toward the front porch, he realized that the metal things were actually pieces of giant, rusted cars. Well…giant compared to the dolls.

He knocked on the front door, harder this time, and thought about the setting for the film. It had to have been a junkyard. And, maybe a coincidence or maybe not, the car that had run over John had been stolen from a junkyard.

"Go away!"

Harley heard the voice through the door and shouted back, "Mr. Henderson. Mr. Sparky Henderson. You're going to want to talk to me. My name is Harley Stephens. I'm with the U.S. Patent Office."

The door opened a crack. "You're from where?"

"United States Patent Office."

"Bullshit. You're from Australia or someplace."

Harley tried to act doddering. He gave a slight tremble to his hand as he raised it in greeting. "The federal government doesn't discriminate, son."

Sparky guffawed.

Harley ignored the criticism. "I'm here to ask you a couple of questions about your claim against the Pipe Shooter."

Sparky squinted. "I thought the case was closed."

"We have some new information. It might even lead to a favorable outcome for you. Mind if I come in?"

"You kidding me?" Sparky opened the door wide, grinning like a fool. "Heck, if you can get those royalty payments coming my direction, I'll even let you sleep with my wife."

Harley stepped through the doorway and into the messiest house he'd ever seen. He glanced around. "Is your wife here now?"

"Nah, she's at her mother's place in Alabama. Gone for a couple a weeks, so I guess you'll have to take a rain check."

"Ah...sure." Harley put a bag on the table and reached inside. "Tell you what, here's the bottom line. If you can identify this pipe shooter, convince me it's one of yours, we'll have that patent-stealing bastard caught dead-to-rights."

"All right!"

Harley pulled out the device, and Sparky started jumping up and down.

"It is one of mine. It is! This one's a bit mangled, but you can see how the pipes connect together. I'm the only one that does it that way. That puke, Josh, uses aluminum to band them together."

Harley narrowed his eyes at the Jethro in front of him. This was the guy. He stilled his shaking hands and coiled his body to spring.

Sparky stopped jumping around and backed away from Harley's stare, noticing a change in the atmosphere. "Wait a sec. What happened to the kindly, old dude? And come to think of it, where'd you get this shooter in the first place?"

Harley waited a moment for Sparky to jump to the right conclusion. "Let's start with the junkyard."

Sparky's eyes grew huge. He dove for the hallway and sprinted down the hall, with Harley right behind him.

A door to the outside was at the end of the hall. Harley waited till they got close, giving Sparky a false sense of hope, then tackled him behind the knees, bringing him to the ground with a nasty thud.

Sparky lashed out with his foot, aiming for Harley's head.

Harley ducked beneath the flailing extremity and jabbed

Sparky twice in the solar plexus, eliciting a sharp grunt but no surrender.

The foot came at him again, so he punched Sparky once in the groin, hard. Which did the trick. The foot finally lay still as Sparky assumed the fetal position.

Harley stood over him and said, "You know something, Sparky. It's up to you, but I kind of hope you don't answer my questions the first time."

Harley pulled a large Bowie knife from a sheath behind his back. The wild-haired man now had eyes to match his hair.

Harley said, "Because we'd have a lot more fun the second time." He turned the knife so the sunlight reflected off the blade, into Sparky's eyes. "A lot more fun."

twenty-five

JOHN half-listened to his mother's phone conversation with a political donor, doing his best to ignore her platitudes, and finished reading the brief about gangs in Los Angeles. He tossed it and picked up one on illegal immigration. "Great job, girls. You're really helping out."

Amber looked up from her keyboard and beamed. Hillary said, "Thanks, Uncle John. You know, this is kind of fun."

John grimaced. He was glad the work wasn't too hard on them, but at the same time he didn't want Hillary enjoying politics. She was too sweet to get involved in this kind of life.

"Anything that helps nail these bastards to the wall is fine by me," Amber said. "Even typing. And hanging with you is a bonus."

Amber, on the other hand...

His mother closed her cell phone and sidled over. "What would you say to..."

"No. It's not going to happen."

At her glare, he decided to explain. "I heard you on the phone. And I don't want to meet with any of the donors. No matter how big they are."

"Don't be a simpleton. That's how it works. If you want to get elected, you meet with the money people, listen to their problems, and cash the check."

"No."

"John, you don't want to piss these people off. They can make sure you don't get elected."

"Most of the time, yes. Running a smear campaign is their modus operandi for getting what they want—and they've perfected the technique. But with so little time before the election, I might sneak in before they get wise. You'll just have to stall them."

Through gritted teeth, she said, "Fine. I'll figure something out."

John almost smiled. His mother was having a hard time not being in charge, but was handling it pretty well. Of course, she handled everything well.

He said, "What about the lawsuit and the election commission? Are you having any luck with that?"

"I'm waiting for a call, but I'm not worried. I've got something nasty on the election commissioner so he won't be a problem for much longer. But I'm having a harder time with the debate. I'm not as connected to the TV world, and the producer won't budge."

Her cell phone rang and she practically snarled with delight. "Ah. The commissioner."

As she stalked off for a little privacy, John shuddered. *His mother, the predator.* She could be scary when she wanted to be. A knock on the door brought him a short reprieve.

He opened it and found an excited Sierra waiting on the stoop.

"Did you know there's a security guard bleeding all over your front porch?"

"Yeah. One of mother's." He shrugged. "And apparently not one of the bright ones. I warned him not to go around back."

"Why? What's back there?"

John gave her a wink. "Booby-traps."

"Wow! Why didn't you mention that in our interview?"

"It's not the kind of image Mother wants me to portray to the public. She wanted the interview to showcase my 'softer side,' whatever that is. Anyway, don't worry about the guard. I gave him some bandages. Come on in."

Sierra stepped through the doorway and surprised John with a small, intimate kiss.

In the back of the room, from Amber's vicinity, there was a sharp intake of breath followed by the words, "You bitch."

Incredulous, Sierra stepped back and turned toward Amber,

who was attempting to shoot daggers from her eyeballs in the manner of all jealous teenage girls.

John ignored the teen and said, "What was that for?"

Sierra turned back toward him. "Thank you *so* much for the exclusive interview after the press conference. My bosses are ecstatic. I think I finally got noticed by the right people. Maybe network."

"Congratulations."

"Thank you. So I did some extra digging around and I've got some great news."

The Barracuda slammed her flip-phone shut and broke in, "I got him. Not only are you staying in the election, but I know who filed..."

His mother stopped and glanced at Sierra. Her lip curled as she said, "Never mind. It can wait till your company has left."

"Mother, she's with us."

"She's with the media, darling. Don't be naïve."

Sierra scowled, muttering in Spanish.

John narrowed his gaze, picturing a vicious catfight between the women. "Disagreeing with you doesn't make me naïve. Sierra is trustworthy. I vouch for her. So enough with the derogatory remarks."

His mother gave her the once over. "I don't want her taping us. Did you check to see if she's wearing a wire?"

Sierra bristled. With a clenched jaw, she said, "No, I'm not, Senator Black. Your son has helped me with my ex-husband and my career. I owe him. I would never tape him without his permission. And by the way, I wouldn't have to record you, Mrs. Black, to write a malicious story. There are plenty of dirty anecdotes floating around if I want one. They're a dime a dozen. Let's just remember which one of us is nicknamed The Barracuda, all right?"

There was a long, drawn out moment where no one said anything. Then his mother barked with laughter. "She's a firecracker, John. I like her."

John let out a breath he hadn't realized he'd been holding.

His mother turned to him. "I like how you've got people who

owe you favors. And you think you're not a politician?"

John shook his head. "What's the news, mother?"

"I've got Barnes by the..." She cupped her right hand then clenched it into a fist, leaving the thought unspoken. "Now he won't brush his teeth without calling me for permission. You'll stay on the ballot until the lawsuit moves forward. And that *won't* be in time for the election."

"Congratulations, I guess," John said. "But who's behind the lawsuit?"

"I can't find out until tomorrow, because it hasn't technically been filed yet. But I know who the attorney is."

Sierra said, "I bet it's Seymour Hertzfeld."

His mother looked nonplussed. "How could you possibly know that?"

"Because Steel is behind the attacks."

John grinned. *Smart cookie.* "That's what we think, too. And now that we know Pfester's top lawyer is orchestrating the lawsuit, we can be pretty sure Steel is our guy. But how did you know?"

"That's why I'm here, I've got good news. Sanchez is out. He's announcing it right before the debate."

The Barracuda cackled.

"That's great," John said. "But why would someone in the lead drop out of the race?"

His mother made the crushing motion again. "Someone's got them in a vise."

John groaned and turned toward her. "What did you do?"

"Don't look at me. I had nothing to do with it. But I hear he's a pervert. That's how I would've gone after him."

"There's more," Sierra said. "And this news is even bigger. When Sanchez makes his speech tonight, he's going to endorse Steel."

"That son of a bitch," Barbara said. "If he managed that, Steel's tougher than I thought."

"You have no idea," Sierra said. She tossed a file folder onto the coffee table. "Here's a story on Steel that never ran. Shows some of his ties to the Russian Mafia. But he's got enough juice that he was able to stop the story before it ever got out."

His mother pounced. "It's definitely Steel."

"Yeah, I agree. He's our bad guy," John said. "But the picture is getting muddier. He's got huge resources behind him. Maybe Pfester has something to do with this. Or maybe the Russian Mafia. Either way, it's going to be hard to get to him."

Sierra's eyes grew round, as if she was just now realizing what they were up against. "No wonder people are dying. These people are used to getting their own way."

John put his hand on her shoulder. "Don't worry. We'll get him."

His mother clapped her hands together. "Hey. With Sanchez gone, that producer can't give me any more bullshit about the debate."

Sierra shook her head. "The producer is Alex Garcia, right? He'll just come up with another excuse. Steel plays golf with him every Thursday so the money's already been exchanged. It'll take more than a bigger bribe to change his mind."

His mother started cursing. "Damn it. Then there's no way to get to this guy in time. If I had another day, I'm sure I could come up with the right strategy."

Sierra snapped her fingers. "Wait. I've got something. Do you know the senator...the guy from South Carolina?"

His mother smiled. "Absolutely. Senator Stratton owes me a favor or two. What do you have in mind?"

"Garcia's *boss* is good friends with the Carolina senator."

The Barracuda cackled. "Girl, let's go make some phone calls."

John watched the two of them retreat to the dining room, wondering if it was a good thing or a bad thing they were getting along so well.

STEEL PAUSED THE TIVO, FREEZING THE IMAGE OF HIS NEW NEMESIS, John Black. Somehow the guy had managed to pull bigger strings than Steel had, because Black was back in the debate. Even worse, the bastard had somehow managed to get a twenty minute "news" piece on the air already, one that made him seem soft and cuddly, if you could believe that shit. Steel chucked the remote against the wall.

He knew damn well that Black was anything *but* soft and cuddly. His assassins were terrified of the guy. Barry had practically wet himself at the sight of a resurrected Black on television. How cuddly could he be?

Keep it together. Keep it together. You're just being paranoid.

Steel took a couple of deep breaths. Barry was the one who should be nervous. He was the one Black was after. The only problem would be if Black caught Barry. The idiot assassin would sell Steel out in a heartbeat.

But that was a problem easily solved.

Steel pushed the intercom button, buzzing his Russian neighbors. "Lexi, you got a minute?"

The speaker buzzed and clicked, making it hard to understand the reply. Steel thought he heard, "Yes...many minutes...Sasha and...on way...to be...seeing you...very bad news."

Bad news? Steel blanched. Why would Lexi have bad news? And why would Sasha deliver it? A niggling suspicion started to form.

Maybe he *was* being paranoid, but for the first time he wondered about the Russians. What if they switched sides if things got rough? Heck, they'd changed allegiance easy enough after the Cold War ended. As soon as their KGB funding dried up, they'd started their organized crime trade, capitalizing on good ol' American business techniques.

It might be best to take some precautions.

He opened his desk drawer and pulled out the lunch sack, remembering Barry's luck escaping from Black, and wondered if the same trick might work for him.

Yeah, right. I'd be barbecued right along with the Russians.

He didn't even like looking at the bomb. Setting it carefully on the desk, he reached further in the drawer for his little semi-auto nine millimeter. It would take several shots to bring down someone of Sasha's girth, but hey, that's probably why it held fourteen bullets in the clip.

He thumbed the safety, put the gun in his lap, and tried to think back to his gun training class.

When Sasha pushed through the doorway, Steel almost dropped the gun onto the floor. But when Sasha made for the far corner, Steel relaxed. If the Russians were coming for him, Sasha probably would've gotten up close and personal. Maybe this was a social call. Lexi sauntered in and took a seat across from Steel.

"We have new problem," Lexi said, handing a fax to Steel.

"This can't be right. There's no way Black could have these numbers this early."

Sasha said, "Is very accurate. Plus or minus four points."

"But no one knows who he is yet. This is impossible."

"Is Pfester's own internal polling," said Lexi. "They are knowing what they are doing."

Steel frowned. It *was* bad news. How the heck could Black have the lead in a three way race between Two-Bits, Black, and himself?

Lexi continued, "Now other Pfester board members are getting themselves worried. They think maybe your campaign is like throwing good money after the bad money."

Steel rattled his brain. *Shit!* Everything seemed to be going from bad to worse. Money from Pfester was the lifeblood of his current lifestyle. Not to mention his campaign.

"Lexi, you've got to reassure them that we've got this under control. I'll torch this guy in the debate tonight. He won't know what hit him. Politically, this won't be a problem."

Steel waited while Lexi mulled things over, then jumped in with a new thought. "The real problem is that this guy is good at ferreting out information, and he's going to follow the trail to the top. So we've got to sever the outside link with Barry and Nails, if you know what I mean. We take care of that and it'll be clear sailing."

Lexi nodded. "Yes, okay. Just make sure you do good debate. And I also concur that Black situation is unraveling. We must make connections to us...disappear. I'm thinking tonight after they meet with rapper would be best time. You agree?"

"Definitely." Steel gestured toward the lunch sack. "You guys want this bomb? I was going to use it to fake an attempt on my life, you know...divert suspicion...but this is more important."

"*Nyet.* Barry and Nails left car with our valet this afternoon. We take care of things then."

Sasha said, "Now associates follow them."

Lexi continued, "Yes. And when time comes, it is big boom for idiots who cause problems. End of story."

Steel snickered. "They actually left the car in your care? God, those guys are dumb."

There was a shout from the corner, startling Steel and Lexi, as Sasha lunged for the file cabinet in the opposite corner. "What fuck is this?"

Sasha picked up a video camera off the file cabinet.

Steel said, "Hey, don't worry about it. That's Nails' camera. He must have left it here this afternoon."

Lexi and Sasha looked at each other.

Lexi said, "You think they're dumb enough to try to get something on us?"

Sasha laughed. "If so, they dumber than ever. Red light on camera is not even on."

He pointed to the little light on the front of the camera, then slammed the camera into the file cabinet a couple of times, until bits of plastic shattered and scattered.

Steel grinned. "Why should they be any better at surveillance than they are at assassinations?"

Sasha guffawed while Lexi slapped his knee. "Ha, ha. Yes. Is truth. Is truth."

They all laughed for a minute straight before Steel calmed down and wiped a tear away. *Death and incompetence. If you can't laugh at that, what can you laugh at? Male bonding at its finest.*

The Russians must've agreed, because Lexi settled down to a chuckle, then looked at his partner and said, "Ah. Good times. Yes?"

Sasha nodded. "Sure beats taking hacksaw to poor Frankie, I'll tell you that."

Steel gulped, tasting bile in the back his throat, and tried to snicker along with the Russians.

But for some reason, he didn't find it humorous.

NAILS WATCHED THE SUN SET ON THE RAPPER'S DIGS. IT WAS ONE of the big-gated homes in the nicer part of Silverlake, with a wall of glass windows in the living room. A cool place from the looks of it.

Nails grunted. Waiting in the microbus sucked, but after the muffed incident with the drive-by, catching Two-Bits without his gun-toting posse was the obvious key to tonight's success.

He heard Barry fumbling with a Zippo and said, "Save it for later. We don't want the flame drawing attention."

Barry put the lighter away without whining, taking Nails by surprise. It was kind of weird that they were getting along now. But having the skinny white boy save him from extinction at the hands of the Russians had earned some respect for the little dude.

Barry said, "I can't believe you left a camera at Steel's place. What, you don't think they'll notice?"

Nails shrugged, the movement shaking the van. "Maybe. But it seems like they might kill us anyway. So why not try it? See if we can get the goods on 'em? The red light is busted on the camera, so I was hoping they wouldn't notice it was running."

"Oh, yeah? That's pretty friggin smart."

"We want to live through this, we *both* better think smarter."

Barry nodded like a bobble-head doll.

Nails began to turn toward the house when something caught his eye. "Did you see that?"

"What?"

Nails pointed down the street. "That dark Chevy cargo van. I'm not sure, but I thought I saw some light, like the burning end of a cigarette."

Barry squinted, then shrugged. "I think you're getting

paranoid." He fanned himself with his hand. "How long we gotta be in this friggin van with no air conditioning? When's Two-Bits gonna split?"

Nails looked at his watch. "The debate starts in thirty minutes. He's got to get rolling any time now."

Barry sat up straight. "There he is."

The black iron gates swung open and two Escalades drove through. Nails watched the cars drive away.

As the gates started to close, he said, "All right, white boy. Go do your thing."

"One alarm, no waiting."

Barry grabbed a small tool kit and hurried from the van, slipping through the gates before they closed. Nails smiled. *Man, that cracker is skinny.*

twenty-six

JOHN stepped into his dressing room and closed the door. *How does Eleanor do this?*

He'd taken a look at the stage, checking for anything out of the ordinary—wires to a bomb, or anything else that might kill him. No worries—business as usual. But when he'd peeked through the curtain and seen the large audience that had already assembled, he'd had a moment of stage fright.

He looked in the mirror, which had a row of lights on top and on the sides, and took a couple of deep breaths. This was stupid, getting worked up over speaking in front of a crowd. He'd faced down the barrel of a gun—he could darn sure face down an audience.

Heck, Eleanor and Mother do this kind of thing all the time.

John smiled. The fact that Eleanor did this for a living was pretty impressive. She was the one who should be here. John had called the doctor on his way over, and even though Eleanor was still out of it, her doctor seemed upbeat about her prognosis.

There was a knock on the door and his mother poked her head in. "There you are." She opened the door further and ushered in a petite woman with a large work box in her hand. "This is April. She's going to put on your makeup."

John coughed. "Ahh. No, thanks. I prefer au naturel."

His mother rolled her eyes. "Au naturel will make you look like a pasty, sweaty corpse under these heavy lights. Don't worry. April knows what she's doing. She can make you look natural, just more of a 'TV natural.' Now, hurry up and sit down. We've only got a few minutes."

John sighed and sat on the chair in front of the mirror. Getting straight to work, April whipped out a brush and a

THE ONE MINUTE ASSASSIN

makeup pad while his mother crowded into a corner, as out of the way as possible in a room the size of a closet.

His mother said, "The media's in a frenzy. One big story after another and now the Sanchez announcement just hit. They smell blood in the water. If you get caught alone after the debate, don't answer any questions."

"You think of them like sharks, huh? I always pictured vultures."

There was another knock and Harley squeezed his way inside. He gave a snort of laughter when he caught sight of John with a powder puff dusting his face.

John said, "Don't start."

Harley wiped the smile from his face and handed John a couple of photographs.

John pumped his fist in the air, recognizing the two scumbags. One was a mug shot, the other a photo of an NFL player. "This is definitely the skinny dude. I'm pretty sure, but not positive about the football guy. I only saw him for a second as I was flying over the car."

"Oh, it's him all right. The washed-up footballer is Dennis Nalen. Affectionately known as Nails. And the rectal thermometer is Barry Jones. Did two years for breaking and entering. Nails is definitely the guy who placed the pipe shooter on your sister's car."

"Isn't 'Nails' the guy who blew out his knee as a rookie?"

"Yeah, that's the one. You want me to take 'em out now, or torture 'em to find out who they're working for and then take 'em out?"

April gasped and dropped her powder puff.

His mother piped in, "Kidding. He's just kidding."

Harley gave a grin and put on his kindly face. "Sorry, love." He picked April's makeup pad off the floor and handed it to her.

She stammered for a moment before Barbara ushered her out the door. Barbara turned a blistering stare toward Harley. "Psychopath."

Harley clutched at his heart as if he'd been wounded, then

grinned. "From you, I'll take that as a compliment."

The Barracuda started to boil over—which John found oddly reminiscent of the times his parents had fought each other. *Better nip this right now.*

"Enough," he said. "We're on the same side here. We all want to keep Eleanor and Hillary out of danger."

"*And* get the scumbags off the street," Harley said. "One way or another."

Barbara shook her head. "There's just one way. The way they get due process under the law."

"Oh, yeah," Harley snorted. "That'll work. Unfortunately, California's proven that if you have enough money behind you, you don't have to worry about a conviction."

"Point taken."

"Besides," Harley said, "my way will save the taxpayers a lot of money. And with the budget deficit that John will inherit, thanks to the corrupt administration preceding him, he's going to need every bit of help he can get."

Barbara's jaw dropped. "Kill the scumbags for budgetary reasons?"

"He's trying to get your goat, Mother. Harley's just showing off his Aussie sense of humor. We're not killing Barry and Nails. Unless we have no other choice. Right, Harley?"

"If that's what you want, John. No worries. But we should find 'em and make 'em tell us who they're working for."

"We already know. While you were finding the trigger men, we found out that our main guy is Steel."

"No kidding? The bastard who used to lobby for a top industrial chemical and pharmaceutical company turns out to be a guy who'd hire people to murder his rivals? What are the odds?"

"And I've heard a rumor he was once diagnosed as clinically paranoid," Barbara added.

"The hard part now is linking Steel to the murders," John said. "And making sure he doesn't have me killed in the process."

They all stared at each other, with matching grim expressions.

Harley said, "On the bright side, Barry and Nails are too inept to worry about. As long as we're vigilant, they shouldn't be a problem."

"But Barry and Nails might not be the main trouble. Steel's got a strong link to the Russian Mafia. From what I hear, they're ex-KGB. Probably good at killing people."

Harley frowned. "Sasha and Lexi Khrushchev?"

John nodded. "Those are the ones."

"That's bad."

There was a knock on the door, and a voice from the other side said, "Three minutes to curtain. Places everyone."

John stood up. "Time to face the firing squad."

When his mother blanched, he said, "Sorry. Poor choice of words. Mother, have your staff pull up everything they can on Steel. We need to find a pressure point. Harley, watch my back during the debate. If nothing happens here, we'll split up. If they come after me, I'll be ready for them. You follow Two-Bits back to his place and see if you can catch Barry and Nails trying to take him out. *Don't* kill anyone without talking to me first."

Harley nodded. "What about your earpiece?"

Barbara said, "No earpieces. They'll think you're being coached for the debate."

John laughed. "After they hear my answers, that won't be a concern."

His mother shook her head. "No earpieces."

"If they go after John tonight, he'll be a sitting duck on that stage," Harley said. "We need the radio. No guns at this event, so eyes and ears are the best we've got going. If the assassins are too far away from my location, I'll need to tell you if someone's coming after you."

"Then signal me. Knock over one of the big lights to get my attention."

With a sigh, Harley nodded and slipped out of the dressing room. John started after him.

"Hold on a second," his mother said. She straightened his tie and picked a couple pieces of lint off his monkey suit. "Are you nervous about the debate?"

"A little. But I can handle it. Sanchez was the only one I was really worried about. The others aren't real politicians. We're talking a rapper, a pro wrestler, and a lobbyist—which is not much more than a glorified used car salesman. I should do all right."

His mother sniffed and said, "Watch out for Steel," then reached out and gave him a hug, surprising him. When she pulled away, her eyes looked moist.

"Good luck. You can do it, son. Win this for Eleanor."

"Thanks. I'll do my best."

He left the dressing cubicle and walked behind the stage to the spot where everyone was gathering, wondering what had just happened. Had his mother actually had a tear in her eye when she wished him luck? Was she actually proud of him? The thought was comforting, yet unnerving at the same time.

He spotted Steel and felt a sudden surge of anger course through his body. He had to fight to restrain himself—to keep from ripping Steel's throat out right then and there.

There was the bastard responsible for putting his sister in a coma. For shooting at his niece. *His niece!* An innocent young woman who had nothing to do with any of this.

John pushed down the violent urge and took three deep breaths, then started to focus on the task at hand. How the heck could he get to someone as connected as Steel? His mother had been committing crimes of corruption her whole political career and she'd never come close to being brought down by her actions. She was way too smart for that.

But was Steel that smart? If he'd tried to kill his way to the top by hiring those goons, then Steel wasn't as intelligent as he thought he was.

John headed straight for Steel, intending to introduce himself. Needing to check him out in person, John placed a hand on his shoulder and said, "Mr. Steel?"

Steel turned around and jumped about a foot in the air. A friendly but obviously fake smile covered his face. "Sorry. You startled me."

Maybe. Maybe not. John kept it cool, but wondered if he'd

just caught a glimpse behind the mask, like he sometimes saw with his mother. Like the guy was scared.

"I'm John Black. Eleanor's brother."

John reached out and shook his hand. John clenched tightly, maintaining the grip, and took a step closer to Steel, invading his personal space.

And there it was again. A moment of terror that was quickly masked. If John had blinked, he might have missed it.

But then the smile and confidence were back.

John kept his grip on Steel's hand. "You remember Eleanor, right?"

"Of course. Eleanor was a hero of mine. You have my heartfelt condolences. A real tragedy."

Condolences! Smug bastard. It took every ounce of strength John had to keep from wiping the smile off Steel's face. Out loud he said, "Thanks for your concern."

There was some squeezing from Steel, in the manner of all men testing each other's grip strength.

John decided to try and rattle him. "It's not much of a tragedy, though. Comparatively speaking."

"What on earth do you mean?"

"Compared to the tragedy that's about to happen."

Steel frowned. "About to happen?"

"Oh, yeah. It'll be so painful, Barry and Nails won't even know what hit them. Before you know it, they'll be sharing information like we're best buddies."

There it was—the reaction he was looking for. Like Steel had taken a punch to the gut.

John almost laughed as a sickly smile returned to Steel's face—and sweat began to show through his makeup.

At the sound of thunderous applause from the auditorium, John turned to find an older gentleman with a headset and clipboard.

The old man ushered John toward the stage, and the pleasure he'd felt from provoking Steel quickly faded.

What am I doing here?

John glanced at the unlikely group of politicians who were being herded toward the cameras. Before he left the backstage area, Two-Bits casually flipped Steel the bird, prompting laughter from Arnold "The Mountain" Schwarzkov, and an outraged grimace from Steel.

John stepped in front of the lights and cameras and approached his podium to the sound of applause.

Don't forget to smile. But it was hard to smile when he was terrified. It was an unusual feeling for him. He tried to think happy thoughts.

Make solid eye contact with the audience, a couple of seconds toward each spot, but never darting movements. Hard to do when you couldn't even see the audience. The lights were blinding. And hot. Very hot. Mother was right about the whole makeup thing. He'd just have to pick imaginary points in space and look at them, pretending there were people there.

He didn't pay attention to the introductions, but instead focused on getting mentally ready. Backstage with Steel had been an enormous success, pushing at him, so John decided to change his strategy for the debate. Try to find another way to needle Steel. See how far he could push the bastard and still stay on topic.

John heard his name from the moderator and decided it was time to pay attention.

"Mr. Black, tell us what prompted you to enter the race at this juncture and what qualifies you for the office of Governor of California."

John cleared his throat and thought, *Here goes nothing.*

"Thank you, Mr. Oswald. That's an excellent question. Indeed, what qualities do any of us have that qualify us for governor? None of us are politicians, though that might be considered a positive since the current administration is being booted out of office under allegations of fraud and corruption. I bring something to the table that is severely lacking in today's politics. Integrity."

John looked toward Schwarzkov. "I've never been arrested for steroid use."

He glanced toward Two-Bits. "I've never worn gang colors. Of course, I've also never written beautiful lyrics, some of which are amazing, by the way." There was a nod from

Two-Bits. "But some of the lyrics seem to instigate violence against our police officers, which I could never condone."

John looked at Steel, who seemed to be holding up all right. *Time to change that.*

"And I've definitely never, ever given legal, yet highly questionable, bribes to our congressmen. Mr. Steel has lobbied for big companies like Pfester Chemicals and Pharmaceuticals—that they should become exempt from environmental regulations. The exact opposite of what I believe. In fact, we shouldn't ever make it easier for big corporations to make money at the expense of everyday people. That kind of thing is just another Nail in the coffin of a flourishing society. I find it Barry sickening."

Steel stiffened, putting on his stock, sickly smile. John turned back toward the audience.

"Maybe that's just my opinion. But the rest are documented facts. Don't get me wrong. I'm no saint. But I do fight for what's right. As someone who specializes in children's rights, fighting for justice is what I do every day. I compile evidence against child abusers and molesters to put them behind bars. I make sure parents pay their child support on time. Little guys don't have the same protections as we do. I believe it's up to us to defend them.

"So that's what I do, day in and day out. And I will bring that focus to bear for the people of California. I will protect them against the corporations that have discarded their health, or lives, in the name of scientific research. With the corruption we've seen in the previous administration, I think that's what California needs."

John saw a flashing yellow light in front of the moderator, signaling that his time was almost up. *Time to drop the bomb.*

"If my sister Eleanor were here, I'd urge you to vote for her. But that's impossible, since another candidate tried to kill her."

There were gasps from the audience.

"So I'm afraid I'll have to do. Please vote for me on Tuesday."

There was a long, pregnant pause before the moderator said, "Tried to kill her?"

"I can't say much at this time, but the incident with her limo was no accident. We have the weapon as well as a prime suspect. There will be more information released in the next couple of days."

John turned his head to the left, away from the cameras, and winked at Steel, who started coughing and spluttering.

The moderator said, "Well...moving right along..."

twenty-seven

NAILS struggled for five minutes straight in an attempt to squeeze his hands into some normal-sized latex gloves. He finally managed, scoring a small victory over the stupid things, and reached into a brown grocery bag full of goodies.

Ugh. This shit's gross. He scattered a variety of freaky sex toys around the room, cringing at a couple of the nastier items. One of the worst "toys" was a leather-studded dildo big enough to pleasure a horse.

But his attention kept wandering and he found himself staring at his surroundings, taking in all the expensive furniture and electronics in Two-Bits' plush digs. Gold statues that looked like overly ornate Tiki dolls. Carved wooden idols sporting gigantic members as big as the statues. A veritable treasure box sat on the dresser, overflowing with bling. *Damn. Brother's got it made.*

He watched Barry attach some fur-lined handcuffs to the bedposts and shuddered, then grabbed a remote control off the nightstand and turned on a huge plasma television that towered over them.

John Black's image filled the screen, larger than life. "So the first step is the special police task force..."

"*Holy crap,*" Barry said. "You trying to give me a friggin heart attack? Shut the Terminator off, all right. Two-Bits is gonna hear the television."

Nails tossed the giant dildo on the bed and gestured toward the TV screen. "He's in the debate, you idiot. This way we'll know when it's over."

Barry grinned. "Oh, yeah. That makes sense."

"But the main idea," John Black continued, "is to increase

economic growth in poverty stricken areas. Level the playing field with the big corporations like Pfester."

Barry nodded. "Abso-friggin-lutely. The Terminator's right on the money. That's what I've been telling you about the rich guys like Steel and Lexi sticking it to us."

Nails felt something moist running down his arm and lifted it toward his face. *Shit!*

Barry leapt toward him and shouted, "You're bleeding again! Don't let it drip. You don't want to leave your DNA all over the place, man."

Nails used his other hand and pulled the tire patching kit out of his coat pocket. He tossed it to Barry, then clamped some pressure onto his upper arm where the bleeding seemed to be coming from. "Hurry, dude."

Barry yanked off Nails' jacket, opened the adhesive tube, and got to work.

From the television, Steel said, "What a crock. You sound like a socialist, Mr. Black. And I'm not sure why you're making these relentless attacks against Pfester. Their medicines have been an enormous help to society."

"Oh, yeah, you're right," John said. "Erectile dysfunction. I've seen the ads."

Nails erupted in laughter. "Now that's the shit right there."

"Among other things," Steel spluttered. "Heart disease…"

John interrupted, "You lobbied Congress, successfully I might add, to reduce the Food and Drug Administration's budget. And this was after your company had been caught… twice…doing illegal experimentation with their new medications. On unwitting subjects."

Nails stood up and clenched his fists. "Is he shitting me? Experimentation?"

Barry shrugged. "I wouldn't put it past 'em."

Nails looked down at the rubber patches that covered his body.

"And now," John continued, "I understand you're on the board of directors of this company. I call that a conflict of interest with the people of California. In fact, even if the public doesn't elect me, the most important thing here is that they don't elect you."

"Now wait a second," Steel said.

"No! Shut the fuck up, both of yous," Two-Bits said, his F-bomb bleeped for television. "According to the yellow flashing light, you white boys had your time. It's the black man's turn to speak. Am I right, Mr. Moderator?"

"Ah…yes. Mr. Two-Bits has the floor. And I would counsel our candidates not to interrupt each other again. Or curse, for that matter!"

John said, "My apologies."

Two-Bits gestured toward John. "Homeboy over there is right about one thing." He waved his hands toward Steel. "This Howdy-Doody motherfucker shouldn't be governor. If the dude is a ho, then he shouldn't be in the show."

"Language!" the moderator said.

Two-Bits slammed his fist into the podium. "But in case you dudes don't remember, the topic was gang violence, so let's get back to it. I agree with some of Mr. Black's proposals, which is hard to admit 'cause he's a white dude. But he's missing one giant piece of the puzzle—state-funded target practice for gang members."

Nails smiled when he heard the audience suck in their breath.

"The biggest problem with gangbangers is that their aim is off. They keep hitting innocent bystanders when they're aiming for rival colors. If we get them some target practice, they'll be taking each other out a lot quicker and solving our gang violence problem a lot sooner."

Nails grunted. *Now that's a ballsy solution. The man will never go for it, though.* Ignoring the TV for a minute, he thought about what Black had said and stared at the new patch on his arm, wondering if Steel was really that connected to Pfester.

Bored, Barry got up and started squirting chocolate syrup and whipped cream onto the bed, his eyes open wide and a grin on his face.

Nails grimaced and started pacing, each step causing a

sharp pain in his knee. *If Steel is one of the guys in charge in Pfester, then I'm getting screwed in more ways than one.* He turned back toward Barry, who was using tweezers to pull some small hairs out of a baggie and scatter them into the whip cream.

"What are you doing?"

Barry smiled. "I got this stuff at a truck stop bathroom. You know, some DNA for the police to find."

Nails shook his head. "That's disgusting."

"Hey, I'm just trying to be smart like you said. I don't want those Russian dudes hacking me into little pieces."

Nails sat on a leather chair. "I'm not sure we're being smart enough."

Barry stopped throwing hair around and said, "What do you mean?"

"The more I think about it, the more I'm convinced. Lexi wasn't deciding whether or not he was gonna kill us. He was deciding *when* he was gonna do it."

Barry sat on the bed, barely avoiding the whipped cream. "You mean even if we get this one right they're still gonna whack us?"

"That's what I'm saying."

Barry said, "Well, that's fucked up."

Nails raised an eyebrow. He'd never heard Barry curse before. It was always friggin this and frig that. "I think we should forget about this job and break into Steel's office. Get my camera back and hope there's something useful on it."

Barry's eyes bugged out. "Hope? That sounds pretty slim."

"You got a better idea?"

"What if there's nothing on the tape? Or what if you're wrong about this thing? Maybe if we do the job right everything will be forgiven."

"And maybe the sky will rain double D women. But it's not likely."

"Hey!" Barry's face turned purple. "You can kiss my rear end. Since when did you become a friggin genius? I'll tell you, the answer is never. You're as dumb as every other football player out there. No, dumber! You let them experiment on you with crazy meds. You're about as smart as that rapper with his 'guns for tots program' or whatever the heck it was. A friggin moron!"

Nails blinked a couple of times, then reached over and started pounding on the skinny cracker.

JOHN STEPPED OUT THE BACK EXIT OF THE THEATER AND INTO THE cool summer night, then took a deep breath of L.A. smog. Miracle of miracles, he'd made it through the debate in one piece. Probably even done himself some good. At least in comparison to the others.

The rapper had been outrageous. Unusual ideas, and some of them good, but nothing that the public would ever go for. But apparently rap was much more popular than pro wrestling, because he still had sizable numbers in the polls. Go figure.

The wrestler had spoken in his thick accent, not even using up his minutes when it was his turn. About all John could understand from the guy were his wrestling catchphrases like "I will *crush* the budgetary problems into tiny pieces." But his favorite one was "I will *destroy* the corpses of the previous administration."

Whatever that meant.

The others had made John look like a political genius, even when he was needling Steel. And luckily his strategy had worked with the bastard. Steel's performance was off kilter for most of the night. And argumentative. It was great.

That was for you, Eleanor. With more to come.

John reached his car and knelt to check the underside for anything unusual. Probably ruining his one good suit in the process, but what could he do?

With everything clear, he got in and started it up, then called Harley on his cell. "I'm out. You find anything tonight?"

"Nothing, mate. Dead end."

John pulled into traffic, watching for a tail that never materialized. "That's bad. I pushed Steel pretty hard this evening."

"No kidding, mate. Crikey, you practically called him a murderer on live television."

"Yeah, that's what I mean. Maybe I pushed too hard. Hard enough he's got to do something about it."

"Don't tell me you're worried about the bozo assassins?"

John hesitated. "No. Well, maybe a little. We still need them."

"Don't beat yourself up. It was a good play, John. Provoking an idiot into making mistakes is never a bad idea." Harley snorted. "And look on the bright side. You earned my vote tonight. That's got to count for something."

Aussies. John shook his head. "If Steel panics, there's a good chance Barry and Nails won't live to see the morning. We've got to find them first."

"I'm following Two-Bits now. If he's their target, I'll get 'em."

"All right. And I'm on my way to Nails' apartment. Hopefully the address you got from the pyro guy is correct."

"No worries. In the end, Sparky was very forthcoming."

Something about the way Harley said that made John hesitate. "Wait a sec. What'd you do with Sparky when you were finished?"

John waited, but there was no response. "Where is he, Harley?"

"You're not gonna like it."

"Humor me."

Another pause, then Harley said, "He's in the bunker."

"You've got him locked in your cellar? Why didn't you hand him over to the police?"

"We might still need him."

John rubbed his temples.

Harley said, "Look, John, there wasn't time before the debate. What difference does it make? We know he's guilty. And the bunker's nicer than a prison cell. It has cable."

John sighed. "Point taken. But as soon as we're done tonight, we'll turn him over and give the legal system a chance to make good. All right?"

"Sure, whatever you say. But you know something, John?"

"What?"

"Due process is overrated."

John gave a wry grin. "Maybe. But that's the same debate we always have. And you agreed to follow my rules when you turned the agency over to me. That means we give due process a chance no matter how often they screw it up."

"They always screw it up."

"Usually. But so what? That's when we step in. *After* the guy ignores the court-ordered child support. *After* he hides his money in an offshore account."

Harley snorted. "Twice as much work that way. My system's faster."

"Yeah. But it doesn't feel right."

"Crikey. You're a noble piece of work, aren't ya?"

John laughed. "Maybe they'll elect me governor."

Harley wheezed, snorted and farted. "That joke gets funnier every time I hear it."

"All right, got to go. I just pulled up to Nails' place."

"Hey. Watch your back, mate. And not just with Barry and Nails. If these guys are really connected to the Russian mob, some Slavic hit men might be headed your way. Ex-KGB. Professionals. Keep a sharp eye out, all right?"

John smiled, hearing the worry in his partner's voice. One minute he was a dangerous, special-ops sniper, twenty years past his military prime, and the next he was the father figure John had needed since his real father had passed away. "You too, Harley."

He turned off the engine and pulled his gun from the special rig under the seat.

Shit. They're not buying it. Steel fidgeted with his tumbler. *I'll be wearing cement shoes by the end of the week. Or however they're doing it nowadays.*

"This'll work," Steel said. "All we need is a little leverage on this guy."

He grabbed the vodka from the limo's mini-bar and poured another round for Sasha and Lexi.

"Forgive me my disbelief," Lexi said. "But you said same thing about debate and that did not go well."

Sasha said, "Is more like he fed you your dog for breakfast, if you take my meaning."

Steel's smile froze on his face as he remembered how he'd once thought it was great to have mob types in his back pocket. "I know it seems like things are falling apart. And the last thing the board wants is to hear Pfester's name blasted on television. I understand. But we can fix this. You guys still need me."

Sasha grinned and downed his vodka in one gulp. "I'm thinking...*nyet*. We don't need bad fuckups in our business. Make life very painful for all."

Steel sat back and gave a half-hearted laugh. "You want Black to win? You want him to make policies that hinder our God-given moneymaking abilities? I don't think so."

Lexi said, "*Nyet*. Black very undesirable. But you can't even keep close fight during debate. Why we put faith in you?"

With the agreement that Black was the wrong candidate, Steel felt the mood tilting in the right direction. Perhaps a little mea culpa was in order. "I'm the best chance we've got. Though I have to admit, I thoroughly messed up. I let the bastard rattle me. But I'm telling you, I'm running a close second in the polls. I can take this guy."

Sasha and Lexi exchanged glances.

Lexi said, "I think biggest problem is lack of professional involvement."

Sasha growled. "I agree."

Lexi turned to Steel and said, "From now on, our people handle everything."

Steel smiled. "You read my mind."

Lexi's bushy eyebrows furrowed in thought. "Our pros already in place for tonight's main action. They will have no problem handling amateurs."

Steel finally knocked back his first glass of vodka, feeling he could join in now that things were more businesslike and less Mafioso.

"Our biggest problem," Lexi said, "will be reining in loose cannon, Mr. Black. Your idea is good one for taking care of this, but only with right people working on it, executing. So let's make plan. Okay?"

Steel grabbed the bottle and poured them another round. "What else do you need to know?"

"More specifics. We only supply muscle," Sasha said.

"*You* supply information," Lexi said. "Tell us more about girl."

twenty-eight

HARLEY waited for Two-Bits' Escalade to disappear into the garage. He'd kept an eye out on the way here, but no one else had followed the rapper home.

Once the garage door closed, Harley's gaze was immediately drawn to the ratty old VW microbus parked in front. "Hello there." He pulled in behind it. "There's no way a homely sheila like you belongs here with the rich folks."

Harley hit the speed dial on his cell phone and called in a favor from his buddy on the police force. While he was waiting on an answer to the VW's license plates, he noticed a dark colored cargo van down the block. It was hard to make out because the streetlight above it was dark, but something about it caught his attention. A moment later it happened again—an ember from a lit cigarette glowed in the darkness of the van.

Harley's gaze narrowed. *Someone's already here.*

His buddy got back on the line and told him the microbus was registered as a junker to a place in Sun Valley. Harley nodded. *Same as before.*

If Barry and Nails were here, that wouldn't leave much time before they made their attempt on Two-Bits. Harley would have to move fast.

But then who was in the cargo van? If it was the Russians, the ex-spies would have already noticed Two-Bits was home. Harley pulled out a map and thumbed through it, in case they were watching him. Figuring he needed to make a better show, he put on a bewildered and frustrated expression, then began waving his hands in the air, gesticulating wildly.

After a moment or two of showcasing his horrible acting abilities, he tossed the map book onto the dash and pulled away, driving toward the dark van. He tried to catch a glimpse of its occupants as he went past, but they were well hidden in the darkness. It was a little too clever for his taste—they'd probably shot out the street lamp.

He took a right turn, out of sight from both the occupants of the van and the house, then took another right and parked. Putting on an earpiece for his cell phone, Harley clipped the handset to his belt, then hit the speed dial and waited for John to answer, drumming his fingers on the steering wheel.

"I haven't found much here," John said. "What's up?"

"We've got problems."

"Tell me."

"Barry and Nails are here, driving another junker from the same yard."

"So what's the problem?"

"They're not alone. I think a Russian hit team is already here, ready to take out our boys. At the very least, they've got the front of the house covered. But there may be more of them that I haven't seen."

Harley slipped out and opened the back tailgate of his Suburban while listening to John swear at the fates.

"Harley, we need these guys alive. Right now they're the only link we've got that Steel is behind these attacks."

Harley unlocked a steel trunk that was welded to the car's frame and grabbed his rifle and a pair of night vision binoculars. He ducked behind a nearby hedge and into someone's backyard, keeping a brisk pace. "I can't get to Nails and Barry before they hit Two-Bits. I won't catch 'em in the act and I definitely can't stop 'em from killing again. If I move fast enough, I might be able to take out the Russians before they can take out Barry and Nails. But even that's an iffy proposition."

Harley stopped at the end of the first backyard and slipped over the fence into a second yard. He was getting closer to his objective so he slowed his pace to a crawl and slipped on the night vision goggles.

"How iffy?" John asked.

Harley whispered, "If they have a smart plan for taking care of Two-Bits they might be done already. And if they're on their way out, I can't get to 'em. It's going to take me at least ten minutes to get into a safe position to cover them from the front door to their car."

Harley heard the sound of a car starting from John's end. "If you're on your way here, I think you'll be late for the party."

"I'm coming anyway. There was nothing at Nails' apartment except the largest pile of pizza boxes and empty beer cans that I've ever seen. There were roaches the size of my fist and you couldn't even see the kitchen through the pile of garbage."

Harley inched forward through the bushes. "In about two minutes I'll need to go silent."

"Roger that. Actually, there was something at the apartment. An enormous amount of drugs."

"Heroin? Cocaine?"

"No, pharmaceutical. More pill bottles than I would've thought possible, and names of drugs I've never even heard of. But they all belonged to Nails and they *all* came from Pfester."

Harley whispered, "I don't see how that helps us right now. We need to stall them to give me time to get in position."

"I know, I know. But we can't shoot out a window or signal them because the Russians might see it and crank into overdrive."

Harley paused in his tracks. "This might sound unorthodox, but we've got their cell phone number."

"Ahh...I don't know."

Harley crept forward. "All we need is a short delay. It's better than doing nothing."

"All right. I'll give it a try. You think Two-Bits is still alive in there?"

"He was a gang leader for five years. He can probably take care of himself. To tell you the truth, I'm more worried about Barry and Nails."

IF THOSE FUCKERS BUSTED UP MY PLASMA I'M GONNA SHOOT THEIR *gonads clean off.* Two-Bits crept into his den, into the music studio, and cocked his head toward the doorway. Whoever the hell was in his crib was still banging up the place.

He dialed open his wall-safe, then reached inside and pulled out his favorite gun—a custom, chrome-plated, .44 Magnum Desert Eagle. Thing of beauty.

He racked the slide and clicked off the safety. *Boom, motherfuckers!*

He started toward the door but noticed the gold medallions around his neck were clinking together, making too much noise. He quickly set down the gun and pulled the necklaces off, stuffing them into the safe. Without the bling he felt kind of naked—but he moved on anyway, eager to pop someone like he used to in the old days.

Two-Bits picked up his weapon and aimed it straight in front of him, holding it sideways like he'd seen in the movies.

The gun was choice—a prime, cool beauty—and the same caliber Dirty Harry carried. But by Two-Bits' way of thinking, the situation was even better 'cause of the new "Make my day" law—the one that applied to would-be burglars. It made it completely legal to execute someone if you were protecting your home.

Legal. Two-Bits cackled, then quickly covered his mouth and got quiet.

It had been years since he'd been able to cap somebody and get away with it. That's what sucked about being respectable. Even when that guy had shot at him last night, his posse got to have all the fun shooting back. They'd emptied their clips in the gangbanger's direction while he'd had to refrain and pretend to be cool about it. All in the name of being governor. But there was nothing cool about being shot at.

Shit. Hope the dogs are okay.

He tiptoed through the living room and sighed with relief when he saw his porcelain dog collection was unharmed.

There was another crash from the bedroom, probably the statues of the fertility gods, and Two-Bits decided to hurry it up. Adrenalin pumping, he slipped off his noisy dress shoes and took off down the hall, his feet whisking over the Moroccan tiles.

Reaching the door to the bedroom, he stopped with his fingers on the handle. *This is it.*

A cell phone rang inside the bedroom.

The thrashing sounds stopped at the sound of the phone ringing. Two-Bits listened for a moment but no one answered the phone. Instead, two people inside seemed to be arguing with each other.

One voice had a nasal quality to it. "I think you broke my friggin nose."

The other voice seemed to come from a big guy—it was really deep with a bass boom like a subwoofer. "You gonna calm down now, cracker?"

What kind of B&E job is this?

The cell phone gave one last ring and got quiet. Two-Bits decided to listen in on the conversation.

"All right. This is hard for me to say, but I'm sorry about your nose, Barry."

"And I'm sorry about kicking you in the nuts. I really am."

Two-Bits heard a chuckle from the bigger one.

"No problem. It didn't hurt that much. But you are one wily little dude. You actually got in a couple of good licks."

"Hey, you mean it? Thanks. I appreciate that."

"Sure thing. But now I want you to listen to me. I don't think we should do this job. I think we should walk away."

Two-Bits frowned. What were they talking about? They didn't want to rob his house after all? It was like one of those sappy TV movies with the hooker with a heart of gold.

The nasally voiced guy—Barry—said, "You know, I think you're right. Why should we do anything if those spooks are gonna get us anyway?"

Spooks? They come into MY house and make racist slurs!

"Besides, with your patches leaking all over the place and my bloody nose...we're leaving DNA everywhere. That's bad news."

Blood? All over my white carpet?

The deep voiced one said, "Then let's get out of here. Shit, we have no idea if Two-Bits is on his way back yet."

"Hey, don't look at me like that. What? Like it's my fault you threw me into the television and busted the darn thing."

Two-Bits' mouth dropped open. *Busted my plasma? Oh, yeah. They gonna die.*

He kicked in the door and aimed his gun at the unusual pair standing at the far side of the room. They both froze in place when they saw him. One was a giant black dude who looked kind of familiar. He was easily three hundred pounds and was polka-dotted with what looked like little rubber patches all over his skin. The other was a sickly-looking white fool with blood leaking from his nose, bug eyes, and skin as pale as a worm living under a rock.

Are these guys for real? They're like creatures from a nightmare.

"What the fuck are you doing in my house?"

The skinny dude's cell phone started ringing again.

The big guy said, "Hey. Take it easy. We were just leaving."

Two-Bits looked around the room at the disaster that had taken place. "Yeah, right."

He cocked the gun for dramatic effect, forgetting that he'd already done it back in the studio. A bullet was ejected from the chamber and fell to the ground, where Barry and the big guy stared at it.

After another ring, Barry said, "You know I bet we can work something out. What if we pay for all the damages? Plus a little interest."

Two-Bits shook his head and smirked, showing off his gold tooth. "Nah. I got plenty of money. We're talking principles, baby. And you can't buy off a man's principles."

The cell phone cut off in mid ring.

He stared at the big man for a second, trying to place him. "Where do I know you from?"

The big dude didn't answer, so Two-Bits racked his gun to show them he was serious. Another bullet ejected from the chamber and clinked onto the floor. The thieves stared at the bullet.

Two-Bits flushed and said, "Never mind. Don't tell me. I'll just shoot you instead."

"Whoa, whoa, hold on there, buddy," Barry said. "We're unarmed. You can't go around shooting helpless people."

"Yeah?" Two-Bits smiled. "I wrote a song about the 'Make my day' law. I know all about what I can and cannot do. All I have to do is fear for my life. Then anything goes."

Barry and the big guy looked at each other.

"Oh my god," Two-Bits said. "I think I feel the fear coming over me right now."

Barry slapped the big dude on the shoulder and said, "Nails! Tell him what he wants to know."

"All right." The big man sighed. "I used to play for the Raiders."

Two-Bits' eyes grew bigger. "I knew I recognized you. Dennis fucking Nalen. Nails. In MY house." He looked him up and down. "Man, what happened to you? You're looking like some kind of freak show."

"It's a long story."

Two-Bits glanced away from the bloody patches. "You know, maybe it's best you don't tell me about it." He turned toward the bed and froze, stunned. Some kind of white and black goo was splattered all over his leopard print duvet. He looked around the room and started noticing all kinds of bizarre things. "What is all this stuff? Don't tell me that's a giant dildo."

Nails looked him in the eye but said nothing, while the skinny dude stared at his feet, his face reddening.

All at once it came to Two-Bits—perversion. White on black perversion. "Aw, man. That's disgusting. Now I'm gonna have to burn those sheets."

Nails shook his head. "It's not what you think."

Barry's jaw dropped. "No way. We ain't homos, man. These are just props to make your death look like an accident."

Two-Bits shuddered, then shook it off and aimed the gun at Barry. "What the fuck did you just say?"

"Uh...uh...we ain't homos, man."

"No. The other thing."

Nails edged further away from Barry like he wasn't with the guy. But when he turned, Two-Bits had a déjà vu, flashing back to the club from the night before and remembering Nails aiming a shotgun in his direction.

His adrenalin started pumping overtime. "You're dead."

As Barry's cell phone started to ring again, Two-Bits racked the slide and ejected another bullet. *Not cool!*

He looked at the bullet on the ground, then ignored it and started firing at the assassins. In the small room, the .44's report sounded like a cannon.

Boom!

twenty-nine

BARRY winced and covered his ears as bits of shattered dildos rained upon him. The sound was deafening.

This is how I'm gonna die...with splinters in my ass? Shot by a rapper with a chrome plated gun?

In three seconds it was over as the barrel of Two-Bits' gun slid backward, locked and empty. Barry felt his body in disbelief. He wasn't hit.

He turned to Nails. It was harder to tell with the bloody patches, but Nails seemed okay, too.

Through buzzing ears, Barry heard the empty clip hit the floor. He turned back to Two-Bits and saw him fumble in his pocket before pulling out another clip.

You gotta be kidding me!

Barry reached into his waistband, pulled out his revolver, and fired three times. He heard Nails get off a few rounds as well. But compared to the big chrome gun, both of their guns sounded like little firecrackers.

Two-Bits' gun fell from his grasp as he collapsed to the floor.

Barry shook his head, trying to clear the buzzing sound from his ears. *Un-friggin-believable. The one guy we decide not to kill!*

Barry stomped over and kicked the limp body. "You idiot! We was gonna give you a pass."

"Hey," Nails said. "Show some respect."

"What are you talking about? He's dead. His body ain't gonna mind. And since we're the ones that killed him...well...I don't want to burst your bubble, but in some circles people would find that disrespectful."

Nails shrugged. "We were going to let him live."

"Yeah, sure. That'd work in court."

"Come on, we were forced to defend ourselves. If he hadn't been one of those gangbangers he was talking about on TV, the ones with the bad aim, the situation might have turned out different."

Barry stared at Nails, but decided that arguing about it wouldn't be worth it. "Let's get our stuff together. With the sound of that friggin cannon going off, the cops gotta be on their way."

His cell phone started ringing again. Barry ignored it and gathered his personal belongings.

HARLEY'S PATIENCE FINALLY PAID OFF. HE'D SPENT THE LAST FIVE minutes perched in an oak tree, scanning the area. And while he hadn't found any others lurking about the house, he had his night vision scope trained on the cargo van the moment the shots rang out.

The shots, big ones followed by two smaller gunshots, startled him to be sure, but he didn't let it distract him. He kept a steady watch on his target. The gunshots apparently startled the occupants of the van as well—chain-smoking Russians from the looks of it—because they immediately jumped in their seats and commenced arguing with each other. Harley recognized a couple of Russian curse words and grinned.

Gotcha.

Then he frowned. The Russian passenger waved his arms wildly, revealing a little box in his hand. The black box had two lights and two metal rocker switches.

Not good.

It was probably a trigger for a bomb. But then again, if they had the house rigged to blow, they would have blown it already. That meant the switch was for something else. Probably the car.

Harley dialed John.

"I'm three minutes away, Harley. But I can't get Nails and Barry to answer."

"It's going down now. Thirty seconds ago, three guns went off inside Two-Bits' residence. Now it's quiet. At least two Russians in the van outside. One has a little black box and his finger on the button. Probably rigged to Barry and Nails' car."

"Any other players?"

"No one out front. But I can't tell about the back."

"Hold on. I'm going to try them again. I'll make it a conference call so we can still talk while I'm waiting."

There were a couple of beeps, then Harley heard a phone ringing through his earpiece.

John said, "What about the Russians? Do you have a shot if Barry and Nails leave the house?"

"Yes."

"And are you sure the Russians are going to kill them?"

Harley sighed. John's question wasn't unexpected, and it wasn't the first time John's morals had made things messier than they had to be. "Reasonably sure."

"You know that's not good enough."

Harley looked through the night vision scope on his rifle. The box was still in the clear. "Tell you what. Box has two switches and right now the lights aren't on. So the device isn't hot. But if I see the Russian arm the trigger when our boys come out, I'll know for sure."

"All right, that'll work. Just stay on the line so we can communicate. With any luck, we'll get 'em out of there alive."

Harley grimaced. "So long as no else joins the party."

Barry picked up the empty shells that had been expelled from Nails' gun and stuffed them into a canvas bag.

His phone trilled again.

Nails grunted. "Either answer the damn phone or shut it off. I don't want that thing ringing while we're trying to sneak out of here."

Barry frowned at the display. The number on the caller ID wasn't familiar. He flipped it open and said, "What is it?"

"Don't hang up, Barry. I need to talk to you."

"Who is this?"

"It's urgent. Life or death."

Barry felt a tingling sensation at the base of his scalp. *"Who is this?"*

He waited for what seemed like an eternity before the voice answered, "Your buddy from the cemetery."

Barry dropped the phone on the hard tile floor and started shaking.

Nails turned toward him and said, "What?"

Barry gestured at the phone and whispered, "It's the Terminator. He's on the friggin phone. And he knows my name!"

Nails picked up the phone and held it up so they could both listen. "How'd you get this number?"

"There's no time. A Russian hit team is outside right now."

Barry whimpered. *Oh my God!*

Nails' eye began to twitch. "Outside of where?"

"Don't play games, Nails…"

Barry whispered, "Oh, crap. He knows your name, too."

John continued, "You're inside Two-Bits' house. Where you just shot him, if I'm not mistaken. And outside are Russian ex-KGB operatives, waiting for you."

Barry whined, "Oh, man, we're screwed."

Nails grunted and turned off the lights, then peeked behind the curtain. "You're John Black, right? Look, I think you're full of shit. I don't know how you got this number, or my name for that matter, but we ain't no punks. And there's no way you'd be warning us about anything."

"If I had a choice, I wouldn't, but our interests are temporarily aligned. I want Steel more than I want you dead. I figured you might agree."

Nails shook his head.

Barry whispered, "Giving up Steel…I could live with that." Then he frowned. "But how does Black know about the Russians? There's no way he could know they want us dead."

Nails covered the mouthpiece. "Don't be a fool, Barry. He's trying to trap us. Or kill us. Maybe both." He took his hand off the mouthpiece. "Sorry, cracker. Whatever you're selling, we ain't buying."

Nails started to close the phone when he heard someone shouting on the other end. He punched the button for the speaker phone.

John said, "Wait a second! Don't hang up!"

"What is it, Black? I told you, no one here is buying what you're shoveling."

"You don't believe me. I get it. But if you hang on I'll give you their location. You can see for yourself."

"Okay, I'll bite," Nails said. "Where are they?"

John said, "Harley, point them in the right direction."

"Down the block, on the west side, in a dark blue cargo van."

Barry jumped back when he heard the new voice.

Nails said, "Who else is listening, Black?"

"That's my partner. He's got a scope trained on the van."

The guy with the gruff, Australian accent said, "If you go to the living room window, you'll get a nice view of the van. And inside the van you'll see the red glow of a burning ash." Barry and Nails heard a snorting sound over the phone before the voice continued, "Idiots are smoking on the job."

Barry shook his head. "No way. That Australian sniper will probably pop us when we show our heads."

Nails covered the mouthpiece again, hesitating. "I don't know. Now I'm not so sure."

"What, you gotta be kidding? *Now* you think they're playing it straight?"

"I thought I saw something earlier. In a cargo van down the street."

"What?"

"Like someone inside was smoking a cigarette."

Barry pounded the bed. "Well, then holy crap! It *is* them! The friggin Russians are all chain smokers. They couldn't stop smoking if they were covered in gas."

"We're out of time, John," the Aussie said. "I can hear sirens."

Barry and Nails looked at each other, then started for the back door. "We're out of here, Black."

"Wait a second."

"Yeah, right."

"Don't go out the back door. We think there's another one out back."

Barry stopped with his hand on the door handle. He looked out the sliding glass door. Darkness. He ducked behind the relative safety of the plastered wall. "Now what?"

Nails shrugged. "Make a run for the car."

John said, "No. Don't get in the car. They've got it rigged to blow."

Nails squeezed the cell phone. "We're not waiting here for the cops to show up."

"Listen. We know where they are out front. In ten seconds my car will be on the street, right outside. If you walk out the front door my partner will cover you till you get here."

Nails covered the phone.

Barry shrugged. "I don't got a clue what we should do here."

"We're damned if we do, screwed if we don't." Nails uncovered the phone. "Fine. We'll go out the front door in five seconds, Black. If you can pull this off and get us out in one piece, we'll give you something you can use. Something on Steel. So don't mess up."

"Deal."

Nails closed the phone, tossed it to Barry, then headed for the front door.

Barry said, "What if they're yanking our chains? And we just waltz up and turn ourselves over to them? We'd be the laughing stock of the prison yard if that got out."

Nails said, "No. We're gonna do this my way."

"Yeah? What's the plan?"

Nails peeked out the glass window next to the door.

Barry leaned over his shoulder. "There's a lot of friggin open space between us and the front gate."

Nails sighed. "No shit."

JOHN RACED DOWN THE STREET, TAKING INSTRUCTIONS FROM HARLEY over his cell's speaker phone.

"You're almost there," Harley said. "The cargo van is thirty yards away at twelve o'clock. Two-Bits' driveway is at your ten."

There. John yanked the wheel to the left and slammed on the brakes, sliding the Suburban and bringing it to a stop almost 180 degrees from where he started. Directly between the van and the entrance to the driveway. At that angle, the bulky SUV provided the most cover possible, but was still positioned for a quick getaway.

Harley said, "Your tire squeals have made 'em nervous. The Russians are feeling antsy."

John ignored the burnt rubber smell and said, "Got it. Our boys are on their way."

He could just make out the silhouettes of Barry and Nails, as lopsided a pair as he'd ever come across. They were moving fast, but the big guy's limp was keeping him from making any real speed.

"They just armed the trigger," Harley said. "You want me to take 'em out?"

"No, wait! Only if they draw their guns. I can get Barry and Nails out without killing the Russians. If they try to follow, shoot out their tires."

"Shit. Now they're keying a radio. Watch your back. Someone else is out here."

John looked down the street, but it was empty. He called out to Barry and Nails, "Hurry up. There's another one coming and we don't have him covered."

Barry and Nails nodded, but instead of veering closer to John's Suburban, they started crossing the street.

Shit. "Something's wrong, Harley."

As Barry and Nails crossed in front of John, he saw a man step out from some bushes next to Two-Bits' house. Something metal glinted in the man's hand as he pointed it toward Barry and Nails. The man was fifty yards away, and a vehicle stood between him and his targets, but it was only a matter of seconds before the gunman would have a clear firing angle.

No, no, no. John pulled his gun from the under the seat. "Harley, I've got one on the east side. He's drawing down!"

"Our bogies in the van are pulling out weapons! And one of 'em is getting out."

"Then go! GO. Take the shot."

Messy. It's going to be messy. As John cocked his weapon, he heard three shots from Harley's rifle and the sound of glass shattering.

Out of the corner of his eye he saw Beanpole and the big guy drop to the ground by an old microbus. John squeezed the trigger right as the hit man ducked behind a retaining wall. He fired off another shot toward the wall then yelled out, "BARRY! NAILS! Get over here."

From the phone, "Got 'em both, John. Where's your bogey?"

"Fifteen yards on the south side, behind a retaining wall. I've got him cornered, but I don't have a clean shot."

John fired again, keeping the guy trapped, then glanced toward Nails, who was in the midst of a heated discussion with Barry.

Nails said, "I'm not getting in the cracker's car!"

"But he wasn't lying! And staying out here is friggin suicide. We're gonna die if we stay out in the open."

There was another sharp crack from Harley's rifle and the retaining wall guy fell away. He hit the ground, his gun clattering into the street.

Finally. "Come on! Let's hurry! There may be more." John opened his car door and walked toward the idiots, who were crouched behind a VW microbus. He heard Nails make a low guttural noise and whap Barry on the back of the head. Barry's eyes bugged out, but his response was interrupted as the microbus exploded in a fiery orange ball of flames.

The concussion knocked John to the ground. A moment later he heard another crack from the rifle.

Harley's voice came from a large oak tree. "Sorry, John. Must've been another hiding in the back of the van. He's out of the picture now."

John heard the sirens getting louder. *Shit. They're close.* He picked himself up and raced over to the van as Harley dropped to the ground and joined him.

Harley had his rifle slung and was pointing his sidearm down the street. "We're out of time, mate. They still alive?"

John felt Nails' pulse. It was faint, but at least it was there. "It looks like it. But they're out cold. You think we can lift this guy?"

Harley flung Barry over his shoulder and said, "This one's easy, but bring the car as close as you can for the big guy."

John stood up and looked at the bizarre patches that dotted Nails' body like a leopard. "Yeah...maybe that'll work."

thirty

NAILS woke to the sound of a nasal whine and rolled over to find Barry doing his best impersonation of an intermittent steam whistle. Not a pleasant sound to behold. But even worse, between snores Nails still heard a loud buzz droning in his head.

He searched his pockets for the magic blue pills but came up empty. *This has gotta be the worst hangover I've ever had.*

He looked around, but the room was unrecognizable. He was surrounded by concrete on all sides but one. And that side wasn't any better—steel bars that completed the dismal-looking enclosure.

Inside the cage with him were a few cots and a porcelain toilet. But outside the cage was a veritable arsenal. Assault weapons, grenades, even a rocket launcher. All locked behind a thick, Plexiglas case.

What kind of prison is this?

He rubbed at the lump on the back of his head and winced in pain. All at once his memory came roaring back. He and Barry had been making a beeline for the hedges on the far side of the street, away from Black. And somebody—probably the Russians—had started shooting at him.

Nails grunted. Being shot at twice in five minutes by different people was a new personal record for him, and a record he hoped wouldn't be broken for quite some time.

Then Black, the guy Barry affectionately referred to as the Terminator, had started stalking toward them. And that's where things got fuzzy. All he could remember was an immense wave of heat and flames, and then waking up with an enormous migraine and a strong desire to beat something to a bloody pulp.

Had the Russians really tried to blow him up?

He fought an urge to attack the bars like they were the blind side of an unprotected quarterback. *Shit. It must be withdrawal from the pain meds.* If he didn't get one of those pills soon, there was no telling what was gonna happen.

A sniffle sounded from the corner next to the toilet as a little homeless-looking guy jumped up. "Hey, Nails. You're awake."

The scruffy-looking dude scratched his stubble and revealed a two-fingered hand.

Nails restrained himself from pounding on the pyro freak. "Shit. What are you doing here, Sparky?"

"The freaky old guy got me."

"What freaky old guy?"

"The guy who looks like your grandpa one minute and an axe murderer the next."

Nails frowned and rubbed his temples, trying to keep his cool. He had no idea who Sparky was talking about.

From the cot next to him, the nose whistling came to an abrupt halt as Barry cried out in his sleep, "No, Lassie! Don't! I'll be a good boy. I promise."

Barry sat up straight, his eyes bugging open.

Nails winced, wishing Barry hadn't shouted, and said, "Relax, dude. And keep it down. Lassie hasn't come home yet."

Sparky sniggered, which earned him a menacing stare. He gulped and said, "Sorry, Nails."

Wait for the blue pill. Don't kill anybody.

Barry slammed a fist into the thin mattress and said, "Wait a second. Those friggin Russians tried to blow us up. I knew it."

"You *knew* it? Well, if you're so smart," Nails said, "what are you doing in this homemade prison cell?"

"Hey, don't get mad at me. I didn't put us here, and I didn't try to kill us. We got bigger fish to fry."

Blue pill!

"Yeah, guys," Sparky said. "Take it easy."

All right. That's it. Nails turned a glare toward Sparky. "I guess you're wanting a little attention, huh Sparky? Well, okay then." He stood up and rumbled toward the little pyro freak. "I'm betting you're the one who put these guys on our tail, am I right? Maybe I should show you just how much I *appreciate* you giving us up."

"No! Wait! I had no choice. The old guy was torturing me."

Nails looked him over. "You don't seem any worse than usual. Not yet, anyway."

Sparky cowered in the corner of the cell. "Okay. Okay. He didn't actually torture me. But you could tell he was going to! You should've seen his eyes. They were freaking me out."

"What can you tell from my eyes?"

Sparky looked him in the eye for a moment before yelping and covering his face. Nails smirked and reached for Sparky. The sound of a gunshot stopped him. It was small and sharp, but the echo ricocheted off the concrete walls, driving a spike into his brain. He turned toward the cell door and caught sight of a white haired, grizzled-looking man with a snub-nosed revolver in his hand.

"No one's going to kill anyone," the old guy said. "Until I say it's okay."

Sparky cried out, "See. That's what I'm talking about."

Nails took a step away from the door. He had to agree, the guy was scary. Once you looked past the white hair, something in the man's eyes warned of the predator lurking inside. Nails felt it on an animal level, an instinctive level.

He decided that the situation probably called for some tact, which was easier said than done. It had been years since he'd tried anything even approaching tact, but hopefully it would come back to him. "If you don't mind, I could really use one of my pain meds about now. They usually make me...a bit friendlier."

The old guy smiled, and the scary look melted away from his gaze. "Sure, mate. Being friends sounds like a good idea."

The old guy walked away from them and opened a locker to the right of the arsenal. Nails spotted his own belt and shoes inside, along with a bunch of other things. He rolled his eyes heavenward and sighed when he spotted the pill bottle.

Magic blue pills.

He moved toward the cell door until the old guy held out a hand and said, "No. Stay behind the white line. It keeps me from having to shoot you out of self defense."

Nails looked at the floor and saw that he'd just moved past the white line. He took a step back and watched the old man put a single tablet and a paper cup on a ledge in the cell door, then step away from the door and wave him forward. Nails rumbled forward and claimed his bounty.

Barry said, "Hey, with that accent you've gotta be Harley, right? Black's partner?"

Harley winked at them as a door behind him opened up and Black stepped through. Nails wanted to laugh when he saw Barry take half a step backwards. Then again, maybe Barry was right about Black being the Terminator. The dude kept coming and coming until he'd caught the two of them.

"You comfy?" John asked. "It's a nice change to see you guys in your natural habitat."

Nails grunted. "Funny."

"Well, it beats chasing you all over the place. I don't know about you, but I don't really care for dodging bullets." John gave a pointed glance to Nails. "Or dodging Chevys for that matter."

"Dodging a bullet always beats catching one," Nails said.

John's gaze narrowed. "I'm sure Two-Bits agrees with you on that one."

"Wait a second," Barry said. "We was gonna leave the guy alone till he started shooting at us."

Nails groaned, wondering if he could get close enough to pop Barry before the old dude shot him. "Shut the fuck up, cracker. Save that shit for the lawyer."

Harley sniggered. "You already waived the right to remain silent."

Barry said, "Hey! Wait up! You can't question us 'cause nobody read us our rights."

John spread his hands and gestured toward their surroundings. "Does this look like a police station to you?"

Nails shook his head. It most definitely did not. He sighed. At least the pill was kicking in. His pain was fading, though with the deadening came clarity about the nasty situation they were in.

Barry said, "Where are we?"

John looked at his partner and smiled. "We like to call this place Harley's Playhouse."

Nails sucked in a breath. *Is he saying what I think he's saying?*

"Now hold on a sec," Barry said. "You can't keep us locked up. It's against the law."

Harley smirked and unrolled a cloth full of shiny surgical-looking instruments.

"You want to talk about the law?" John grimaced. "It's against the law to kill your fellow citizens. Yet you managed to send Odie, Two-Bits, and Crenshaw to meet their maker."

"Crenshaw?" Barry asked. "No, no…that dude had a heart attack. We had nothing to do with it."

"SHUT UP," Nails said.

John spoke through clenched teeth. "It's also against the law to try to kill my sister. And my niece. And me. So you've already turned your back on the law. I don't think I'll lose any sleep worrying about what the law says."

Shit. Nails kept his eye on Harley and his surgical instruments. The old dude looked gleeful. *Not good.*

"Whoa, whoa," said Barry. "Let's calm down. And let's try to remember that all your family members are still alive. We never actually shot you, no matter how hard we tried."

Harley snorted.

John said, "Is that supposed to comfort me?"

"I don't know," Barry said. "I'm just trying to point out that we have our good sides, too. And it's not like we wanted to kill anybody. Steel and the Russians forced us into it."

"Is that right? You're a victim of circumstance?" John asked.

Harley pulled out a long, serrated hunting knife and started to clean his fingernails with it.

Barry's eyes widened.

Sparky whimpered in the corner and muttered, "Not the knife again."

Nails ignored them and said, "We're not saying we're blameless. Just that we were stuck between a rock and a hard place. There were mitigating circumstances."

John said, "Well, now you're stuck again. On the one hand, Steel and the Russians just shot at you and blew up your van. So that pretty much tells you what they're thinking. And on the other hand, I have to admit the thought of you guys expiring makes me feel kind of tingly inside. So where does that leave us?"

"Hey, look," Barry said. "I think we're all on the same side here. Steel and the Russians tried to kill us. Let me tell you, that does *not* inspire any employee loyalty. So that's strike one against those guys."

Harley said, "Just one? Sounds like a strikeout to me."

"Abso-friggin-lutely. And by the way, not to kiss up or anything, but I want you guys to know how much I appreciate you saving us from the Russians. That's a marker we mean to repay."

John turned to Nails. "What about you? You going to make good on the deal we made back at the house? Something on Steel in exchange for rescuing you?"

Nails thought about it for a moment, weighing his options. Keeping a deal was important to him, but he'd made a deal with Steel first. Then again, that asshole had reneged as far as he was concerned. Big time. And at least Black seemed to be a straight shooter. "Yeah. You'll get what I promised you."

"Good. What do you have?"

"In a minute," Nails said. "First, we got something else to cover. I want to make us another deal. One that gets us out of here."

Harley snorted.

Barry said, "Hey, let's open our minds a bit. I'm sure we can work something out."

John said, "That's not going to happen."

"Ah, come on. Why not?" Barry whined.

"First off, Harley and I believe in balance and justice. And you've killed people. The only way to balance out something like that is to save lives, and somehow you don't seem like the lifesaving type. So that leaves justice as the only way to balance things out."

Sparky piped in, "What? Is that a Karma thing?"

John shook his head. "Kind of. But you're missing the point. You won't get any help from me until you follow through on our first deal. Keeping your word is important to me. After that, if what you give me is good stuff, I'll see what I can do to help get you a lighter sentence. That's the best I can do."

Nails squinted. "But *how* will you help us?"

"I don't know. But I'll figure something out. Maybe I'll help you get evidence of the Russians' coercion. Maybe I'll testify that you helped us out. Or maybe, when I'm elected governor, I'll exert a little influence with the judge to get you the lightest, legal sentence possible."

Barry's jaw dropped. "That's right. This dude could be governor. Heck, Nails, that's not a bad guy to have on our side."

"*If* he's on our side. That's the big question. How do we know he doesn't hold a grudge about his family?"

John said, "I do. But it's even more important to have balance and justice. Do something decent. Give me a reason to be on your side."

Nails thought it over, but wasn't sure how to respond. "Can you give us a minute?"

"Sure."

Nails huddled with Barry and Sparky against the back wall and started whispering.

"Shit. Do you believe this guy or do you think he's going to kill us anyway?" Nails asked.

"I believe him," Sparky said. "Hell, I would've voted for him." He glanced over his shoulder. "But I don't know about the old guy. He gives me the creeps."

Keeping his voice low, Barry said, "What choice do we

have? I say we help these guys and try to win them over to our side like the man said."

Nails shook his head. "I don't like being trapped. When I'm cornered it makes me want to fight back instead of trusting 'em. If the three of us work together we can take 'em when they open the cell door."

"Are you kidding me?" Barry said. "They've got us locked up in some kind of nuclear bunker and you're worried about trusting 'em? I'm worrying about that white haired dude going 'country' on us and doing us like in that *Deliverance* movie."

Sparky's face paled. "I never even thought of that."

"You guys make me sick," Nails said. "If we don't work together, we won't be able to bust out of here."

Barry and Sparky shuffled their feet and looked at the floor.

Nails growled under his breath. *Assholes.*

John called out, "All right, that's enough. You guys have three choices. Option number one is telling me everything I want to know. Option two is tying you up and dropping you off outside the Russian's place. Who knows, maybe you'll get lucky and they'll only take off a few body parts. And option three is having Harley take care of you boys right now. That way, at least some form of justice will be served."

Nails, Barry, and Sparky looked at each other.

"So which is it, boys?" John asked. "Door number one, door number two, or door number three?"

thirty-one

"THIS is it," John said. He glanced up at Steel's third floor window, but the rooms behind the glass were dark.

The interrogation of Barry and Nails had been successful, though entirely unsatisfying. Everything they'd found out about Steel and the Russians pointed to the same conclusion—the motive for the entire assassination scheme had been to horde *more* money and power.

More. How original. Like they didn't have enough of both already. John shook it off and focused on the task at hand. One locked office, full of goodies—ripe and ready to be plucked.

Harley drove past the office building and parked a block away, out of range of the street lights. "You really think Nails has a video camera in there? That Steel hasn't noticed?"

"I know it's kind of thin. But, yeah, I do. It sounds like the kind of inane plan Barry and Nails might try. They're not rocket scientists. To tell you the truth, I'm more worried about following in their footsteps and doing something stupid ourselves. If we get caught breaking into Steel's office, the press will have a field day. Another Watergate."

Harley smothered a laugh. "We're collecting evidence against a killer. Your conscience should be clean enough, mate. Going in there to spy on your opponent is *not* the point of what we're doing."

"I'll be sure to tell the police that when they arrest me."

John slipped on a pair of black leather gloves, then grabbed a small toolkit from the backseat and got out of the car. Harley fell into step beside him, similarly attired in a black jumpsuit and black gloves.

About twenty feet from the front door to the office building, John picked up a rock from the gutter and hurled it toward the exterior light. With a crash and the tinkle of broken glass hitting the concrete, the entryway went dark.

Harley pulled his lockpick set from his coat pocket and got to work. John watched for a moment, marveling at Harley's skill, then turned his attention toward the street.

Nothing. At one in the morning there weren't many cars to be found.

"Got it." Harley opened the door with a grin, then pulled on a black ski mask.

John followed suit, making sure the eyeholes were in the appropriate places, and headed inside. He and Harley took the stairs to the third floor, keeping the pace slow and deliberate enough to remain silent. There wasn't supposed to be anyone there, but experience had proven that it was better to play it cool than get caught unaware.

On the top floor, John paused at the door to Steel's place, imagining the potential evidence inside. *Come on. Be here.*

Harley finished the lock in no time and reached for the handle, then stopped with his hand an inch from the metal.

"What's the matter?" John asked.

"Hand me the voltmeter."

John tossed it to him, then groaned when Harley got a reading.

"Sneaky little bastards," Harley said. "It's just a trickle, but it's there."

"Can you get around it?"

Harley hesitated, "I think so. Give me the bag."

Five tension-filled, sweaty-palmed minutes passed before Harley triumphed over the alarm. And then they were inside, with pencil beam flashlights, searching the office. John took Steel's desk and computer while Harley searched the rest.

Four fruitless minutes went by before Harley whispered, "Crikey. I guess it wasn't much of a hidden camera."

John looked up from Steel's appointment book as Harley pulled a twisted heap of metal, plastic, and videotape spaghetti from the garbage can. John turned his flashlight on the tape and saw that a lot of it was crushed, and some of it burned. "You think there's enough left to get anything useful?"

"It's possible. Some of it is in good shape and some of it is destroyed. It depends if the good stuff has anything important on it."

"Not good enough, Harley. I hate to say it, but we're going to have to go through the whole office. As long as we're here, we should try to find some evidence that hasn't been destroyed."

"The cleaning crew hasn't been here yet. They could be here at any moment."

"Then we'll have to hurry."

Harley sighed. "I'll keep an eye out. Anything in his desk?"

"Nothing connecting him to Nails and Barry. But his appointment book has meetings with petroleum companies, the energy taskforce, Pfester...you name it. A veritable 'Who's Who' of people wanting to line Steel's pockets. Those bastards will do anything to get friendly leadership from the governor's office. The funny part is that they've all got little dollar signs next to their names, like a code to say how much cash they've slipped him. Reminds me of elementary school, when the teacher found the girls' list of boys with hearts next to their names."

"Somehow I doubt that'll hold up in the California legal system," Harley said. "We need to speed this along. I hate to say it, but what about the Barracuda?"

John grimaced. "Yeah, she might be able to help."

"Give her a call. I'll keep looking."

John took a seat at the desk and pulled out his cell phone.

On the first ring, his mother answered. "What is it, John? Everything all right?"

"Everything's fine. Hope I didn't wake you."

"You had me worried there. But wake me? Come on, I'll be lucky if I sleep at all before the polls close on Tuesday. Even the girls are still up."

John frowned. "Don't work them too hard, okay? This isn't their fight."

"Are you serious? Hillary and Amber have vivid memories

of being shot at. They *want* to do everything they can to mess with this prick. And this is something they can do."

"You're right, Mother."

"I usually am."

John flipped to the next page of Steel's appointment book. "Look, the reason I called is because I need your advice."

"Really? Do tell."

"Hypothetically speaking, if someone happened to be in a...rival politician's office...what would you look for if you were trying to get evidence?"

"What are you saying, John? No. Wait a minute. Don't tell me. Cell phones make it easy for others to listen in, so it's probably better to keep me in the dark. The police have already given me a hard time about your bombshell in the debate tonight. And now that Two-Bits has been killed, there's a full-blown investigation going on. Feds, too."

"About time."

"I agree. But you touted your idea about murder on television, so of course they want to know whatever you know. The police commissioner's been poking his nose so far up my ass looking for clues, he's bound to get an infection."

John cringed. "Nice image, Mother."

"Don't get all high and mighty on me. Of the two of us, I get the impression that only one of us is keeping within the law tonight."

"You're saying it's you?"

Harley cried out, "Gotcha."

"Hold on, Mother." John covered the mouthpiece. "What?"

Harley grinned and rolled a giant filing cabinet away from the wall. Behind it was a large, forbidding wall safe. "When I saw that the cabinet was on wheels..."

"Can you open it?"

Harley nodded. "It's an older model. It'll take me about half an hour, but I can do it."

"Then don't just stand there." John put the phone back to his ear. "Good news. With any luck we'll be able to crack this...uh, case...in thirty minutes."

"Good. And by the way, John, I want to tell you what a great job you did in the debate. Your sister would've been proud of you." He heard a sniffle on the other end. "I mean, she *will* be proud of you."

"Thanks. I'm trying."

"I know. We all are. Even Hillary and Amber. Right, girls?"

John heard the girls call out, "Hi, Uncle John."

Harley started drilling, so John went into the outer office, closing the door behind him. He kept to the shadows, with his gaze on the outer hall and stairs.

His mother continued, "Right now I'm working on your speech for tomorrow morning at the courthouse."

John groaned. "I'll probably be up all night. I won't be in any shape for a speech tomorrow morning."

"Suck it up, I don't want to hear it. There's no way out of this one. I got the state senate leader to join and support you, which is a pretty big coup since you're known in most political circles as a pariah. I worked my tail off to get you this endorsement. And it's been well publicized already. You're going."

John sighed. "All right."

"And after that we need to turn things over to the police. We've got until noon tomorrow to hand over our files, or they're going to bring you in for questioning."

"Can't you buy us more time? We're very close. If this doesn't pan out tonight, law enforcement will interfere with my investigation."

"I did buy you more time." From the tone of her voice, John could picture his mother pursing her lips in anger. "That's why you get until noon tomorrow. Well, I guess that's noon today since it's already morning. And my political chops are why you don't have to go down there in person."

"Okay, okay. No offense intended. And back to why I called, what do you think people could find in a dirty politician's office?"

He heard his mother laughing on the other end.

"Nothing, if they know what they're doing. These days, politicians don't keep records lying around, John. Too many people have been burned by curious staff members or plants from rival politicians."

He tried to think of a way to get his point across in an inconspicuous way. "What about in a...*safe*...place?"

"Hmmm. I don't think most people would know how to find and get into a *safe* place."

"But if you could?"

"It would probably be too hard to decipher what's important and what isn't. Especially if you're in a hurry. A lot of it could be legal mumbo-jumbo. I'd just grab everything that was in there and sort it out later."

"All right. See you at the courthouse at nine."

He hung up, then noticed that the drilling sound had stopped. He stepped back into Steel's office. "That was quick."

"Yeah, no worries. It just needed a little tickle to open up."

As Harley reached for the handle, they both heard it at the same time. A siren.

John turned off his flashlight and raced to the window.

Harley loaded his tools back into the bag. "I don't get it. I'm sure I disabled the alarm on the safe."

John watched the police car speed past the building and disappear into the night. He gave a nervous laugh. "False alarm."

Harley opened the safe, then whistled at the contents. "There's gotta be half a million dollars in here."

John started pulling out bundles of cash from the top shelf. Underneath the stacks were a handful of filing folders, stuffed with papers, including ones on Pfester. One thick file was entitled *John Black*. That was to be expected. But another caused a hitch in his breathing.

"Shit! Why would he have a file on Sierra?"

"I don't know. Here, take a look at that one while I take a peek at the rest."

John stepped away from the safe and thumbed through the file. A lot of info seemed to be from her ex-husband, but some came from a P.I. firm in Santa Monica. And there were a dozen handwritten notations scattered throughout. The worst part was a notation with a date and time. It had been circled in red, and the time was for nine a.m.

Today.

"I can't believe this. Supposedly, he's got an appointment with Sierra this morning."

"Then maybe that's what this is for."

Harley stood by the safe, holding a brown paper sack. He pulled out an electronic device and a baggie full of sparkly powder. "Look familiar?"

John's stomach sank. "These guys are sick puppies. Bomb happy. Before this week I'd never even seen a bomb. Which is the way I like it."

Harley put the device back in the safe. "What do you want to do?"

"Find out what she's doing." John pulled out his cell phone and punched in Sierra's number.

Harley said, "We shouldn't hang around."

"Just give me a minute."

After a couple of rings, Sierra answered, "What time is it?"

"I'm sorry to wake you but I have an important question to ask you."

"It's all right. What's up?"

"Do you have anything scheduled with Steel this morning?"

"Yeah. I have an interview at nine in his office."

"Cancel it. He's going after you. For some reason your ex-husband told him you and I are an item. He probably wants to use you as leverage against me."

"Why?"

"I don't know. Because he knows I'm getting close. Because he's paranoid. It doesn't matter why."

"But I can't get out of the interview. Believe me, when we settled on Steel as the leader, I called my boss and tried to get out of it. But he told me he'd can me if I refused the assignment. Steel requested me."

"Your life is worth more than your career."

"Come on, John. People know I'm going there. It's not like I can just disappear. They'd know it was him."

John looked at the bomb in the safe. "It's not worth it. And I can't be there to protect you. I've got to play politician this morning."

"I don't need your protection. My cameraman is a black belt."

John shook his head. *A black belt doesn't protect you against a bomb.*

"I have to, John."

"Can you change the location?"

"Only if he wants to. I don't have much to say about it."

John stared at the bomb. "All right. If something happens that changes his mind, do the interview in the studio. That way you'll have plenty of friends around. Plenty of witnesses."

"But what would make him change his mind?"

John grinned. "Good question. That kind of instinct is what makes you so good at your job."

"You're dodging the question."

"You'll know soon enough. I'll talk to you tomorrow."

John hung up and turned to Harley. "We'll kill two birds with one stone. We'll piss off Steel and keep him from getting to Sierra." He grabbed the bomb from the safe. "How much gasoline would it take to render this floor unusable?"

Harley's eyes lit up. "I dunno. Maybe a gallon. I've got a container in the car."

"Get it."

JOHN AND HARLEY SAT IN THE CAR, WAITING. JOHN THUMBED THROUGH the files, but was having a hard time making heads or tails of most of it. The most interesting thing that caught his eye was a piece of legislation that Steel and his pals at Pfester had written. Why big corporations and lobbyists were able to write laws was anybody's guess. To John's way of thinking, it was a dysfunctional system.

Harley said, "I still don't get why we piled the money around the bomb? It's a crying shame to destroy it."

"There was nothing else to do. It's ill-gotten money. And we damn sure couldn't let Steel keep those bribes."

Harley snickered. "Maybe it'll provoke him again. Losing half a mil would do it to me."

"Hopefully."

Harley looked at his watch. "And three, two, one…"

The blast blew all the windows out on the upper floor, and most of the windows on the lower floors. For two seconds a massive fireball lit up the area brighter than Dodger Stadium, before fading away to a few small flames.

Harley blinked. "Oh, yeah. That'll definitely provoke him."

"Wow." John gave a short whistle. "I think you used too much gasoline."

thirty-two

"DAMN it! These are my offices!" Steel growled through gritted teeth.

"I'm sorry, sir. But it's also a crime scene and we haven't quite finished yet."

From the hallway outside the lobby, Steel watched the plainclothes detectives and the lab-coated guys scurry around the blackened carcass that used to be his office.

He glanced at the badge of the uniformed officer who was impeding his entry and said, "Officer Leary, I've had my campaign offices demolished mere days before the election. And I've spent the last half hour answering stupid questions posed by your L.A.P.D. bosom buddies—as if *I* knew anything about the horrendous attack on *my* office. And every second I waste talking to you is another second of my life that I'll never see again. So let me make this clear. If you don't let me into my office immediately, I'll make sure that my first official act as governor will be calling your boss and ensuring that your miserable existence gets sucked into the deepest level of hell that Los Angeles has to offer. Am I making myself clear?"

Governor was a bit of a stretch, but for the moment Steel pretended that Black's poll numbers weren't climbing. While the peon in blue thought over his options, Steel fumed, picturing Black's head sizzling on a platter—fajita style. *That bastard has to be behind this! Stealing my governorship isn't enough—he has to rub it in my face.*

Steel mulled things over until L.A.'s finest showed he had some brains after all. Officer Leary scrunched up his face and said, "Okay, then. I'm gonna let you inside, but I'm afraid I'll have to escort you through the premises."

Steel pursed his lips. "Fine."

He shouldered his way past the officer, surveying the extensive damage. *Goat raping bastard.* It was unbelievable.

Steel felt a moment of dread wash over him as an unpleasant thought trickled through his brain. *What if it wasn't Black? But it couldn't be Sasha and Lexi...could it?*

As he looked over the blackened rubble, his fury turned to trembling. Blowing a target's office was straight out of the old KGB handbook. *Shit.* Maybe they did want him dead! If Sasha and Lexi decided to cut their losses, that was it. Game over. Collect your coffin at the door.

Of course, Barry and Nails had managed to avoid their fate, although they were pretty much the only ones to avoid death last night. The execution of Two-Bits was all over the news. But the headlines weren't reading home invasion or gangland murder—the large body count of Russian nationals littering the street had pretty much destroyed that option.

Steel walked past blackened and blistered walls, fervently hoping that his safe had survived the blast. If the Russians were trying to kill him, five hundred thousand dollars would make for some nice "walking around" money. Because the more he thought about it, the fact that Sasha and Lexi's buddies were taking dirt naps didn't bode well for his future.

He wasn't sure which was worse—the dead Russians, or that somehow Barry and Nails were *not* among the deceased. Instead of taking the fall, the Dynamic Duo had managed to pull off the execution and take out an entire KGB death squad.

Maybe he'd underestimated those guys.

Maybe. But that kind of logic was hard to swallow.

When he reached his private office he almost lost his breakfast. The safe door was wide open and bits of charred money were scattered amongst the debris. He dropped to his knees and covered his mouth. *Five hundred grand!* He tried to keep from puking, but wasn't successful. Officer Leary had the grace to avert his gaze.

Those bastards!

Steel wiped the back of his mouth on his sleeve. There was no way Lexi would blow up that much cash. So it had to be Black. Only a do-gooder putz would do something so stupid.

No. Wait! That's just what Sasha and Lexi want you to think! There wasn't five hundred grand worth of burnt bills lying around. They probably kept the rest and had blown up a token amount to avert suspicion. Smart!

Steel shook his head. He'd have to figure out a way to outfox the foxes. But first things first, leverage on Mr. Black. It was time to see if his Russian "friends" would follow through with Sierra Rodriguez. That could be a good start to getting things back on track.

Steel heard a chuckle from the officer standing next to him. Leary picked up a blackened sliver of a hundred dollar bill and tapped on the face of Benjamin Franklin. "Looks likes you'll be joining me in the deepest level of hell, am I right?"

Steel just stared, pulled his PDA from his pocket, and jotted down the peon's badge number.

SIERRA STOOD BEHIND TERRY AND WATCHED AS HER RED-HAIRED cameraman got some great footage of the destruction. *Wow.*

"This election just keeps getting better and better." Terry panned his camera across the police cars, then tilted it up toward Steel's office. "This is great stuff, Sierra. If you nail this interview with Steel, you'll be going straight to the top, baby. No candidate interview ever had bomb footage for the B-roll material."

Sierra frowned. She should have felt elated, but instead she worried about John. The situation seemed to be escalating out of control. The identities of the men outside Two-Bits' house had just been reported. And they weren't merely diplomats for a small province in Russia—they were ex-KGB. Bombs, assassinations, KGB—where would it end?

For some reason, John was worried about her, when he should have been worrying about himself. She started back toward the news van but stopped when she noticed a heavy-set man in an expensive suit leaning against the brick wall of a Laundromat. She backed away, noting his thick bushy eyebrows, and her mind immediately jumped to KGB. She was ready to call 9-1-1 when the man closed his cell phone and walked away.

Sierra let out the breath she'd been holding. Maybe she should be worried.

She jumped when her BlackBerry vibrated, then snatched it from her purse, attempting to get her overactive mind back to business. She scrolled through a message from her boss that said: "Due to damage at Steel's office, interview moved to Luigi's—one block to the south." Sierra looked down the street and spotted the restaurant, then glanced at her watch. "Let's go, Terry. We've only got five minutes to set up the lighting."

JOHN TURNED HIS ATTENTION FROM THE ROAD AND BACK TO HIS NOTES, doing his best to ignore Hillary and Amber's discussion about the abs of a cute guy from school, but also trying not to dwell on Eleanor lying in the hospital. At least Hillary and Amber seemed safe now that he was the primary target. Hopefully, Sierra was exercising caution as well.

His mother poured a finger of single malt scotch, then rapped her knuckles on the side window of the limo. "Girls, keep it down. Give your uncle a chance to learn his speech."

"Sorry, Uncle John," said Hillary.

"Me, too," Amber said. "We shouldn't distract you from your speech. How else will you drive another stake through Steel's heart? That debate was so sweet!"

John said, "I shouldn't be doing this speech, Mother. We've applied pressure to Steel as much as possible with verbal jousting, but it might not be enough. We've got to push till he breaks."

"Don't be silly, you are pushing. Our internal polling has you ahead by one point. It's within the margin of error, but you're still ahead. And the way you pressure rich people is to threaten to take away what's important to them—their money and power. For Steel, every speech you make is another shove toward the edge of a cliff."

"I prefer the old fashioned way. Pictures of misdeeds, logbooks with incriminating notes, witnesses that'll testify against them. That sort of thing. This politics stuff is nasty."

His mother barked with laughter. "That's what makes it fun. And that's why your sister and I like it so much."

"Well, you guys can keep it. Our seven-thirty with the lobbyist made my stomach turn. Guy's a snake oil salesman."

"Of course he is. But it's just for show, John. You're not committing to anything. You and I both know you won't take graft from those vultures, but the last thing you want is for Big Industry to unite against you to keep you from office. And if they don't think you can be bought, we're sunk."

"I know, I know," John growled. "But I don't have to like it."

"If you did, I'd think aliens had put an imposter in your place."

Amber said, "Can I have one of those 'John imposters'? You know what I'd like to do with him? Here's a hint, John—it involves a spanking."

Hillary laughed but rolled her eyes. "Now there's a picture."

Ignoring Amber, John turned toward his mother and said, "Anything good in those files I gave you?"

"You mean the files that were blown clear from Steel's office and miraculously landed at your feet, even though you were miles away?"

John smiled. "Yeah. Those files."

"Unfortunately, no. As I told you, most politicians are pretty good about keeping their tracks covered. I'm still looking, but I'm not very hopeful. Maybe you'll find something on the videotape."

"I don't know. Most of it is too far gone. Right now the only complete parts haven't turned up anything useful. But we might work a different angle, even if we don't get any solid evidence. Maybe we can bluff, show him some hidden camera footage. With any luck, he'll be worried about what's on the rest of the tape."

"I know I would."

"Look, Mother, so far all we've got is a bad tape and some reluctant witnesses with criminal connections to Steel. Witnesses who may or may not be helpful in a court of law. I need more time to work the case. I need less time spent on these speeches."

"All right. While you're giving the next speech, I'll make some calls and see if I can free up some time for this afternoon. Will that work?"

John looked out the window as the car pulled to a stop. "It's a start."

SIERRA FUMED. IN ONE SENSE, THE INTERVIEW WAS GOING WELL. THE story would go national for sure.

But on the other hand, Steel was coming off like a saint. His "I'm the victim" slant was working great and might swing the vote back a percentage point or two.

So far, the only good part of the interview had been a flitting reaction from Steel when she'd mentioned John's name. The facial tic was enough to show that John was getting under his skin, but was too quick to make good television. Then again, maybe they could slow it down in editing.

"You have to wonder," Steel said, sporting a charming smile, "just why the establishment doesn't want me to be Governor of California. I think they're running scared. Scared of a man who'll take them to task and grind out the corruption that's filling politics today."

Sierra barely retained control of her facial expression, keeping it neutral instead of gagging on the pure nonsense being spewed. She gave Terry the cutoff gesture, and he switched off the camera and the nearest light.

Steel rose to his feet. "Thank you, Ms. Rodriguez. That was a delightful interview. Maybe we can do a more... in-depth...interview later."

Oh, God. Is he making a pass at me? "That would be nice, Mr. Steel. Have your people talk to my people and we'll set it up."

They shook hands, and Sierra had an immediate urge to wash hers. Instead, she switched off her microphone and started wrapping the cable while Terry put the small lighting kit back in its case.

Harsh words caught her attention, and Sierra turned toward the back of the restaurant where Steel was having a heated discussion with a couple of heavyset men with bushy eyebrows and expensive suits.

She covered her mouth with her hand. Either one of them could've been twins with the man outside. Worse, she recognized them—Sasha and Lexi Khrushchev. Mafia *and* KGB. *And* pharmaceuticals. A trifecta.

Oh, great. John had told her to meet Steel in a public place, but he probably didn't have the Russians' restaurant in mind when he said that. What should she do?

She could picture a gun pointed squarely between her shoulder blades.

Calm down, calm down. They can't shoot you with witnesses around.

She glanced around the restaurant and noticed that the few patrons there seemed to be from the same heavyset, bushy eyebrow family.

Not good. But at least there's Terry.

She turned to find Terry walking toward the back of the restaurant. "Terry! What are you doing?"

Terry stopped. "I've gotta take a leak."

"No! You can't."

Terry's brow furrowed. "What?"

She ran over to him. "Please. We have to get the tape to the station. It's only ten minutes away."

"Are you kidding? I can't take a leak?"

She pointed at the bushy-eyed men. "Please. Let's go."

"Yeah, okay."

He grabbed the camera and the lighting case and walked toward the front door. Sierra followed right behind him, sticking as close as possible. Too close—she bumped into him, prompting a grimace and some harsh words under his breath. She backed off a half step but still kept right behind him. As she exited the door, she snuck a glance back at the gruesome trio of Steel and the Russians.

They seemed unhappy.

Sierra smiled as she hit the sunlight, then glanced around for the Russian who had been loitering near the van. He was not in sight.

A half block later, Terry opened the van doors and put the equipment away. Sierra put some cables in the van and paused, wishing she hadn't driven her own car today. "Would you mind waiting for me, Terry? I'm kind of jumpy today."

"No problem." Terry closed the back door of the van and leaned against it. "I'll stay put till you give me the high sign."

"Thanks."

She walked a couple of car lengths back to her Buick, her gaze darting all around, but there was no sign of anyone. She pressed the remote that unlocked the doors, then remembered a couple of bad horror movies and checked the backseat before climbing inside. But there was nothing there.

She shook her head and laughed. *Paranoid. You're getting as bad as Steel.* She turned the key and shifted into drive, waving at Terry as she went by. She locked the doors and relaxed.

At the next stoplight, she heard a thump from the backseat. Her heart raced as she turned to find the rear seat folding down, exposing the trunk, as well as a heavyset Russian who poked his head out.

She gave a scream as the man pointed a gun at her.

His brows met together to form one long, giant caterpillar crawling across his forehead. "You will please to be turning left at next light," he said, his heavy accent making him hard to understand. "And no more of the noises, okay? Or I will be forced to make you quiet."

thirty-three

THEY *want me dead.* Steel shuddered, picturing a bull's-eye painted on his back as he fingered the leather strap of his shoulder holster.

There was no other explanation. Why else would the Russians want him here when they brought the kidnapped reporter to their warehouse? They knew he couldn't stomach that kind of thing.

Because the bomb in his office had gone off too early. That had to be it.

Thank God he'd brought his gun.

It was the first time he'd ever carried. Sure, he kept one in the nightstand like every other Los Angelino smart enough to realize what kind of world they lived in, but this was the first time he had one strapped to his chest. The weight was oddly comforting.

Of course, they hadn't said they wanted to kill him. And everyone acted like they were his buddies. *But since when do Mafia guys ever give you advance warning they're going to kill you?*

He paced the warehouse floor, stepping around the Russians who always seemed to be underfoot. There were only a half dozen of them, along with Sasha and Lexi, milling about or seated at a card table backed against a stack of crates. But it felt as though he was surrounded.

Lexi said, "Steel, stop moving about. You make me nervous."

"Da," Sasha said. "Girl will be here any moment. Make still your body or I will make it still for you."

Steel squinted. *I bet you would, you sonofabitch!* "Yeah, sure. No problem." He fidgeted for a minute before heading toward the lone office in the giant building. "I've got to take a leak."

"Thank you for sharing," Lexi said. "We all appreciate this intimate knowledge."

Steel closed the office door behind him, wishing there was an exterior exit but knowing there wasn't. He stepped into the bathroom, keeping the light off and the door cracked so he could see if anyone came in. With trembling hands, he whipped out his phone and dialed Barry's phone. For the fifth time this morning.

Damn it. Where the hell are these guys? He needed an ace up his sleeve! An hour ago he'd had the unpleasant thought that once the Russians picked up the girl, it was game over. That they might think they had enough leverage against Black they wouldn't need Steel anymore. After all, how many gubernatorial candidates did you need in your back pocket?

But if Barry and Nails were able to take out an entire KGB hit squad, he might be able to turn this thing back to his advantage.

Damn. Voicemail. Again.

He cursed up a storm, waiting for the beep, then took a couple of deep breaths and peeked through the crack in the doorway. "Barry, I don't know where you guys are but I'm running out of time here. So listen up and do exactly as I say. If you do this right, not only are we square, but you and Nails have got two hundred thousand coming your way. I need your pal, Sparky, and I need your cousin's junkyard. And I need you to rig this place to blow. Here's what I want you to do..."

"Crap, Nails. You're bleeding all over the cards."

Nails grunted and leaned back against the cement wall, pressing a bandage against his arm. "Don't get me started."

"Why not?" Barry wiped the queen of hearts on his pants, slid the card into his hand, then dropped a reject on the pile. "You should kill those rat bastards. I can't believe they're doing experiments on you. That's gotta be illegal."

Sparky picked up a card and grinned. "I got Gin."

Growling, Barry tossed his cards onto the little table. "You got the luck of the devil, you know that?"

Sparky gestured at the cell bars. "You're kidding, right?"

From his workstation, Harley shouted, "I told you guys to pipe down."

Barry rose from the cot and ambled toward the bars. "Sorry, old man. We're just bored out of our minds in here."

"Get used to it," Harley rasped.

Barry felt his whole body tremble. "No way. You never get used to it. And I don't wanna go back. Ever. There's gotta be something we can work out here."

He waited for an answer, but the creepy old man kept silent. It figured. Seemed like everywhere he went, everything he did, he was at the whim of someone with more power than he had.

There was a series of beeps from a cell phone on the counter. Harley broke away from his computer and picked up the phone. "This yours?"

Barry nodded, happy to keep things friendly.

"Then who keeps trying to reach you?" Harley showed Barry the caller's number.

"That's Steel. His private cell number."

Harley grinned. "He left a message. What a sociable bloke."

Barry shivered. The words were friendly enough, but the glint in the old man's eye was downright scary.

SIERRA STRAINED AT HER ROPES, BUT THEY DIDN'T BUDGE. SHE'D BEEN bouncing around in her own backseat for the last hour, feeling scared and sorry for herself, and the only thing she'd managed to do was move her blindfold up a quarter of an inch.

At last the road sounds changed as the tires rolled onto a smoother surface.

Finally. We can get this over with.

She gulped, realizing the implications of arriving at the intended destination.

There was a screeching sound from the tires that echoed

as the car came to a stop. She shook her head. Better pay attention.

All right. The echo means we're inside a building—a big build-ing—with a smooth surface. Probably a warehouse.

The car door opened and large, rough hands hauled her from the car and marched her across the floor. With her blind-fold raised up the tiniest bit, she could make out items that were at her feet. Big wooden crates and a smooth concrete floor. The echo was pronounced—definitely a warehouse.

She saw the wooden chair a half-second before the Russian behemoth shoved her into it.

"Don't move, girly."

"Okay."

She felt a thump on her head and winced.

"And don't talk or I make you quiet."

She kept silent and waited, tapping her heels together. *There's no place like home. There's no place like home.*

Eventually, shoes entered her field of vision. Lots of scuffed black shoes that seemed like they were all identical. As the footwear shuffled around, they appeared to interact with each other and mill about—as if they were guests at a conven-tion, making small talk. She almost laughed. Was she getting hysterical?

Then one pair of shoes, finely polished, stepped closest to her. Were these from the leader? Or the lonely nerd of the party?

A thick Russian accent came from her right, and not from the owner of the polished shoes. "Yuri, take off her blind-fold."

No. Don't give them an excuse to kill you. "You don't need to do that. I don't want to see who you are."

Again she felt a whack on the back of her head.

"No one speak to you yet, so be quiet."

"Maybe she's right. Why do you want to let her see our faces?"

That time it was the polished shoes talking. And it was Steel. No doubt in her mind.

"Because, Ms. Rodriguez is very intelligent woman. I am

sure she already knows who she is dealing with. Your voice, right now, very famous. And for us, I think our accents might be big clue."

With those words light blossomed as the blindfold was lifted. But her spirits dimmed at the sight. Tied up, coming face to face with the Russian Mafia, pushed any happy thoughts to the background.

"Besides," Lexi said. "*If* she leaves here alive, there's no reason for her to think we can't make her dead at any point in the future. And *if* she is not intelligent as we think and she try to finger us anyway, I am sure she understands we have witnesses saying we never here."

If?

Sierra looked at the big Russians surrounding her and settled her gaze on Steel. "You putz. Is this how you'd run California?"

Sasha wheezed and slapped his knee. "See. She very intelligent. She interview you one time and already know you are big putz."

"Hey," Steel said. "I think you should tone it down, comrade."

"Quiet, putz." Sasha shifted his weight, as though he was going to launch himself toward Steel, who immediately raised his hands in mock surrender.

Now that's interesting. The Russians are in charge.

"Okay," Lexi said. "Enough small talk. We require for you to call boyfriend, Mr. Black, and inform him of our demands."

Sierra held back a laugh. John—her boyfriend? Not that she hadn't thought about it. "I'm afraid you've been ill informed, Mr. Khrushchev. My relationship with John Black is professional, not personal."

Sierra frowned as Steel started fidgeting.

Lexi leaned in close enough for her to smell the borscht on his breath. "Please not to be lying. My brother is very impatient man."

Sierra stammered, "I...I'm sorry. I don't know where you got that information, but it's wrong."

Sasha's face darkened and he growled. Lexi gave Steel a questioning glance.

Steel cleared his throat a couple of times. "She's lying," he said. "I have a source who videotaped them together. He's positive they're an item."

Sierra racked her brain, trying to figure out where this was coming from, until it hit her like a ton of bricks. That sonofabitch Gil. Conspiring with Steel.

"And you believed him?" she asked. "Lying comes as naturally to my ex as any other politician, present company included. Plus, Gil would do just about anything to screw me over."

Steel's jaw dropped, showing she'd scored a direct hit.

Lexi scowled. "Is this Gil your source?"

Steel remained silent. Sasha glowered at Steel and pulled out a silencer, snarling in Russian as he married the silencer to his gun. Lexi moved in front of Sasha, exchanging harsh words with his brother in their native tongue.

With a sigh, Sierra took a deep breath, happy to have the focus on someone else. Steel looked ready to faint, the poor bastard.

After a few tense moments, Lexi nodded, bringing a smile to Sasha's face and a look of alarm to Steel's.

Sierra's eyes widened. *Oh my god. They're going to kill him right in front me!*

Lexi said, "I'm sorry you and I could not come to arrangement, Ms. Rodriguez."

He gestured to Yuri, who immediately brought out his own silencer and approached Sierra.

Oh my god. They're going to kill ME!

Sasha advanced toward Steel, prompting a shout from the politician, "*Sierra!* Tell them the truth!"

Sierra groaned. *I'm going to die.*

She snapped to attention, trying to think of a way out. "Okay, okay. There's more to the John story than I've told you."

Lexi held out his hand and Yuri stopped cold. His brother kept moving until Lexi yelled out, "Sasha! Wait a moment."

Sasha grimaced but held fast.

Lexi said, "Please, Ms. Rodriguez. Don't tell me you were lying about Mr. Black. That would be problem because I believed you first time."

"Of course not. I was telling the truth, but I didn't really give you the whole story."

Lexi arched one of his caterpillar eyebrows. "Yes?"

Thinking fast, she said, "John and I are definitely into each other. We haven't acted on it during the campaign, but he has very strong feelings toward me. He'll definitely bargain with you to keep me alive."

Steel piped in, "See? I wasn't lying."

Lexi said, "And why should I be believing either of you?"

"Let's call him. He's on speed-dial number eight on my cell. The phone is in my purse on the front seat."

Lexi's brows crinkled. "Yuri? You left cell phone in car?"

Steel shook his head. "And you guys call me a putz. At least I know they've got GPS on cell phones nowadays."

Sasha glowered at Steel but headed for the car. "We must hurry and make call. Then we dump cell phone far from this place."

Lexi smiled at Sierra. "I hope, for your sake, that he wants keep you alive."

JOHN STRODE INTO THE BUNKER, IGNORING THE CARD GAME IN THE cell, and approached Harley at the computer station. He perused the screen as Harley paused the video from Steel's office.

"Did our geniuses manage to tape anything useful?" John asked.

"Probably. But there's not much left. A few tantalizing bits and pieces, but any of the really good stuff has been destroyed."

"Then why were you so excited on the phone?"

Harley grinned. "Because Steel wants our boys' help to double-cross the Russians. And I know where and when he's gonna do it."

John pumped his fist in the air. "Show me."

Harley went to another file on the computer and hit the "play audio" button. "I got this from Barry's cell phone about twenty minutes ago."

John listened to the first part about needing Sparky and his bombs at the junkyard. In the cell, the boys edged toward the door and listened, too.

Steel continued, "I didn't want to do this over the phone but you guys aren't answering. *Why* aren't you answering? I know you're not dead because the Russians are plenty pissed that you got away from their hit squad. I want you to know that I had nothing to do with that mess. It's all Russians. And now they want me dead, too."

Barry snickered. "Serves him right. No one is buying his line of crap anymore."

John shushed him.

Steel said, "I have to tell you I'm pretty impressed that you got away. Ex-KGB guys are tough. But if you do what I'm telling you and we work together, you're gonna walk away from this nasty situation. I guarantee it."

Harley switched off the audio playback.

"Like his guarantee means anything," Barry said. "Why should we help him?"

Nails grunted. "Because the Russians want us dead."

John listened to the exchange, trying to think up a good way to use the cellmates. To his dismay, an old Wham! song rang from his pocket. He snapped the phone open, silencing the song.

Sierra was on the other end. But she sounded far away, or maybe on a speaker phone. "Honey…"

John scratched the back of his neck. *Honey?*

"Are you there, honey? I've got a problem and I need your help."

"Sure…sweetie. What's the problem?"

He heard a small scream that got cut off quick. He gripped the phone tight.

A deep, muffled voice, speaking heavily accented English, came on the line. "Mr. Black? We have proposition for you."

John put the phone on speaker and placed it on the table, motioning for Harley to start recording. "Is this Mr. Khrushchev?"

"Don't take me for stupid man, Mr. Black. Do I need to grab your interest by doing something unpleasant to your girlfriend?"

Girlfriend? "No. You have my complete attention."

"Good. We require your immediate withdrawal from governor race. Or bad things will happen."

Shit. John grabbed a pad and pencil and started scribbling.

"Mr. Black? You still there?"

"Yes. I'm thinking over your proposition."

John angled the pad toward Harley: *We need to set up a meeting with these guys. Do the exchange in person.*

"Don't think too long, Mr. Black. This is one time deal. Expires in thirty seconds."

Harley showed John his note: *Junkyard?* He pointed at Barry, Nails, and Sparky. John nodded.

The Russian continued, "You disappoint. I'm sorry we could not do business together."

Over the speaker, John heard the sound of a gun chambering a round. "Take it easy. I'm on board. But I need Sierra before I'm willing to bow out."

"There you go, thinking I'm stupid. Again."

"Right back at you," John said. "I'm not stupid, either. We need a neutral exchange or this isn't going to work."

"No. Too risky. You are in position to demand nothing. Goodbye, Mr. Black."

John was going to jump in, but was beaten by a new voice on the other end. One without a Russian accent. It was muffled, too, but he was almost certain it was Steel.

After something incomprehensible, John heard, "How about a junkyard in Sun Valley?"

It was Steel all right, trying to screw over the Russians. *How appropriate.* John said, "A junkyard works for me. Walls of cars will keep out any prying eyes."

Muffled, heated whispering could be heard.

John said, "I'm scheduled for a press conference in ninety minutes, right near Sun Valley. I can make a statement to the press, but before that I'll bring you a notarized statement resigning from the race and I'll even bring a video camera. We can tape my withdrawal so you guys will have it official when we do the exchange. Then you hand over Sierra and we'll have completed a successful transaction."

"We reject your counteroffer, Mr. Black. We have other options we will pursue."

Steel said, "But I like the offer."

Another Russian voice growled, "Shut up, putz."

"Shit. We're losing her." John covered the mouthpiece and whispered to Harley, "Cue up some dialogue from the video-tape. The best you've got."

He took his hand off the phone and said, "It's your loss, Mr. Khrushchev. Because I've got something that would have sweetened the deal."

Harley hit the play button on the computer screen and Lexi's thick, Russian accent played over the speakers. "Yes. And when time comes, it is big boom for idiots who cause problems. End of story."

On the recording, Steel's voice answered, snickering. "They actually left the car in your care? God those guys are dumb."

Listening in, Barry and Nails seemed to be getting agitated. John snapped his fingers a couple of times and shushed them. Harley switched off the playback and John turned his attention back to the phone. "Sound familiar? Do I have your attention? Or do I need to do something *unpleasant* to grab your interest?"

Silence, followed by heated whispering. Finally, "Where you find such tape?"

"Would you believe this loose spaghetti of a videotape fell from the sky? Shortly after the explosion in Steel's office?"

"*Nyet.*" Another long silence. "But if you will bring tape to exchange, along with resignation papers, then we have deal. Hey, putz, give Black location of junkyard."

"Neville's Auto Parts in Sun Valley."

The grumpy Russian growled again. "One hour, Black. Then we start cutting."

There was a click as the line went dead.

John grabbed his phone and shoved it in his pocket, then paced the length of the room. "An hour's not enough time to set the place up. They'll probably have a lot of men."

"At least eight, including Sasha and Lexi," Nails said. "Maybe more."

John looked up, noticing the information had been freely offered—like they wanted to help. John glanced at Harley, who nodded his approval.

John said, "All right, guys. Here's how it's going to be. The intel you gave me on Steel's office was legit, so you've got my promise that I'll ask the prosecutor for leniency. That was our deal. But I'll go you one better. If you guys help me save Sierra's life, I'll let you go."

Nails looked skeptical, Barry hopeful, and Sparky was just plain excited.

John continued, "Temporarily, of course. You've killed people so I can't let you go scot-free. But if you help me save one life, you get to walk out of that junkyard on your own. I'll give you a two day head start before I come after you. And who knows, maybe you'll get lucky and manage to stay free."

Barry and Nails looked at each other. Barry whispered, "I believe him."

Nails shook his head and looked down at the tire patches on his bleeding arm. "I can't believe I'm saying this, but I do too. And it might give me a shot at some of the bastards responsible for experimenting on me."

"You guys in?" John asked.

Barry nodded, grinning like a fool.

Sparky piped up, adding, "I've already got some bombs set up for my Bondage Barbie flick that I'm working on."

John blinked. "Are you serious?"

Sparky giggled like a schoolgirl, then nodded his head.

Harley snorted. "Atta boy, Sparky. You just became my new best mate."

thirty-four

TWENTY minutes later, John and Harley followed Barry, Nails, and Sparky down a meandering path that led away from the west gate of Neville's Auto Parts. Each man carried a red, gallon-sized container full of gasoline and had various weapons slung over their shoulders—taken from Harley's bunker.

John checked the battery level on his video camera—full power—then put it back in its case and looked up at the towering walls of smashed cars on both sides. It was like walking down the Grand Canyon of junkyards. Majestic, if not for the waste of resources.

Harley leaned in and whispered, "You really going to drop out of the race, John? When that's just what Steel and the Russian Mafia want?"

"Not if I don't have to. But if that's what it takes to keep Sierra alive, then you bet. I'm not going to throw away someone's life to help my sister get elected governor."

Sparky stopped at a small clearing. "This is the spot."

John surveyed the area. A couple of other aisles snaked away from the clearing, leaving a couple of exits if things turned sour and the Russians got nasty. *Not bad.* A few straggler cars were lying about, giving a fair amount of cover if necessary. Harley scanned the skyline, no doubt looking for sniper positions.

"All right," John said. "Which cars do you have rigged? We don't have much time before they get here."

Sparky pointed at various spots surrounding the clearing. "Trunk of the 'Vette, front tire of the Torino, hood of the Cougar, bumper of the Mustang, and the whole dang microbus—they're all rigged to blow. If you each take a car, we can have these set up in two minutes. Just pour in your container of gas and connect the loose black wire to the black metal nub on the device."

"Whoa, whoa, whoa," said Barry. "I don't wanna be connecting no wires. That's insane."

Sparky laughed. "Don't worry. Nothing can blow until I rig it to the battery. And I won't do that until everyone is clear."

Harley said, "Where's the other end of the wires? Your center of operations?"

Sparky pointed to a junker ten feet away.

"No good. That's too close." Harley pointed up toward the top of a tower of cars. "Extend your line to the trunk of that Caddy up there. That's where you and I will hide out."

Sparky nodded and handed his gas can to Nails, then ran toward the junker.

John pointed to a straggler Skylark, sitting across from the microbus that was loaded for bear. "I'll wait there for the Russians. That'll leave them the microbus as the logical place for their position. Just where we want them."

Harley nodded. "Good idea. Unless your position is too close to the microbus." He yelled out, "Sparky! Is this Skylark too close to the big one?"

Sparky looked up from his wiring. "Should be all right."

Harley and John looked at each other.

John said, "Not very reassuring."

"No." Harley looked down the aisle between the cars. "We want to make sure they come down the same path we did."

"No problem," John said. "We'll text message Steel from Barry's cell phone. After we get set up."

Harley clapped a hand on Barry's shoulder and pointed out spots on each of the other pathways through the cars. "After you fill your bomb with gasoline, I want you each to take one of these roads to yourself. Hide behind the third car down your aisle."

Barry piped up, "Hey, why don't we get a lofty perch to shoot from? You got one."

"Don't forget I've seen you shoot, mate. At the cemetery."

Barry reddened.

Harley continued, "You need to be closer to your targets in case you have to take a shot. That's why you stay down here."

"The main thing," John said, "is saving Sierra's life. So don't shoot unless you get the signal from Harley or me. And you won't get the signal unless things turn to shit."

Nails grunted. "What do you mean? We aren't going to take these guys out? It's a perfect setup."

"We don't kill people unless we have to, Nails. It's a radical idea, to be sure, but one I live by." John patted his video camera. "This baby will record the whole thing. That's all we'll need to put them away. So we won't have to kill them if they play it straight."

Nails growled, "They don't play straight. Or haven't you noticed that?"

"If they don't...then they don't. That's where you'll come in. You're the safety net for this show. But if they do, and I hope to God they do so Sierra and I aren't in the middle of a firefight, they'll be rounded up by the police later today."

Nails grumbled, but kept quiet as he stalked away and worked on filling his bombs with gasoline. John thought he heard him mumble "naïve cracker" under his breath, but chose to ignore it.

"Okay, Barry," John said. "Let's send a text message to Steel, then get these bombs ready."

STEEL SAT IN THE BACK OF A BLACK VAN, ON THE METAL FLOOR, bemoaning his sorry state. That it had come to this—riding in a cargo van instead of his precious limousine, next to a trussed up kidnap victim, half a million poorer after his office exploded, and on his way to his own execution at the hands of the Russian Mafia—the notion seemed beyond impossible. *And* he wouldn't be governor.

Yuri snickered with his Russian buddy, as though he was aware of Steel's distress.

Steel grimaced. *Where the fuck are Barry and Nails?*

His hands were sweating like crazy. He had his gun, but there was no way he could take out all these guys, even if he wanted to try.

His phone vibrated, alerting him to an incoming message. The IM was from Barry, and he about peed himself he was so excited.

The message said: "Everything is set up. Come in west entrance. Stop Sasha and Lexi at light blue microbus. When things get nasty, run away from microbus! Fast! How far are you now?"

Fingers trembling, Steel dropped the phone into his lap and messaged back, trying to keep it casual so Yuri wouldn't notice. "Be there in three minutes. Blow bus when I shout Bug-a-boo."

He had to fight hard to keep the grin from his face. It wouldn't do to show his enthusiasm. He wasn't going to die! And he *would* be governor after all!

Now, if he could just get his half a million back, he'd be in business.

Lexi turned from the front seat of the cargo van. "Yuri, did you make sure jamming device working?"

"Yes, boss."

"Good. Turn it on as soon as we arrive at junkyard."

Barry's hip started vibrating like a rattlesnake was tied around his waist, and he nearly dropped the gasoline can on top of the detonator. *Darned vibrate mode!* He read the message on his cell phone and felt his pulse quicken. He yelled out, "They're right on top of us. Three minutes. Tops. And he wants us to blow the cars on Bug-a-boo."

Harley yelled back, "Hide your gas cans and get in position."

Barry heard Harley's voice shouting from above. He turned to look, and sure enough the crazy old man was pulling Sparky into the trunk of car that sat on top of a huge pile of cars. *Glad I'm not locked in a trunk with that dude.*

John stalked past him, and he overheard John telling Harley not to blow on Steel's command, but to wait for John's command. *Bug-a-boo? What kind of word is that?*

Barry started toward his hiding spot, but stopped when he caught sight of Nails waving him over. He crossed the clearing and headed down the aisle with his partner.

Nails clapped a meaty paw on his shoulder and pulled him closer. "We're not letting them walk away."

"What are you talking about? Steel? They're gonna put him behind bars after we get through this thing and rescue the girl."

"Don't be stupid. There's no way Steel, or the Russians, will play it straight. So we need a preemptive strike."

"Whoa. Think about what you're saying. You want to shoot at the Russians? We'll be dead meat for sure."

"We're dead if any of them get away, too. Either way, they'll be coming after us. You think the two-day head start Black is giving us will help with that? The odds will go up if we shoot first."

JOHN WATCHED THE DISTANT CONVERSATION BETWEEN BARRY AND Nails, then keyed his headset and whispered, "Harley. Our boys are up to something."

"Crikey. That's the last thing we need. Want me to put a bullet in 'em right now?"

"No. If things get ugly, we'll need the extra guns. Just keep an eye on them."

"Two eyes. The rat bastards."

"Is Sparky ready?"

"Close. He's still wiring away. And it's getting hot as Australia in the winter in this trunk. Another ten minutes, Sparky and I will be having ourselves a sauna." Harley paused. "They're here, John. Two black cargo vans coming through the gate."

John shouted, "Barry, they're here! Get back in position."

Looking around, John spotted one last gas can out in the open. He raced over, scooped it up, and flung it out of sight. Moving next to the Skylark, he pushed the record button on the video camera and tucked it behind hubcaps they'd piled up for camouflage.

A dark shape came whizzing toward his head, falling from the sky, and John had to jump to the right. A Barbie doll that looked like it had been to hell and back landed at his feet.

Sparky's voice rasped over his radio, "Sorry, John. I guess Bondage Barbie wants to see the action up close, huh?"

"Whatever floats your boat, Sparky. Now shut up and get back to work."

He backed against the Skylark's door and waited, watching Barry slink over to his position—looking like a dog that had done something wrong. John heard the crunch of tires on gravel as the first van rolled into view.

He casually keyed his microphone. "Harley? Is Nails still in position? Barry is looking awfully guilty."

"Yeah, mate. Don't worry about Nails. Worry about the Russian Mafia. And maybe Sparky. He's only got three out of five cars completely rigged. If you can stall the Russians for a couple of minutes, it would help."

John took a deep breath. And waited.

The first van pulled to a stop. Doors flew open and half a dozen burly men, wearing coats that were far too hot for summer in the valley, exited and spread out. No Sierra.

And no Steel. The only one he recognized was Sasha, the nastier of the two Russian brothers.

His earpiece clicked, and Harley's voice whispered, "Don't worry, mate. Sierra's in the second van."

Sasha and another Russian stopped across from John, thirty feet away and next to the microbus. *Good.* The other four split up, two each stopping at the aisles between the cars. Stopping directly in front of Nails on one side and Barry on the other.

Even better.

Out of the second van came Lexi and Steel, the latter

looking uncomfortable and nervous as if he wasn't really enjoying the situation. Finally, Sierra marched into view, pushed along by yet another Russian. They stopped with the others by the microbus.

Sierra was blindfolded and her hands were tied, but she seemed unharmed. John breathed a sigh of relief.

Lexi said, "It's good to meet you, Mr. Black. Though circumstance most unfortunate, to be sure."

John held up an envelope. "I have the resignation right here. And the tape. Hand her over and let's get this done."

Lexi smiled. "Let us not be hasty. You have friend nearby? Your white haired partner, perhaps?"

John smiled back. "You know Harley?"

"We've never had the pleasure. But our files tell us that he goes where you go. So your sniper friend must be here somewhere, yes?"

"Yeah. He's around. If everything goes smoothly, you'll never have to meet him."

Lexi shook his head. "No. *Nyet.* Let's show our cards to each other. Make deal go faster."

Sasha pulled his gun and rested it by Sierra's ear.

John heard a click in his earpiece and hesitated, waiting for Harley's response. But all that came across the radio was static.

"Harley?" John started to sweat. *Why static?* Could they have taken out Harley without John knowing about it? That seemed impossible.

Then it hit him. These ex-KGB guys must have some of their spy toys with them. So not only was John's communication cut off, the video was probably no good either.

Shit!

Sasha made an impatient face and cocked his weapon.

John said, "Hey, ease up on the trigger. I'm having a hard time raising my partner on our radio."

Lexi spread his hands. "Very sorry. Jamming device only supposed to affect tape recordings, but it sometimes disturbs other signals as well."

John tried to play it cool. "Jamming device?"

"What can we say? They are necessary evil in this line of business. Maybe you better shout to partner before Sasha loses patience."

"Harley!"

John waited, trying to think of a way to take the Russians down while still keeping Sierra safe. Up above, the trunk kicked open and Harley stood up, showing empty palms.

Lexi grinned. "Dressed in black, he look like vulture waiting for us to die."

John said, "So now you know where he is. You can keep an eye on him but he won't come down from there. Let's do this."

"Okay." Lexi turned toward his comrades. "Sasha, go make exchange. Yuri, you only watch birdman and no other places. Shoot if you see movement."

Sasha led a trembling Sierra toward John, crossing the distance at a rapid clip.

Come on, come on! John kept his gaze moving from Russian to Russian, each step of Sierra's moving her further away from danger. Fifty feet more and she would be out of the worst of it.

John shook his head—the bad guys would still win. They'd get everything they wanted. Keeping Sierra safe was only part of the plan, but it wasn't enough. With no video camera to record the exchange, John tried to think of another way to put Steel and the Russians behind bars. *Any* way! Chances wouldn't get much better than this.

His attention was drawn by Steel as he edged away from Lexi and the microbus. *Oh, yeah. Bug-a-boo. If I let the bus blow, the Russians will think I did it and come after Sierra and me.*

But if I get them fighting amongst themselves...

Ten more steps brought Sierra and the Russian gangster to a halt. John handed Sasha a bulky manila envelope and embraced Sierra. He pulled off her blindfold and gave her a small kiss, acting the part of a boyfriend, then leaned in close and whispered, "If the other shoe drops, dive to the right and take cover behind the car."

Sierra nodded.

John called out, "Hey, Steel. Where are you going?"

Steel froze in place as Lexi turned toward him, brow furrowing. "I like to pace when I get nervous," Steel said. "Is that a crime?"

"You worried your partners are abandoning your joint venture?" John asked.

Lexi scowled and said, "Get back here."

Steel ignored Lexi, taking another couple of steps away from him. "Now why would I think that, John? Just because this whole mess has turned into a *bug-a-boo*?"

At Steel's yelp, the Russians stared at him like he'd just grown a second head.

"Don't get paranoid," John said. "I'm merely thinking out loud, Dick. I don't know, maybe you're worried because they know how to make bombs and someone just tried to kill you."

Lexi said, "Get over here, Steel. Don't listen to Black. We still partners, you and me."

"Maybe Steel doesn't want to be partners, Lexi. Maybe he's got his own explosive plans."

Steel screeched, then shouted, *"Bug-a-boo,"* and ducked down, covering his head with his arms.

Lexi frowned and pulled his gun. "Get up, putz."

Steel looked around and called out, "Bug-a-boo, bug-a-boo!"

Lexi cocked his weapon and said, "What means bug-a-boo?"

As if in answer, four shots rang out, echoing off the canyons of twisted metal. The two Russians near Nails dropped to the ground.

Shit! Nails!

Sasha pulled his weapon and aimed it at John, who raised his hands and said, "It's not me!"

A moment later, the two Russians near Barry were dropped by six shots. As Sasha turned toward Barry's position, John yelled out, "Bug-a-boo," pushed Sierra down, then leapt toward Sasha.

Beetle-browed Russians dove for the cover of the surrounding cars.

Sparky let out a war whoop and blew the first bomb, followed in rapid succession by each of the other four. Bits of Corvette and Torino scattered everywhere, propelled with explosive force. One Russian slumped in the dirt, a ragged fender jutting from his chest. The remaining Russians scurried away from the cars, shooting wildly in every direction, as bits of Barbie dolls rained upon them.

The bottom half of a Barbie hit John in the chest as he barreled into Sasha. John grabbed it, using one hand to shove the Barbie into Sasha's mouth, and the other hand in an attempt to knock the gun from his grasp.

Sasha gagged on the doll, leather-clad legs poking from his mouth, but his grip held firm as he brought the gun around. *Shit!* John picked a secondary target, the elbow near the gun hand, and moved inside.

It was risky, John knew, because in two seconds Sasha's proximity, and his heavy mass, would give him the edge. John worked fast, and in half a second dislocated Sasha's elbow.

The pain loosened Sasha's grip on the gun, but the Russian used his bulk and jumped on top of John. As they tumbled to the ground, John managed to aim the gun, turning it toward Sasha's midsection. They hit the ground with a thud and a bang, John's body pinned beneath the now lifeless Russian. A saliva-covered Barbie, complete with bigger and better battle scars, escaped Sasha's mouth and fell to the ground.

Wriggling, John tried to get free from Sasha's corpse. Several Russian bodies littered the junkyard, but two others were still firing away, hitting anything and everything. A couple of extra rounds went into Sasha's body.

John heard several sharp reports from Harley's rifle, followed by cursing from his Aussie partner. "Steel's hoofing it! Quit messing around, John. Most of the bogeys are lights out, and I'll get the last two buggers I've got pinned down, but Steel's getting away."

John squirmed, slowly making his way free. The ground shook as Nails rumbled past, right through the middle of the firefight, gun in hand and trailing blood behind him. He was followed a moment later by a skittish Barry, coming from the other side.

Two more shots from Harley and everything turned silent.

Three seconds later Sparky started whooping and hollering, jumping up and down in the trunk of the Caddy. Harley climbed down the junked cars and vaulted to the ground as John finally got to his feet.

A low moan came from behind him and John turned to find a wide-eyed Sierra clutching her stomach, a blood stain spreading across her blouse. He rushed to her side. *"No!* Shit!"

Harley slung his rifle over his shoulder. "Stay here with her. I'll go after Steel."

NAILS PASSED THE VANS AND PAUSED. HE COULD SEE A HUNDRED yards from this position, straight to the gate, and Steel was nowhere to be found.

There were only two places he could be—hiding in the vans, or down the only other aisle between the piles of cars. The path curved to the right so Nails couldn't see if Steel was down that way or not.

Not used to running, Nails groaned. His knee was killing him so he tried to pop the cap on his bottle of blue pills. No luck. His hands were too slippery with the blood that always seemed to leak from his skin.

Damn it. There's no way that Pfester bastard walks out of here!

Barry pulled up, stopping right behind him. "Where is he?"

"Open this bottle for me. I'll cover you."

"Yeah, right."

Nails growled and tossed him the bottle. "Now, Barry."

"All right, all right."

Barry shoved his gun in the waistband of his pants and popped the top, cringing at the sight of blood. Nails scarfed down all the remaining pills, chewing 'em up.

"You shouldn't take so many. Those things will kill ya."

Nails looked at his blood-streaked limbs. "No shit. You check the vans. I'll search this aisle."

"All right." Barry pulled his gun and put a hand on the first van's door.

Nails took off, wincing at the pain, but pushing his pace as fast as possible. It wasn't long before he hit a straightaway the length of a football field, and no sign of Steel. He hadn't passed any other pathways, either.

So where is he?

The tall fence was to Nails' left, with a pile of cars leading up to it, stair-stepped like a pyramid. *Would he try to go over the fence?*

A scuffling noise from the top of the pile of cars made the decision easier.

Nails started climbing the giant stairs, one crushed car at a time. He was a couple of cars from the top when Steel stood up, revealing his position on the top car.

"Hey, Nails. You were great with the bomb thing. Good job. I didn't even mind having to wait for the blast. Probably a technical glitch, right?"

Nails kept silent and moved up to the next car as he watched Steel put a fake smile in place.

"Can you give me a hand, Nails? I want to get over this fence."

Nails grunted and moved up to the top car, a grim expression on his face.

Steel, apparently sensing trouble, backed up to the other end of the car, about twenty feet from Nails.

"What's the problem, Nails? Hey, don't you want the money I owe you?"

From the bottom of the pyramid, Barry called out, "Heck, yeah. I want it! What are you doing, Nails?"

Nails ignored Barry. "Take a look at my skin," he said to Steel. "You notice anything unusual?"

Steel looked at the blood and tire patches, flinching. "Frankly, you look like shit."

"That's right." Nails took two steps closer. "I do. I'm a walking dead man."

"Use some of the money I owe you to get fixed up. I know some great doctors."

Nails clenched his fists. "The day I meet another Pfester doctor is the day I go on a killing spree."

"I've got nothing to do with Pfester any more." Panic etched Steel's voice as he backed up to the edge of a forty foot drop. "Barry, come talk some sense into your partner. He's going nuts."

Barry started scrambling up the cars.

Nails took two more steps, up onto the crushed white roof. "You don't like what I've become? I've done some bad things in my life—but before two weeks ago I'd never killed anybody. Now I'm a pro."

Steel put on his most charming smile. "I know we've had some bad times, Nails, but I'll be elected governor in two days. Surely we can work something out. Whatever you want—it's yours!"

Nails paused, two arm lengths away from Steel. "I want my life back!"

Steel opened his mouth to speak, but nothing came out.

"But since you can't do that," Nails continued, "I want *your* life."

Steel yelped and tried to draw his gun as Nails bullrushed him. One step from Steel, Nails slipped in his blood and hit the deck of the car. Grabbing Steel's left ankle, Nails' momentum carried them off the edge of the car.

Barry reached the top car in time to see Nails and Steel go flying out into space before dropping like stones. He heard Steel's yell come to an abrupt halt as he hit the ground. Barry raced to the edge and peered over the side, cringing at the sight below.

It must've been the drugs and the thin skin, 'cause it looked like Nails had been dropped from a skyscraper instead of forty feet.

Barry tried not to hurl. For some reason, his mind raced

back to the first kill—Nails lifting Odie over the edge of the balcony. It was like things had come full circle.

Like...poetic justice or something.

Barry jumped when Harley knelt next to him. *Crap! The crazy old man.* "I had nothing to do with it."

"No worries. I know you didn't."

"You're still gonna let me go, right? You said I get two days head start."

"Sure, mate. Sparky, too."

With a sigh, Barry slumped against the car.

Then Harley grinned. "But two days is nothing, Barry. Nothing at all."

thirty-five

JOHN paced the hospital room, keeping a close eye on Eleanor, and doing his best to ignore the din. His mother barked on her cell phone, yelling at her aides, and generally trying to make sense of the exit polls. Hillary and Amber alternately chatted and listened, both glued to the constant analysis spewing from the television. Occasionally, they jumped and shrieked for joy when a commentator predicted a victory for John.

Only Harley stood silent, though the smirk on his face spoke volumes.

John waved him over. "You got a lead on Barry and Sparky?"

Harley snorted. "The trail's a mile wide. Crikey, even a 'roo could follow it. But as promised, they've got until tomorrow afternoon to enjoy their freedom. After that...they're mine."

John nodded, relieved the last loose end would be tied up soon. But for some reason, the tension that kept his muscles tight didn't dissipate. Between the election and Eleanor's health he felt like he was going crazy.

Harley stalked away, throwing a "Looking good, governor" over his shoulder.

John frowned. *How the hell did I get here?*

The last thing he wanted was to be an elected official. He glanced down at Eleanor's still form and shook his head. *No. The last thing I want is for Eleanor to be lying here like this.*

Thank god she's getting better. There'd been an uptick in brain activity the last couple of days. A good sign, according to the doc, so Mother had decided to hold the election vigil at the hospital in case Eleanor woke up.

But the hospital setting just made the vigil more surreal than it already was.

His mother hung up the phone with a predatory smile. "I think you did it."

Before he could answer, Sierra burst into the room, her stomach wound dressed and her left arm in a sling, but a wide smile beaming from her face. "I just got the word. My station is going to call the election for John!"

The room erupted in shrieks—hysterical teenaged shrieks. Somewhat out of character, his mother made a fist pump as his niece and Amber jumped in his arms and hugged him.

"Ohmigod!" Hillary said. "Congrats, Uncle John. You deserve it!"

John gave her a rueful smile. "Your mom deserves it."

"You both do."

Hillary broke off and hugged her grandmother. Amber squeezed him tighter, making John a little uncomfortable, before Sierra pulled her away. "That's enough, Amber. Leave something for the rest of us."

Amber shot her a glare, but backed off.

Sierra leaned in and whispered, "I know you're not looking forward to this post, but as one of your constituents, I think things can only get better with you on the job."

She gave him a lingering kiss, but his warm response was cut off by a clap on the back from his mother.

"You did it!" the Barracuda said. "Don't let this go to your head, but I've never been more proud."

John shook his head. *Proud, huh?* And all it took was winning Governor of the state of California. "Not bad for someone who hates politics, right? Though I have to admit, it wasn't difficult after the Steel fiasco hit the media. Russian Mafia and politics make for good copy. And, of course, Sierra's story of my 'heroism' certainly didn't hurt."

"Hey," Sierra said. "Don't blame this on me. You're the one who saved my life. I just reported it."

His mother shook her head, then wiped away a hint of a tear. "In my lifetime, who would have thought that John could actually become a media darling?"

John's mood darkened. The idea of the media hounding him held no appeal.

But the idea of hounding politicians was very appealing. "Not for long, Mother. I hate to break it to you, but the day I'm inaugurated, I'll be going after the corrupt politicians. And once they see what's coming, they won't stop till I'm destroyed or out of office."

The Barracuda gave him one of her famous predatory smiles. "Let them come. You don't mind getting your hands dirty if you have to. And I'll be there to watch your back."

Harley snorted his response from across the room. "That's my job, mate. As always."

John smiled. From a political standpoint, there weren't many stronger than his mother. And from a danger standpoint, there weren't any scarier than the Aussie assassin.

Not a bad duo if you wanted to go after the most powerful and corrupt of the politicians.

In fact, it might be the best of both worlds.

Troy Cook has worked on more than 80 feature films, writing and directing his first at age 24. Shooting films in exotic locations led to brushes with the Russian Mafia, money launderers, and murderers. After surviving an attempted coup, riots, and violent demonstrations, he's decided it's safer to write novels.

His first novel, *47 Rules of Highly Effective Bank Robbers*, won several awards and was selected by *Library Journal* as one of the best debuts of the year.

You can visit Troy at www.troycook.net
or
www.myspace.com/troycook47rules